TH
FAM
AT
NO. 23

Kathryn Sharman is a British author of domestic suspense novels. She has a degree in English Language & Literature and an MA in Creative Writing. Her work has been shortlisted for the international Bath Novel Award. Having previously worked as a journalist and copywriter in London, she now lives in Yorkshire with her husband and three children.

KATHRYN SHARMAN

THE FAMILY AT NO. 23

HODDER &
STOUGHTON

First published in Great Britain in 2025 by Hodder & Stoughton Limited
An Hachette UK company

This paperback edition published in 2025

The authorised representative in the EEA is Hachette Ireland, 8 Castlecourt
Centre, Dublin 15, D15 XTP3, Ireland (email: info@hbgi.ie)

1

A CIP catalogue record for this title is available from the British Library

Paperback ISBN 9781399747158
ebook ISBN 9781399747165

Typeset in Plantin light by Manipal Technologies Limited

Printed and bound in Great Britain by Clays Ltd, Elcograf S.p.A.

Hodder & Stoughton policy is to use papers that are natural, renewable
and recyclable products and made from wood grown in sustainable forests.
The logging and manufacturing processes are expected to conform
to the environmental regulations of the country of origin.

Hodder & Stoughton Limited
Carmelite House
50 Victoria Embankment
London EC4Y 0DZ

www.hodder.co.uk

For
C. F. and B.

I

The café is crowded this morning and Iris has to raise her voice to be heard above the scourge of the coffee machine and the shouts of the baristas. One of them wears a leather apron, his hair caught neatly in a topknot. A scroll of brown paper hangs from the wall with words such as 'cortado' and 'macchiato' handwritten on it. She sighs, remembering when she used to be able to buy her entire lunch for the same price as a cup of coffee. But it's Laura's favourite, located on her side of town, so this is where they arrange to meet. They've known each other since the NCT days when they bonded over mugs of tea and *Elle Deco*, preferring to discuss paint swatches rather than the colour of their kids' poo.

'I'll have to get back soon,' says Laura, checking her smartwatch. 'Sofa delivery.' She stirs sugar into her flat white and foam slops around the sides of the cup.

'So, are you all settled in now?' Iris asks, dutifully. She'd hoped to avoid house talk today.

Laura rolls her eyes.

'Oh, you know. It's like the bloody Forth Bridge. Never-ending.'

'I'm not sure why you had to move in the first place. Your old house was amazing.'

There is an uncomfortable pause as her friend takes a sip of her coffee and shrugs.

Iris will never forget the day Laura had told her they were moving. Having shared school runs and nights out, she had thought their lives were following parallel lines. Their sons, Freddie and Ben, were the best of friends too. Thrown together during CBeebies benders and soft play sessions, they'd clung to each other like driftwood on their first day at school. By the time they were entering their final year at Grove Park Primary, they were walking themselves to school; dark-blonde heads drawn together to discuss Pokémon cards. She had taken it for granted that the boys would continue on to the local comp together. It wasn't the best – a recent Ofsted inspection had seen its rating downgraded from 'Good' to 'Requires improvement' – but she and Laura had always joked that a decent salt-of-the-earth secondary school had never done anyone any harm.

But then, about a year ago, Laura had announced that she and her husband, Ivo, had put their house up for rent. A 'recent windfall' from a deceased relative, combined with their 'dream house' becoming available on the other side of town meant they'd snapped up their 'forever home' in a chain-free sale. With every pat phrase it felt like another domino had fallen. 'And it means we'll be in the catchment area for Toppingham.' Crash. The final blow. Iris had been floored, her imagined future rewriting itself before her eyes.

'So, is Ben definitely going to the high school?' asks Laura, as though reading her thoughts. She knows this is a bone of contention between them now. Conversations about school have become terse and difficult.

'Well, it didn't feel like we had much option.' Iris pauses to sip her coffee, which is too bitter and strong for her taste. 'Ben's still a bit worried about who he's going to hang around with, now that Freddie's not going to be there.'

Laura looks down into her coffee but then leans forward across the table and gives her hand a squeeze.

'Look, why don't you just have another stab at Topps? You can appeal, you know. Or put Ben's name down on the waiting list, see what happens. I know a couple whose daughter got in the other year and they live even further out than you guys.'

Iris feels her jaw clench reflexively. She hates the way Laura talks like this, as though she thinks they live in some wasteland now, beyond county lines. But it might as well be true. This town is your typical middle-class commuter haven – leafy, rich, privileged – but like most places, it's divided into the 'haves' and the 'have-nots'.

Iris takes another look around the café, at its pale reclaimed wooden floorboards and the chalky grey walls. It's mainly greasy spoons, chemists and vape shops on her side of town.

'Yeah, maybe,' she replies. 'I'll talk to Steve tonight, see what he says.'

'Worth a try,' says Laura and gives her another encouraging smile before she downs her coffee and stands to leave. 'Got to go. I mustn't miss my delivery slot.'

Iris watches her friend through the window, her bouncy pony-tail and designer trainers disappearing down the tree-lined street with purpose. Laura always looks so well, as though nothing could ever cause her harm. Smooth-skinned, sparkly-eyed, dark hair like a mirror. It makes Iris think of a shiny new coin. Lucky.

Reaching for her coffee again, she tries another mouthful and winces. But she can't leave it. That would be even more of a waste of money. And they have to watch every penny. So she swallows it down and thinks of her son, Ben. He's a bright boy, or so his teachers say. Sensitive too. But then she's always known that. Even now he knows when she's sad or tired. He will pick her a flower or make her a cup of tea, unasked. An only child, it's not surprising that he's the centre of her world. But he's different to other boys. A boy like Ben doesn't belong at the local comp. He might not survive. He certainly won't thrive, that's for sure.

She gives her coffee one more sip before pushing it away. Perhaps she's being unfair. After all, she and her husband, Steve, went to similar schools and they turned out all right … didn't they? But the thought of Laura and Ivo in that beautiful new house. Their son going to the best school; it has curdled something in her recently.

The coffee machine lets out another high-pitched screech. It sounds like an alarm bell ringing in her head, the whistle blow of a train about to leave the station. A young woman with headphones and a hoodie approaches the table and Iris is brought back to the moment.

'Are you going to be much longer?' she asks. 'It's just that I'd like to plug in my laptop.' She gestures to the power socket beneath the table and Iris apologises, gathering her coat and bag.

Outside, the street is quieter. The pavement is sun-dappled today, a gift for April. There is no grind of traffic to dull the sound of birdsong in the nearby trees and Iris decides to let herself wander. She admires the local independent shops that line the street with their striped awnings. A man emerges from the nearby florist holding two enormous bouquets. As she wonders who the lucky recipients might be, an inquisitive cockapoo crosses her path. She stops and crouches down to stroke the dog, reading Barney on the name tag before the owner continues onwards. She and Steve have never indulged the idea of pets. Ben has allergies and they have to be careful. But the feel of the dog's silken pelt and its warm tongue remains on her fingertips.

She walks on and the shops give way to larger stretches of pavement punctuated by tall, established trees. By autumn, these streets will seem paved with gold as yellow and orange leaves line the walkways.

Her eyes are downcast, contemplating this thought, when she hears a muffled cry and the dull clang of metal banging to the ground. A satsuma rolls along the pavement towards her feet and Iris looks up to see an old woman lying prone on the path ahead. A shopping trolley lies beside her, up-skittled.

'Are you okay?' she calls.

There is no answer. She's unsure what to do, so picks up the spilled fruits – apples, pears – and deposits them back in the basket. 'Can you hear me?' Iris tries again. 'I think you've had a little fall.'

'You don't fucking say,' comes a voice from within the pile of grey curly hair and faded navy mac. The old woman lifts her head to regard Iris and a drop of blood leaks from her temple.

'You're hurt. Perhaps you should lie still?' Iris says, looking up and down the street. In the past, when she has seen someone taken ill like this, she's always been relieved when the victim is receiving assistance from passers-by and she can carry on. But the street looks deserted. Not a soul is around.

'Just give me a minute,' the old woman says breathlessly. 'I'll be all right.' She pulls herself up to a sitting position and brushes down the lapels of her coat. 'These bloody pavements will be the death of me. I've written to the council but do they do anything?'

Iris blushes at the colourful language.

'You're bleeding,' she says, pointing.

The old woman puts a hand to her head and looks with mild interest at the blood, smearing it between her fingers.

'Oh well, could be worse. Give me a hand, will you? Set me right on my feet.'

'I really think you should wait until we've had you checked over for any broken bones.'

'I'll be the judge of that, missy.'

She heaves herself upwards and Iris is forced to lend an arm in support. Testing her legs, the old woman shifts her weight from one foot to the other. She gestures towards her shopping trolley. Her hands are grazed like a toddler's.

'At least let me help you home,' offers Iris. 'Do you live far?'

'Just around the corner.' She nods, setting her mouth in grim determination.

As they walk side by side, the old woman leans heavily on her trolley, using it as a walking aid. Slowing her gait to match, Iris considers the rows of Victorian terraced houses. They are on Riddleston Road, she realises, not far from Laura's new place. This street is spoken of in hushed tones of reverence, one of the most prestigious addresses in the area. Each house reaches three storeys high, the smart gabled roofs painted in black and white. Tiled garden paths unfurl from pastel-painted front doors. Wide sash windows stare outwards from the brick facades revealing a hint of the salubrious interiors within.

'This is me,' says the old woman eventually. They have nearly reached the end of the street when Iris catches sight of a thickly overgrown privet hedge and a gate that hangs loosely on its hinges. She tries not to stare but the disparity is obvious. The front garden is a tangle of weeds, obscuring a path of crazy paving. The window frames, once painted blue, are weather-beaten and peeling. Grey, dust-laden net curtains conceal the rooms inside. There is no tantalising glimpse of fashionable middle-class decor. The house looks uninhabited, dead. A rotten tooth in an otherwise gleaming smile.

'I've let the old place go a bit,' she mumbles.

'Let's get you inside, shall we?' Iris says. She is wishing, not for the first time, that someone else was on hand to deal with the situation but the street is empty. 'I'm Iris, by the way.'

'Rosemary,' comes the reply as a key is fitted to the door of number 23 and the blistered wood gives way to reveal a dark hallway and a musty smell.

'Oh, two flowers,' Iris says, trying a smile, but the old woman moves past her into the house and the door closes behind them.

Piles of mail, mainly takeaway flyers and local papers, lie strewn underfoot but not so much that Iris can't appreciate the original tiled porch, its tessellating colours of white, blue and terracotta still beautiful. The hallway leads to a chink of light towards the back of the house. She looks up at the high ceilings and corniced walls. Once white, they are now yellowed and dusty like a piece of old wedding cake. Ahead is a wide staircase, the wooden ribbon of a banister winding up and up, and she can't help wondering at the rooms above, sealed with ages of dust and paint. The place is a mess; cluttered, grimy but as they say, good bones.

'I know what you're thinking,' Rosemary says, following her gaze. 'How can someone live like this?'

'No. Not at all,' Iris demurs. 'I was just thinking what beautiful old houses these are.'

Rosemary shrugs and purses her lips.

'I've lived here most of my life. You get used to the same old walls. I really should have moved on when my parents died but didn't have the heart to sell up.'

'You had no family of your own to pass it on to?'

She's being nosy, but she can't help asking. So much of property is inherited now, passed down from generation to generation. It's one of her and Steve's bugbears. The fact that honest, hardworking people like themselves don't stand a chance of getting on the property ladder, but carry on paying all their wages to wealthy landlords.

'Never married,' confirms Rosemary. 'Why would I want to saddle myself to a man and brats?'

The tone takes Iris by surprise, as though the old woman has looked into her own life for a moment and sneered at her choices.

'It's such a big house for just one person though.'

'Says who?'

'Well, I just mean—'

'I can still manage the stairs perfectly well.'

Iris catches sight of the blood on Rosemary's forehead again and reaches for a tissue in her bag. The old woman takes it from her silently and presses it to the skin above her temple, which is beginning to bruise.

'I'm sorry. I meant no offence.'

Rosemary reaches out a hand towards the newel post as if to steady herself but the gesture appears proprietorial.

'You know, Iris, it's just a house. This one has been a blessing and a curse.'

Easy for you to say, Iris thinks, but she smiles and nods.

'I'll just rest in my chair for a bit,' says Rosemary, taking off her mac and wincing at some ache or pain. She seems a bit unsure on her feet suddenly and Iris reaches out a hand to help her but it is shrugged off.

'Is there anyone I can call for you? A relative or friend, perhaps?'

Rosemary gives a bitter laugh at this and shakes her head. 'I don't have any. There is no family. They're all long gone.'

'What about next door? Your neighbours?'

She tuts at this. 'Never set eyes on them. I don't even know their names. Foreigners, most of them. Always coming or going. I think one spends half the year in another country. They couldn't give two hoots.'

'But surely there must be someone?'

Rosemary turns to look at Iris then. Her eyes might have been a deep chocolate brown once but they now appear faded.

'No. There is no one.'

Iris pauses. 'Look, I really think we should get you checked over. That bang to your head ... maybe I should call an ambulance—'

'No!' declares Rosemary with a force that takes Iris aback. 'I don't want all that circus. People, strangers coming in here. They'll only want to put me in hospital. A home. I won't go. I want to stay here. In my own house.'

And with that she moves off in the direction of the front room.

Iris finds herself alone, dithering in the hallway, wondering what to do. Perhaps she should just go. Steve has a work trip tomorrow, will need clean laundry, and Ben will be home from school soon. She likes to be there when he gets back. But something makes her pause. She is loath to leave, it feels churlish. And besides, a part of her wants to stay a little longer. Call it morbid curiosity but this house intrigues her.

'Why don't I make you a cup of tea then, while you put your feet up?' she calls. 'It's the least I can do.'

She hears Rosemary make a grunt of assent so she wanders down the hallway, looking for the kitchen.

It's as bad as she expected. The kitchen cabinets look like they were fitted sometime around the Seventies but most of the fixtures are original; the same high ceilings and corniced walls, albeit papered with faded roses and covered in a layer of greasy grime. The dirty lino flooring covers what she suspects might be lovely quarry tiles underneath and a wooden dresser resides along one wall, filled with china.

As she stands at the sink filling the kettle, Iris looks through the window onto the garden beyond and considers the jungle of trees and plants. The lawn stretches out behind the house, bordered mainly with grasses and wildflowers and some long-established shrubs in desperate need of pruning. Tall trees stand looming, blocking out much of the natural light; a haven for birds.

She puts the kettle on to boil and leans against the work surface. Next to canisters named 'tea' and 'coffee', a calendar is nailed to a wall. Each page has a painting of a different bird and the RSPB logo. Few engagements are marked, the dates of the month empty. Surely there must be doctor's appointments, a WI meeting or something like that? She peers closer and lifts a page of the calendar but nothing is planned, just a couple of odd reminders such as 'visit cemetery', 'buy corn plasters', 'water plants'. There is a date the following month marked 'birthday' but it doesn't say whose it is.

Iris drops a teabag into a mug she's found in the cupboard overhead. In the fridge is a carton of milk as well as individually wrapped cheese slices, an iceberg lettuce and some pickled vegetables in jars plus a half-empty tin of tuna, turning brown and crusted. She sniffs the milk and looks around the kitchen again and that's when she sees two small bowls on the floor; one for food, one for water. They are close to the back door, in which there is a cat flap. *So there is someone*, Iris thinks, splashing milk into the mug.

'Here's your tea,' she says, opening the door to the lounge but there is no response. Within this room there are more florals, spilling out over the fireside rug onto the curtains and the cushions. It's as if the inside of the house, like the exterior, has been left to grow wild, untamed. Iris briefly thinks of Sleeping Beauty's castle and its forest of thorns, the enchantment that lay over it all. And in a way, a strange spell has been cast over her too. As every minute passes she is fascinated and appalled in equal measure, at this house, this woman, which seem to not quite exist in the real, everyday world.

'Rosemary,' she tries again, in a stage whisper.

Perhaps she's nodded off so Iris places the tea on the nest of tables beside her chair and gently touches her arm. The old woman's mouth falls open, as though in shock at such an act of kindness, but no sound passes her lips. Moving further around to face her, she realises Rosemary's eyes are open. They stare into the middle distance, at something far beyond. There is a stillness, a finality to her body.

This is what a dead person looks like, Iris thinks. She takes a step backwards and looks away. But her eyes are irresistibly drawn back to Rosemary's face; the fine down on her cheeks, the way her eyebrows have settled into a look of slight surprise.

Should she feel for a pulse, press her fingers to the fine delta of blue veins at the wrist? Or even try mouth-to-mouth or CPR? But the look of acceptance, almost serene amusement, on Rosemary's face won't allow her to consider such a disturbance. Not that Iris has really got the stomach for it, if she's honest.

She walks out into the hallway to locate her handbag where she left it earlier, but also because she doesn't want to be in the same room as a dead body. The hairs are standing up on her neck and she feels suffocated by the musty, airless atmosphere of the house. She reaches into her bag for her phone. She should call someone. Who would that be? Not 999, that's for emergencies and this situation is no longer urgent. Is it the police to whom she must report a death? Should she run outside and start banging on doors to locate a neighbour? But then Rosemary's words come back to her: 'There is no one'.

And that's when she leans on the newel post, just as its owner did a little while earlier. She runs her hand over the smooth dark honey-coloured wood. It would only need a little buffing to bring it up to a high shine again. Iris looks down at the phone in her hand and then up and around at the gaping hallway. There is no one, she thinks. No one would ever know.

2

SIX MONTHS LATER

Iris steps back to admire her handiwork. She has just finished giving the hallway a second coat of paint – a soft grey – which makes the white skirting boards and cornicing really pop. Her gaze travels upwards where all is newly decorated, pristine. Beneath her feet, the mosaic of tiles spreads out in a chorus of colours. There weren't too many that needed replacing in the end and the rest have cleaned up nicely. The turquoise winks at her amid the terracotta, black and white and she wonders whose feet have stood here before over the years. Who lived in this house? Who died in it? Pushing the thought away, as she must always do, she lifts the paint roller and tray and takes them to the kitchen to rinse them out.

She looks out of the window. It is there again. The tortoise-shell cat that haunts the garden despite the fact she has sealed up the door and removed any traces of food. She hates cats and while Ben is still allergic to animal hair she's not taking any risks. When they first moved in, it could be heard mewing plaintively on the doorstep at various times of the day and night, but when-ever she opened the back door to shoo it away, it would already be gone. Steve had questioned its persistence to begin with but she had passed it off as just another neighbourhood moggy. 'Probably tries it with everyone on the street,' she'd joked.

The cat stalks the lawn now before settling on a patch of grass – always the same place by the laburnum tree that overhangs from next door's garden. Why does it have to choose that very spot? It sits there and stares out towards the kitchen window, its eyes blinking in slow motion, watching the house. Iris stares back for a moment, willing herself to face up to this presence, wondering who might break first. The cat wins. Cursing, she fills a jug of water, opens the back door and strides out, opening her arms to make herself appear larger.

'Get away,' she shouts, emptying the jug, water leaping from her hand like a lasso. At the last moment, the cat hisses and dives through a gap in the fence, disappearing. Iris finds herself standing on the new patch of grass by the tree, staring at the spot where the cat was just sitting, its absence like a negative in a photo.

When Iris opens the door, Laura is standing on the front porch, her arms filled with flowers and a bottle of Prosecco. Her hair is caught up off her face, with a pair of large sunglasses acting as a makeshift hairband, and she is wearing a pair of colourful dungarees with a discreet label on the front pocket. Iris makes a mental note to google the brand name later.

'Ta-dah!' says her friend. 'I thought you lot had been in the new place long enough so I'm inviting myself round to help you warm it.'

'Oh,' says Iris, trying to keep the surprise out of her voice. She hates nothing more than unexpected visitors. In her book, it's just rudeness dressed up as spontaneity.

'Seriously, you don't mind, do you?' says Laura. 'Only I was just passing and I couldn't wait any longer.' She steps over the threshold. 'I still can't believe we're neighbours again. And the boys are at school together. Ivo and I were so pleased to hear that a place came up for Ben in the end. It's great!'

Iris closes the door and watches her friend as she appraises the hallway, her voice echoing upwards.

'Wow!' she calls over her shoulder.

'Ignore the state of the kitchen,' says Iris, following on after her. 'We still need to finish getting it sorted.'

'Of course. Rome wasn't built in a day. But you must have done so much.'

Iris shrugs. 'Amazing what you can do with a bit of Polyfilla and a few gallons of paint.'

'It's incredible. And such a find.' Laura dumps the flowers and the bottle on the work surface. 'I mean, I knew these houses were nice but I had no idea.' She continues to move around the kitchen, looking out at the garden. 'And you say you just stumbled across it, the day it went on the rental market? I'm surprised it wasn't sold at auction, a place like this!'

Iris takes a vase down from a cupboard, finds some scissors and begins to unwrap the flowers. She can feel her shoulders rising as she snips at the stems.

'My lucky day, I guess? I think it helped that we were a family and prepared to commit long-term. And spend some money on it.'

'But still. This could have gone for a fortune on the open market.'

Iris slams down the scissors, her hands shaking.

'What are you saying, Laura? That we don't deserve to live in a house like this?'

Her friend spins around, eyes pulled back from where she has been gazing at the walls, and frowns. 'Hey! No. Of course not. I'm thrilled for you. You and Steve have worked so hard. I know that,' she says, her voice soft and concerned. Then she cocks her head to one side. 'Are you okay? Moving house, it's tough. Don't underestimate the stress of it all.'

'I'm fine,' Iris says, smiling tightly as she arranges the flowers into place. They look like they've come from the fancy florist's on the high street.

'Okay, well aren't you going to show me around? I'm dying to see the rest of it.' Laura walks back along the hallway and moves as if to enter the front room.

'Not in there,' says Iris. Laura pauses, her hand on the door, a swatch of rose-clad wallpaper just visible through the gap. 'We haven't got round to that room yet. I'll show you upstairs.'

As Iris leads Laura to the next floor her friend continues to make appreciative noises, running her fingers along the shiny mahogany handrail, exclaiming at the light, the space. She pokes her head into the main bedroom – 'so big, you could even install an ensuite' – and then briefly into a smaller room, which is now Ben's.

'How's he getting on? It's a shame the boys aren't in the same form, isn't it? Still, I guess they can always meet up at lunchtime or after school.'

Iris nods, thinking about how Ben spends most of his breaks in the library now, hiding out within the stacks, his nose in a book, while Freddie is on the rugby pitch, his trousers greening at the knees, his blazer already bearing the signs of rough and tumble. Ben, on the other hand, would appear to have shrunk, grown paler, withdrawn into himself. He now nurses his bookishness, his ineptitude for sports, his predisposition for coughs and colds. She will just have to make sure they arrange lots of get-togethers in the holidays. She'll suggest it to Steve tonight.

'We still have a bit of work to do,' says Iris, changing the subject. 'The bathroom is a mess, although the shower works so it will do for now.'

'I can imagine,' laughs Laura. 'I remember driving down this road a few times and this house always stuck out like a sore thumb.' Iris bristles, ignoring the comment. 'Still, what a project. I guess the previous owners must have been here a long time and the place got beyond them?'

Iris nods. 'An elderly lady, apparently. Had it for years before she passed away.' She curses herself inwardly. She's already said too much.

'Oh God. Do you think she actually died here?'

'I wouldn't know,' says Iris, leading the way back downstairs, eager to distance herself from this line of discussion. 'Tea?' she calls over her shoulder as she walks into the kitchen. She sees Laura eyeing the bottle of Prosecco on the kitchen counter but declines to open it. She's not in the mood for alcohol or effervescent, celebratory explosions. She'd like to get back to some more DIY before Ben arrives home from school.

'No, I'm fine, thanks,' says Laura. 'Already had way too much caffeine this morning. We'll have to celebrate properly at Halloween though. I'm throwing a party.'

She looks out of the kitchen window onto the back garden, her attention snagged by the cat who has returned to stalk the lawn once more.

'Bloody thing,' mutters Iris. 'Can't get rid of it.' She bangs on the pane of glass, harder than she means to. 'Shoo, piss off,' she shouts.

'Oh, go easy. Looks like a sweet old thing. Do you think it's a stray? Maybe you could adopt it?'

'I think it's adopted us, more like. Won't bugger off. Besides, I can't let it in the house. Ben's allergies.'

'I thought he was growing out of that now? He used to be okay around Freddie's rabbit.'

'Yeah, but I don't want to take any chances.'

Laura nods, a trace of a smirk on her lips as she turns away. 'Well, I think you might be stuck with it. Looks right at home out there.' She takes her jacket from the back of the chair and leans in for a hug. 'Congratulations, again. It's just what you've always wanted.'

3

Laura pulls the garden gate to and casts a glance over her shoulder. They've done their best to tidy up the front garden, she notes. The congregation of weeds has been beaten back into abeyance, the door furniture has been replaced with shiny chrome, the peeling window frames painted in a bright white – she'd spotted poor old Steve up a ladder several weekends on the trot.

They do everything themselves, on a shoestring budget. It must be bloody exhausting, she thinks, but fair play to them, no one works harder. Iris could look happier about it, though. Laura has seen her friend grow more tense, more strained as the years have gone by. She fusses over Ben like a clucking hen. No wonder Steve works away so often these days, it must be unbearable.

Laura looks up at the houses she passes as she continues to walk down Iris's street. Now that is a bizarre thought. This street and Iris. She never thought she'd conflate those two things. They are gorgeous houses though, always have been. Apart from that eyesore her friend moved into six months ago. She had been flabbergasted, she won't lie. Unable to keep the shock from her face, her amazed silence stretching out a beat too long when Iris had given her the news. But she had quickly saved face, arranging her features into delighted surprise, eager to know more.

Iris had been quite evasive, even more than usual. Her friend is nothing if not a closed book. Rather, it is she who peers into the pages of Laura's life, poring over the details, noting everything, memorising it seemingly for future reference. It's true, she has always enjoyed the fact that Iris is a captive audience, a doting fan who reinforces her choices and decisions. It helps to justify some of her more outlandish purchases or flagrant exhibitions. She is thinking of the rather self-indulgent fifteenth wedding anniversary party that involved the hiring of a Bedouin-style marquee in the back garden with catered food. She smiles to herself even now as she pictures the kilim rugs underfoot, the rosewater and pistachio cake, the jewelled lanterns. Even the dress she wore; a sexier version of her original wedding dress yet still the same size.

Still, it is a bit odd. This house situation and Iris. Laura is happy for her, of course. But God knows, she wouldn't want that albatross around her neck. It's looking miles better but that place needs a fortune spending on it, which Iris and Steve don't have. While they have never been explicit, Laura suspects they have quite a bit of debt between them, and modest salaries both. Which is why she's never understood why they would spend so much time and money on a property they don't even own. Though not everyone can afford a mortgage, she concedes, and Iris and Steve have never had any help from their parents. But there is something a little off about the whole thing, a bit out of whack and she can't put her finger on it.

She'd tried scouring the real estate websites and local estate agents' windows as soon as Iris mentioned they were moving but she couldn't find any trace. Which makes sense, she supposes, if the house was never advertised, even as a rental. Nobody in the area knows anything either. Iris had been characteristically vague when she'd pressed her on the name of the agent, citing a private rental firm before changing the subject, asking Laura for wallpaper recommendations.

But it's weird. She'd said as much to Ivo, but he hadn't so much as raised his head above his laptop. 'Not really any of our business, is it?' he'd said and she had felt reprimanded.

He always teases her about being a busybody. A show-off. Little Miss Fancy Pants had been his nickname for her when they'd first started dating at university, which had seemed cute when he'd actually been easing off said underwear. Whereas now it feels like a criticism. But someone has to make an effort, keep up appearances – even in the lingerie department. And he does still notice when she wears an expensive new set. Though she doesn't really wear it for him these days.

Perhaps her husband is right though. What does it matter? None of their business. She just hopes that Iris and Steve haven't taken on too much, got themselves in over their heads. And therein lies the rub. The reason she had felt the telltale creep of envy as she was viewing the house. The fact is, Iris and Steve don't have the money (or the style – there, she admits it) to pull off a project like that. An old house like the one on Riddleston Road could be magnificent in the right hands, and with the requisite budget, and she can't help wishing that she and Ivo had spotted it first.

Swallowing this thought and pulling her coat closer, she walks the rest of the way home and considers her to-do list. As a freelance photographer she can pick and choose her projects, working around the school holidays and Ivo's commitments. She has two shoots coming up this week – one engagement and a couple with a new baby. They'll go out into the local park and take advantage of these beautiful autumnal colours before they all disappear.

Reaching down, she picks up the spiky green casing of a conker. Inside, its flesh is creamy and tender revealing the mahogany seed, polished like a nugget of wood. And she remembers the feel of her fingers earlier on the smooth balustrade of Iris's home. Her feet eagerly climbing the stairs, up and up. She thinks: I wonder if the previous owner really did die in that house? She thinks: wouldn't there have been a death announcement in the paper?

4

Standing in the window bay of the shop, Iris wrestles a dress onto a mannequin, trying to ignore the gawkers on the pavement as she briefly inhabits this goldfish bowl. Low autumn sunshine slants through the glass, blinding her. She feels a prickle of sweat as she tugs the garment onto the wooden torso.

She breathes, wiping the sheen from her brow and steps down out of the display. Trying to dress a squirming toddler was easier than this. But she doesn't mind working part-time in the boutique. It has allowed her to make some money and still be around for her son, while also keeping on top of the house. The idea of a proper career has fallen away over the years, though sometimes she regrets giving up her old job. She used to work as an estate agent, managing viewings, driving around to different properties. She enjoyed the briefest of interactions with clients, not to mention looking into other peoples' homes. And she was good at it. But then she became a mum. Ben was always a sickly child and someone had to be there when Steve was away, driving the lorry.

She checks her watch. Her shift is nearly over. Avoiding any eye contact – she doesn't want to get embroiled with a tricky customer at the last minute – she makes her way down to the staff room to collect her bag and coat.

Back home, she sets to cleaning the house. She tries to keep herself occupied, doing anything to distract herself these days. Because it comes to her unbidden, at any given moment; the image of Rosemary's face. She must guard her thoughts closely but they come rolling upon her like a wave, her stomach clenching, her face turning hot, her legs jellied.

When Steve had come home that night, six months ago, she had considered telling him. About Rosemary. The house on Riddleston Road. The way the day had taken such a strange and dark turn. Already it feels as though this all happened a very long time ago, to someone else, in another lifetime. Besides, if she had told her husband, what would he think? To just leave that poor old woman, abandoned, would be unforgivable.

Yet it is exactly what would have happened if Rosemary had died on her own, without witnesses. You hear about it all the time on the news, in the papers. She would have remained sitting there in her chair, undiscovered. For how long? No, Rosemary died as she lived; alone. Sadly, it happens to so many. It's a shame but it's not Iris's fault, it's not her responsibility. But the weight of it hangs on her, like a stone around her neck. A vision of moist earth, the slice of a dull moon, the smell of her own sweat mixing with the stale tang of urine – it flashes across her brain as though the scene is momentarily illuminated by a sheet of lightning before all is dark again.

In the end, it was all quite straightforward. Steve was away for a week overseas and by the time he returned she'd managed to pack up their old place and move lock, stock and barrel. She'd arranged a clearance company to sort out Rosemary's house; both vans overlapping in the space of one day while Ben was at school. She explained to Steve on the phone how this amazing rental opportunity had come along and they needed to move fast, before anyone else snapped it up. That she would organise the finances through her personal account as she did with all the household budgeting. After all, the majority of his wages are swallowed up each month by his own debts.

He had been a little taken aback when he came home to discover the smart location of his new home but less so when he realised how much DIY would be involved. But he agreed, it was quite the find. And, more importantly, it was great news that this meant they could reapply to Toppingham; their new address bumping Ben's name straight to the top of the waiting list. In fact, Iris had been surprised at how easily he had accepted the abrupt change in their circumstances. But then Steve seems to just acquiesce these days. She's the one who has to get stuff done in this marriage.

Like most things in life, it wasn't the act itself that was difficult but the days and weeks and months that followed it. Iris had gone back to Rosemary's house late at night, under cover of darkness. Returning with tools and overalls, the door still open on the latch, she had worked quickly. Digging the hole in the garden took longer than she imagined, even with her work-hardened body and the momentum of fear and adrenaline to propel her. It was small – Rosemary didn't take up much space – but deep. Hopefully deep enough not to be disturbed by dogs or foxes.

The overgrown chaos of the garden provided a welcome disguise. The house was at the end of a terrace, the next door neighbour away for months on end. Rosemary had no friends, no relatives. No one would ever know. This is what Iris told herself as she dug, her head covered with a black hoodie, her hands gloved.

The hardest part was handling the body itself. She had ventured upstairs and found Rosemary's bedroom; the dressing table with its matching vanity set, the smell of rose water, the single divan. Iris had stripped the bed, taking the pale pink sheets and folding them neatly. Next, she had made an efficient search of the cupboards, the wardrobes, the drawers, looking for any of Rosemary's personal effects. Apart from the usual old lady ephemera – talc, slippers, hair nets, a box of tissues – she had found nothing else, no photographs, apart from a black and white one of an older couple, presumably her parents.

But under the bed, she discovered a black metal box with initials painted in gold. A padlock was attached but the key was already inserted. Inside, Iris sifted through papers; legal documents, her parents' last will and testament, all confirming that Rosemary was the sole heir to the property. Iris had scanned them feverishly, looking for a codicil but there was no mention of anyone else. Perhaps the old woman really had been speaking the truth, after all?

In amongst these papers was a fat bundle of correspondence; hand-written letters, all with Rosemary's name and the address of the house: 23 Riddleston Road. Some of them looked very old indeed, the paper yellowed and frayed at the edges, as though the envelopes had been handled many times, the contents read over and over again. Iris's hands itched to open them. But she was conscious of the time and the packet of letters was tightly bound together with a pink ribbon. There was obviously something deeply personal rather than professional about these letters. She wondered if they didn't have a romantic attachment to them; a former boyfriend, a fiancé even, a love affair that fell by the wayside over the years. In any case, it could have nothing to do with the house.

Gathering up the bedding and the box, she moved downstairs, checking her watch for the time. It's just a body, she told herself, an empty shell. A few years ago, she had briefly worked at an old people's home where she had to deal with elderly bodies; their smells, their frailties, their decay and delicacy. And she had found it was easier not to get too close to any of them or to even learn their names. It was a job, like all the others, a means to an end. Money in the bank to help her family make ends meet. So this is how she decided to think about Rosemary as well.

She wrapped her up in the pink sheets. The body, though stiff and awkward, was small and lightweight and she carried it like a swaddled child out to the garden. Lowering it carefully into the gaping maw of the ground, she then returned to the house to fetch the strongbox, which she placed alongside. Any other personal items could be destroyed, donated or passed on to the house clearance company and sold on.

The night was still and black as she paused, listening to her own ragged breathing. Her back ached, her blistered hands throbbed and for a moment these things threatened to pierce her conscience, to make her stop and realise what she was doing. Was it too late to change her mind? To carry Rosemary back to her chair, return the bed sheets and the other effects. To break the madness of this spell somehow and return all to as it was. She could still go back to her little rental, her beautiful son, asleep at home in his bed. She hated herself for leaving him all alone.

But the thought of Ben had strengthened her resolve. He deserved better. Isn't it every parent's duty to try and rise, to give your children more than what you had? Besides, wouldn't Rosemary want to help a family like hers, to help a boy like Ben – the grandson she never had? No. This was for the best, she told herself. And before she took up the shovel again, she had bent to pick a rose from the garden. Its perfume was deep and redolent in the cool of the night as she dropped it on top of the body. She had pricked her finger in the process, she noticed. There was blood on her hands, of course. But it was done now and like every other task Iris had ever set her mind to, this was just another that must now be completed. So she began to fill in the hole with earth. She needed to get back to Ben soon, before he woke, before the sun came up.

5

'Great class, thanks!' Laura calls as she tucks her yoga mat under her arm and grabs her water bottle. She checks herself in the full-length mirrors of the dance studio and contents herself with the fact that the slight flush to her cheeks is the right side of healthy glow. Some of the others had suggested they go for a coffee afterwards but she needs to do some food shopping for the forthcoming Halloween party this weekend. She's invited the whole street as well as a few couples from Freddie's new school.

The gym car park resembles the forecourt of the Land Rover dealership, so she's always grateful when she casts her key fob around in the air and her car obediently beeps at her in response. Dumping her gear on the passenger seat, she tightens her dark ponytail and slicks on some lip balm. Eschewing the queue of traffic winding into the centre of town, she turns right, peeling away from the other cars. Soon, the high bronzed hedges and green fields she loves are streaming past the windows and she relaxes her hands on the steering wheel.

As she brings the car to a halt at the local farm shop, she glimpses the nearby field covered in trammelled lines of mud and straw and a wooden sign painted with the words 'Pumpkin Patch – This Way!'. They used to bring Freddie here when he was little. Her heart quakes briefly at the memory. How she thought those early days of motherhood would last forever, strung together in a never-ending chain of joy, exhaustion, magic and banality. But then, once her son started school and she began her photography business, everything had sped up somehow. Overnight, her high-pitched, dinosaur-loving son had morphed into a taller, deeper-voiced boy who wouldn't let her cut his hair any more. And that was that. That whole part of her life was over; the door slamming abruptly shut just as she realised she'd forgotten her keys.

She and Ivo had tried for more kids. She would have loved to have had three or even four. That greed now seems laughable. No brother or sister showed up for Freddie. Perhaps he had been a miracle all along. Or perhaps something had shifted since he was born. Laura went to the doctor for some initial tests, which suggested all was normal, and Ivo had said they should be patient, let nature run its course. As the years spun out and still no siblings, Laura had wanted to try IVF – they had the money after all.

But it was the one time she and Ivo had violently disagreed. He didn't want to subject either of them to painful, invasive procedures with no guarantee of success. The more she argued or tried to cajole, the more he held fast. It had been the first and last time he had ever said no to her. But of all the little and large luxuries – the house, the cars, the holidays – this was the thing she had wanted the most. And he had denied her. Now, at the age of forty-four, when her period does turn up, it feels like a pointless show of red in her calendar. A reminder of so many wasted opportunities.

The entrance to the farm shop is a cornucopia of produce. Wreaths of pale straw and faded grasses interwoven with dried flowers are hung about the place and she considers buying one for the front door. It's not enough now to have a festive wreath at Christmas; you need one that evolves to reflect the changing seasons, all year round. Ivo might say it's a bit much but then she juts out her chin and thinks *why not? He can't say no to me.*

Inside, she wheels her trolley around the fruit and vegetable stands. Selecting armfuls of apples, she decides not to calculate the cost. They are a bit pricey considering they're to be used for party games. She also grabs several red and white cabbages to make slaw, toppling them into the trolley before she then heads to the organic butcher's counter. She has several shoulders of locally-reared pork on order, which the shop assistant in his striped apron and white hat duly collects for her from the back.

As she stands in the queue for the checkout, she considers her guest list for the party. She is aware that for the first time this year, it will be a very mixed crowd, new friends and old overlapping, and she allows herself a moment of doubt as she thinks about Iris and Steve. It's the first time in ages she's had them over to the house as a couple and Laura feels her stomach give a small flip of guilt, in spite of herself. She will have to play it carefully. And then there's Freddie and Ben. God knows whether they're even still friends.

She still feels Iris is acting rather strangely these days, not replying to her messages immediately, no longer as available for coffee as she used to be. Could she be feeling it too? This shift between them all?

There was a time in the past when Laura felt she could drop round on the spur of the moment but the other day Iris had been quite cagey about showing her around the new place. But then perhaps she's just trying to get the house as presentable as possible before she gives everyone the guided tour. Besides, Iris and Steve have always been quiet, introverted types. As a couple, they are a little hard work, she thinks disloyally. But then Steve doesn't have it easy with Iris. She's not sure how he's put up with it all these years. And there are definitely some skeletons in that marriage, for sure. She looks up then to see the shop assistant is watching her expectantly, eyebrows raised.

'Oh, sorry,' says Laura with a shake of her head. 'Miles away.' She packs the groceries into her cloth tote bags and taps her watch to pay. She didn't catch what the amount was but instead swings the bags into the trolley, scrunching up the till receipt and throwing it into a nearby bin as she passes. On top of the groceries, carefully balanced, is the resplendent seasonal wreath. She can't wait to get it up on the front door.

6

Iris is up early as usual, unable to sleep. She dips her hand into the warm soapy water and allows the sponge to bloat before she lifts it to the front door and sluices down the woodwork, polishing up the new knocker and letter box until they gleam in the cool morning sunshine. The house is looking so much better since they gave it all a fresh coat of paint, she thinks with pleasure. But before she can clamp down on it, an image comes to mind of Rosemary's aged hand, the thick wormy veins as she had lifted the key to the door and let them both in all those months ago. How the Virginia creeper, climbing up the house like a disease, was so overgrown you had to push past it to gain entrance. It was one of the first things she had told Steve to get rid of, ripping its clinging form from the brickwork, poisoning it with chemicals at the source. All that was left of it now were scarred traces, an imprint left on the stone.

She stretches again, standing on the balls of her feet to reach higher. Her sleeve lifts to reveal a livid scratch along her wrist and she thinks of the cat again. The other day, she had reflected on Laura's words and decided to try a different tack. Perhaps if she couldn't beat it into retreat, she could capture it and take it to the Cats Protection League. She had crept across the lawn, her voice a low murmur, her hand proffering some disgusting fishy-smelling treats she'd bought from the supermarket. The cat, sitting proud in its usual position by the tree, had looked at her with insolent eyes, refusing to move. As Iris approached, she found herself resorting to the old cliched refrains. 'Here, puss-puss. Here you are, kitty-kitty,' she had coaxed. The cat had allowed her to get within arms' reach before it leapt, claws unsheathed, lacerating her arm.

As she continues to wash down the front door, another thought enters her head, so ridiculous and far-fetched that she laughs out loud and gives herself a small shake. But it remains there, nestled in her brain, a small voice whispering, 'It knows. The cat knows.' And she is so lost in this train of thought, the surreal yet disquieting nonsense of it, that she doesn't register the sound of someone walking up next door's path and standing at the opposite front door to her own.

'Nice. *Bello*!' comes a disembodied voice. It is a melange of accents; Italian, with a London twang overlaying it. Iris starts, looking about her, trying to locate where the voice is coming from before she looks across the fence dividing the two houses. A short, tanned, well-built man, with a beard that is showing signs of silvering, stands on his doorstep clutching a newspaper and a pint of milk to his chest. He nods towards the front of the house and smiles at Iris. '*Tutto bene*. I like.'

'Oh,' replies Iris, looking back to the house as though she no longer knows why she is here, what she is doing in front of this door with a wet sponge in her hand. 'We moved in a few months ago,' she says eventually.

He nods again. 'Tell me. Where is … what is happening to the old woman?' He makes a gesture as though he is searching for something.

'Rosemary,' supplies Iris, before she thinks better of it. 'I don't really know,' she says with a shrug and a forced smile. 'She must have moved on,' she adds.

'Yes. I see,' he says. '*Claro*.' And he makes a lopsided gesture of regret.

'Have you returned from holiday?' asks Iris, trying to keep the nerves from her voice as she wrings out the sponge into the bucket by her feet.

'Yes, forgive me,' says the man with a hand to his chest. 'I am Gianni. I live here but I have been away.' He flings a hand out casually at something beyond his shoulder as he says this. 'At my home in Pisa. I travel a lot for my business, *oggetti d'antiquaritato*,' he adds before clarifying, 'antiques, artefacts.'

'Right,' she says and nods with enthusiasm. Her hands are growing cold now as the wind blows at the wetness of her fingers, turning the water frigid.

'By the way,' he says. 'I must discuss the tree with you.'

'Tree?' she asks, turning her head in the direction of the street lined with the old horse chestnuts and sycamores she has always admired. 'Why?'

'No, no. *Scuse*,' he says. 'My tree. In the back. It is getting very large, I think. Too much. I worry about it when I am away so long.'

'Okay,' she says, remembering the laburnum that straddles the boundary fence. She had enjoyed its cheerful yellow blooms when they first moved in but then she had done some research and discovered that its seed pods can be poisonous.

'It is to be cut down. Soon. Better for both of us, I think?' suggests Gianni. 'The roots go too far underground, I am told.' He makes a gesture with his free hand, his fingers splayed. 'Both sides. Me and you! So the tree doctor comes, today. He will need to work your side too. Is okay?' he asks with a raise of his eyebrows, his tanned forehead wrinkling. He smiles encouragingly as if he is doing her a great favour. Iris imagines the tree again, its branches dangling down over the patch of freshly laid turf there. The new seed of the lawn meshing with the old, until they almost appeared the same.

'Oh,' she says again, her voice falling down the word as it slides from her lips, the realisation dawning on her.

'*Alora. Bene*,' he says with a nod, taking her silence as agreement, and he bids her good day as he opens his front door and disappears inside.

She stands, repeating the conversation to herself, trying to understand what has just happened. The wet sponge now feels icy and she looks down to see her hands shaking, whether from cold or the fresh shiver of fear biting into her, she's not entirely sure. Her mind reels; an image of tree roots stretching deep underground, a shallow grave and an absent neighbour who is now very much present.

7

Iris sits at the kitchen table nursing her morning cup of tea and sends up a silent prayer of thanks that she is not working in the shop today. Saturdays can be so hectic and she resents giving up her weekends. Not to mention the fact that they have agreed to go to Laura's Halloween party, or 'gathering' as she is now describing it, tonight. It will mean mingling, talking to random strangers, and fielding questions about what they do for a living, league tables and local politics. At least Ben is at the good school now and she doesn't have to face all those withering looks. But she doesn't want to discuss the house.

Mentioning her new address makes her feel raw and exposed. She thought it would be a triumphant flag she'd wave proudly once they had moved into Riddleston Road but she lives in fear of meeting someone connected with Rosemary. Yet six months down the line and it's like she never existed. Most people raise their eyebrows with mild interest when she mentions the location of the house, but that's all. The old woman was right: there really was no one. And once again Iris feels a pang of guilt before reminding herself that this is exactly why she did the right thing.

Out of nowhere, a grinding buzz starts up in the back garden and she slops her tea in alarm. She lurches to the kitchen window. The cat, omnipresent, can be seen darting across the lawn and into the undergrowth. To the right she can see the overgrown laburnum tree shaking, its branches appearing to tremble with fear. And she finds that her hands also have a tremor to them.

Winding her cardigan tighter around her and shoving her feet into her slippers, she unlocks the back door and tramps outside.

'Hey, hey,' she shouts, waving her hands in the air to attract the attention of the tree surgeon. He is up a ladder with heavy-duty ear protectors clamped to his head. 'Stop! Please!' she continues. He sees her and reluctantly switches off the chainsaw he is wielding, though not before a sizeable limb is lopped from the tree and falls to the ground.

Climbing down the ladder, he pulls the ear protectors from his head and asks in a way that sounds really quite unhelpful, 'Can I help?'

'Is this really necessary?' she says, her arms folded.

The tree surgeon shrugs. 'Just doing my job, love.'

Iris thinks of how Laura had once said how nothing infuriates her more than when people – usually tradesmen – call her love. 'It's just the same for men, only they get "mate",' she had countered. 'Yes,' replied Laura, 'but one is jovial and the other is patronising. There's a difference.'

'You're not taking down the whole thing, are you?' asks Iris, gesturing to the butchered laburnum, which now looks to be listing to one side.

He nods in confirmation.

'But it's a perfectly healthy tree. I could report you. To the council or …' she casts about, 'to Greenpeace.'

A smirk crosses the man's face now and he hoists the chainsaw back into position. 'The owner has every right if the tree is becoming a nuisance. Private property.'

'Right, well you'll have to stay on that side.' She points over the fence. 'I don't want anyone trespassing on my land.'

'I'll need to treat the roots,' he replies in exasperation.

'No chemicals in my garden!' she shouts.

He gives a shake of his head, muttering something about 'bloody hippies' under his breath, and the chainsaw strikes up its ferocious growl again.

Iris looks down at the ground beneath her. Her feet are damp from the dew clinging to the patch of new grass, the freshly laid turf, which appears to be flourishing. She curls her toes and stomps back into the house. Steve is in the kitchen, clearly having witnessed the whole exchange from the window.

'Why are you making such a fuss about the tree?'

Iris spins, rounding on him. 'Don't you start.'

Steve raises his hands in mock surrender. 'Jesus, what's got into you this morning?'

'It's just a shame, don't you think?'

'I thought you said it was dangerous. Poisonous or something?'

Iris lets her shoulders sag. 'Maybe I was overreacting. It's not like Ben's a baby any more.' Steve mumbles something indiscernible and drinks his tea. 'Anyway, trees are supposed to be good for us, aren't they? Lungs of the streets and all that? And I don't like the idea of a load of chemicals leaching into the ground.'

'So why did I go to all that bother getting rid of that stuff growing on the front of the house?'

'That was different,' she says, her back to him as she continues to watch the garden. 'It was damaging the brickwork, overrunning the place.'

'So is that tree,' replies Steve, looking up from his phone. 'Blocking out a lot of light. And it's one thing we haven't had to pay for ourselves. By rights, the landlord should be doing this kind of thing for us.'

Iris tenses. It brings her up short when Steve talks like this, sending a trickle of cold water through her. She thinks of this house as their own now and sometimes she could forget that he doesn't know the truth. It's fine, she thinks, breathing through her nose. It's just while they get Ben safely through school. A few more years and they might move on. And they have right on their side.

She'd looked it up one day on the internet, fingers shaking on the keyboard as she'd typed the words 'What happens to property when someone dies with no family?'. Apparently, if no relations come forward after twelve years, the house would be awarded to the Crown. Which is hardly bloody fair, is it? What about squatters' rights? They are even maintaining the place for future generations. What could possibly be wrong about that?

She turns around to face her husband.

'What are you wearing for Laura's Halloween party tonight?' she asks, changing the subject.

Steve hangs his head and emits a low moan. 'Oh God, do we have to? You know I can't stand those things. Laura is getting worse. And you know I don't really get on with Ivo.'

'We've got to go. I've already accepted. And more importantly, Freddie has invited Ben. It's a chance to make some new friends at the school.'

'For him or us?' says Steve with a cocked eyebrow. He runs his hands across his head, exposing his receding hairline, and Iris moves forward to pull his hair back into place.

'It's fancy dress too, remember?'

'Fuck! No.'

'But Laura will think we've let the side down if we don't make an effort.'

'No, babe, I refuse to jump to that woman's impossible standards.'

'Well, I'm just wearing a black dress and that old witchy hat from years ago,' she says, playing with his hair absentmindedly.

'Easier for women, isn't it?' he says, batting her hand away.

'Why don't you wear your old Alice Cooper T-shirt and some jeans then? Laura won't mind. She's always had a soft spot for you.'

Steve frowns. 'Don't be daft.' But then he smiles. 'Okay, I'll dig it out, just this once.'

That night, the three of them huddle together against the cold as they walk the short distance to Laura's house a few streets away. Ben is quiet and morose, notes Iris, but then when isn't he these days? He is dressed in a white T-shirt and tracksuit bottoms, his hoodie drawn up around his head and a *Scream* mask in his hand, ready to don before they arrive.

As they approach Laura's porch, it's clear that she's gone all out this year. A ridiculous amount of carved pumpkins, their triangular eyes and jagged mouths illuminated from within, are positioned on the steps leading up to the front door. As Iris lifts the heavy brass knocker and allows it to fall, she eyes the wreath; all expensive, artfully arranged corn, grass and dried berries. She remembers now how Laura had texted her last month to wish her a 'happy autumn equinox' and she feels her eyes roll back involuntarily.

But when her friend opens the door, Iris can't help but feel a rush of genuine warmth. The house is lit in a pink, rosy glow and the smell of caramelised sugar and meat juices greets them, immediately setting her mouth to watering.

'Oh thank God!' says Laura, throwing her arms around Iris's shoulders. 'Normal people at last.' She breathes the last words into her ear and laughs her wicked, cackling laugh. 'Come in, come in,' she beckons. 'Hey, Ben, good to see you, honey!'

Iris looks around to see that her son is now wearing the mask. She whispers to him, 'You can take that off whenever you like, you know.' But he merely nods silently and Iris has to banish the eerie feeling it gives her.

'Guys, you're welcome to try the mulled cider if you like but there's also beer, wine, whatever you fancy.'

'Beer, thanks,' says Steve.

'Is there a bottle of red open?' asks Iris. 'I'll just have a small one.'

Laura takes their coats, admiring their outfits. 'Look at you two!' she drawls.

Iris and Steve, in turn, both take in Laura's lithe, lissom form in a fitted catsuit, complete with ears and tail. Predictably, Steve says nothing but continues to gawp, mouth open.

'You look amazing,' says Iris.

'Oh, thanks. God knows how I'm going to get to the loo in this thing.'

An hour later, Iris finds herself stationed next to the kitchen island, glass of wine in hand and a tight smile plastered to her face. Steve is chatting to a man who has bonded with him over a shared love of IPA and the salty snacks. His phone beeps a notification, and she watches him as he reads a message, and then pockets it again. Meanwhile, Ben has disappeared down into the basement to join Freddie and the others. Earlier, when Iris had hovered at the top of the staircase, she could hear the raucous sounds of laughter below, a TV blaring, the crack and fizz of cans being opened and something about ordering in pizza. She had reached into her handbag to check again that she'd packed Ben's inhaler and EpiPen as well as antihistamines; the touch of these things reassuring to her fingertips.

Looking about Laura's kitchen now, she admires the tasteful cabinets and industrial-style lighting. She wonders where Laura's husband, Ivo, is and then hears him before she sees him. He is officiating over some large basin filled with water and apples in the lounge. It is all very loud and macho to Iris's ears and she wonders why some men never seem to give up the desire to compete and compare. He is wearing a devilish costume that lends itself well to his dark curly hair and rakish goatee beard. She inclines her head further to look and confirm that yes, he is in fact holding a stopwatch and is recording scores on a blackboard.

She doesn't recognise any of the other guests, she realises. Iris had hoped there might be one or two parents from the boys' old primary school (not that she had ever really got to know many of them other than Laura), but it all seems to be new acquaintances, unfamiliar faces.

'Hi, I'm Sarah-Jane.'

Iris turns around to see a tall blonde woman, inexplicably dressed as an angel, with her hand thrust out. She's always a little flummoxed when people offer to shake hands; the physical touch of a stranger. She is also trying to process two names at once. Double-barrels make her nervous, especially when she is expected to remember them.

'Hello, I'm Iris,' she manages in response and takes a large slug of her wine, which will, appropriately for the occasion, be staining her teeth black.

'Great kitchen, isn't it?' Sarah-Jane gestures with her wine glass around the room. 'I think they used Tavistock & Jones.'

Iris raises her eyebrows in feigned interest but is none the wiser. Instead, she nods appreciatively and runs her hand along the work surface for effect.

'It's so important, don't you think? To personalise your home, go bespoke. We used the same company for our kitchen, my husband wouldn't consider anywhere else.' She laughs as though the alternative would be ludicrous. There is a pause in the conversation where Iris realises she is meant to reciprocate but her knowledge is limited and she already needs the toilet.

'Do you know where the bathroom is?' she asks.

'Oh, I think there's a cloak somewhere on the ground floor. Or one at the top of the stairs, I believe.'

Iris thanks her, and moves in the direction of the hallway, wondering why this stranger seems to be more intimately acquainted with her friend's house than she is, but then she reflects that it has been a long time since she accepted an invitation to Laura's, especially since they moved.

Inside the downstairs loo, she bolts the door and sinks down onto the toilet gratefully, hanging her head between her legs and breathing deeply. She wonders how long she can legitimately stay in here before someone else needs to use it. Emptying her bladder, she cranes her neck round and examines the walls. They are covered with photographs of Laura and Ivo over the years; rowing at university, throwing mortar boards into the air, in black tie and a ball gown, their hands clutching champagne coupes and cigarettes. Further up – tucked away discreetly, but still visible – are framed copies of their university degrees; Laura's first from Oxford, Ivo's law certificates.

Iris has noticed this before, the humble, shambolic display of achievement by the upper middle classes. It doesn't make sense to her. Why hide it away in a cubby hole, as though it's a slight embarrassment? As though it is nothing. When really, Iris thinks, it is everything.

Standing up, she flushes the toilet and washes her hands, breathing in the floral perfume of the soap, drying her hands on the Moroccan hammam-style towel. Glancing in the mirror, she realises her gothic 'smoky eye' make-up is disappearing down her cheeks and into her crow's feet. She licks a finger and wipes away at her face. Her straight mousey hair is tied back in a low ponytail, a few strands pulled down to frame her face underneath the cheap nylon witch's hat. Whoever invented fancy dress deserves to be shot, she thinks. At least the black dress and opaque tights are both warm and slimming and lend themselves well to her black knee-high boots. Steeling herself, she takes a deep breath. She can hear shouts on the other side of the door. Someone announces that the meat is ready. She wonders what Ben will be eating. He knows he has to be careful around food.

As she steps out into the hallway, a couple of people walk past carrying a portable karaoke machine and her heart sinks a little further. Tentatively, she sticks her head into the lounge where a few guests are sitting about on Laura's enormous squashy sofas. A silent version of the *Rocky Horror Picture Show* is projected onto the far wall, but no one seems to be watching it. Instead, a huddle of parents is standing around discussing the pros and cons of tracker mortgages and high interest savings accounts.

Iris turns away in disgust, acidic bile rising in her throat. Perhaps she needs to eat, to soak up the wine. She tracks back to the kitchen where a woman appears to be helping herself to something inside Laura's fridge and a man, complete with unravelling toilet-roll outfit, is pouring a large packet of peanuts into a bowl he has just taken from a cupboard.

Iris feels herself bristle.

'Excuse me, hi, sorry.' She leans towards him. 'I don't know if Laura and Ivo mentioned this but my son has a nut allergy.'

The man stares at her for a second, dumbfounded.

'So tell him not to eat these then?' he says eventually.

'The thing is, it's not that simple. Sometimes, just being around an open packet of nuts can set off an attack.'

The man looks around him. 'I don't even see any kids. Where is he, then?'

Iris tries to keep her voice low and measured. 'Downstairs, with his friends. But I'd just like to be on the safe side.'

The man laughs. 'Are you for real?'

'Please. This isn't a joke. These could make him seriously ill,' she says, gesturing to the bowl in front of her.

'But I'm doing the high protein, low-carb thing. That's why I brought these especially.'

It is Iris's turn to stare at him now, her mouth working while no words seem to formulate. Instead, she grabs the bowl of nuts and looks about the kitchen, trying to guess behind which cupboard door the bin is invisibly disguised.

'Fuck's sake,' she hears the man say behind her. 'We've got a live one here, lads.'

In the end, Iris gives up and chucks the nuts and the bowl into the nearby sink before she spins around, shouting 'wanker' in the man's general direction. A loud cheer goes up in the lounge and she can't help feeling that everyone is laughing at her.

Her cheeks are flaming red now, her face flushed from the wine and the heat of the kitchen. She looks around for Steve but he is nowhere to be seen so she marches down the hallway to find her coat. Her eyes are stinging, whether it is from the thick kohl of her make-up or the brink of tears, and blindly she barrels straight into Laura's arms.

'Hey, hey. Iris. It's me. What's up? You're not leaving already are you? I was just about to serve the pulled pork in brioche rolls.'

She stares into Laura's wide, clear, perfectly made-up eyes. Why is her friend always so calm, unflustered? Immaculately in control of every situation. And that's when she hears it. The sound of her son, Ben, downstairs. Something is wrong, she knows it.

8

Laura checks her make-up in the mirror on the upper landing. Her cheeks look a little flushed. There is a sparkle to her eyes, her hair a little mussed. But to anyone else she looks ever the perfect hostess. She leans in and corrects a couple of smudges around her mouth, smooths her hands down her waist and turns to inspect her silhouette. She can hear the sound of Ivo and his friends chanting in the lounge, can smell the pork, about to turn the wrong side of caramelised and burned. Was this costume a mistake, she wonders, unsure if she can really get away with it.

Straightening her seams, repositioning her feline ears, she hears another voice above the general noise. It is Iris. She recognises her peculiar blend of forthright emotion, teetering somewhere between fury and tears, as she seems to be most of the time these days. And then the word 'wanker' – loud enough to carry clearly up to the next floor.

As Laura hurries down to the bottom of the stairs she is just in time to catch Iris in her embrace. She sees the tracks of tears running down her friend's face, ruining the ill-advised make-up, her eyes red and sore within the ashen pallor of her skin.

'Iris, you're trembling.'

'No, I'm not,' she replies. 'I'm just fucking furious. How long, Laura?'

'What?'

'How long are you going to keep this up?'

Laura feels her heart beat a little faster, her conscience sending up a flare of panic as she clings tight to her friend's arms. She searches the bloodshot eyes for clues.

'What do you mean?'

'This.' Iris signals behind her with a tilt of her head. 'These people.'

'Oh, I see,' breathes Laura, her relief palpable. 'I know, one or two are a bit much, aren't they? But it's more for Freddie's sake. We're just trying to help him settle in to the new school, y'know. Feel a bit more a part of the community. Besides, some of them are okay when you get to know them.'

Iris opens her mouth, about to say something when the sound of a choked, gargled groan can be heard emanating from the floor below.

'That sounded like Ben.'

'I expect it was just the movie. They're watching a horror film.'

'Have you checked on them recently, Laura?'

'They're fine. We can just leave them to it these days.'

Iris breaks free of Laura's clutches and moves back along the hallway to stand at the top of the stairs leading down to the basement.

'Ben,' she calls out speculatively.

At this, Freddie responds from below.

'Mum?'

Something about his tone makes Laura catch Iris's eye.

'Everything okay?' she shouts, keeping her voice cheery, light-hearted.

There is a pause and another louder, more insistent groan can be heard. Laura watches as Iris launches herself down the staircase and then follows on behind her. In the basement, the flashing party lights she had erected earlier continue to pulsate in the dark. The movie plays across the flat-screen TV although someone has now turned down the volume. Freddie and the others are standing in a semi-circle, their backs turned, but they quickly part to reveal Ben, kneeling on the floor. It looks like a glass has been spilled and a dark pool of liquid has soaked into the carpet.

Iris crouches down in front of her son and gently calls his name. Laura sees her slowly lift up his head. He is still wearing the mask and as Iris whisks it away, there is the remains of vomit on his chin and the front of his T-shirt. Laura turns to Freddie and the other boys.

'What happened?'

No one answers. Their faces only register embarrassment, mild shock, distaste.

'Freddie?'

'I don't know, Mum. He seemed fine. He was just sitting on the sofa, watching the movie.'

'What has he eaten?' asks Iris. 'Ben, what is it, love? What's wrong?'

'He didn't eat anything,' replies Freddie. 'He just had a glass of Coke.'

'Have you little shits put something in his drink?' shouts Iris.

'Hang on a minute,' says Laura. 'I don't think—'

'No, of course not,' says Freddie. 'One minute we were playing a game of Truth or Dare. It was just a bit of fun but then Ben got all weird and threw up.'

'Freddie,' scolds Laura.

Iris slowly raises Ben to his feet. 'He's shaking. Ben, do you need anything? Your pen? Can you breathe, love?'

'It doesn't look like a normal attack,' says Laura. 'Maybe he's just got a bug or something?'

Iris looks at her with contempt. 'Nothing about Ben's condition is normal. You know that, Laura.'

'You can say that again,' mutters one of the boys from within their close huddle and another one sniggers.

'Right, everyone upstairs, now!' says Laura. 'Freddie, bring me some kitchen roll while you're up there.'

The boys trudge upstairs in single file, heads bent.

'Iris, I'm so sorry. I don't understand what happened. You know I'm always careful around Ben.'

'Not careful enough, obviously,' she replies and leads Ben upstairs. 'Come on, darling. Let's get you home.'

Freddie passes them on the stairs on his way back down.

'Sorry, Mrs S. Can you ask Ben to message me when he's feeling better?'

But Iris doesn't answer, just moves past him, stony-faced. Laura gives him an encouraging smile and mouths 'don't worry' as she takes the kitchen roll from him. Tearing off handfuls of paper, she begins to mop up the spillage. It is only when she tidies up the piles of wet tissues that she realises they are, in fact, soaked with urine. Leaning back on her haunches, she recoils with disgust and then her shoulders sag as she contemplates the events of the evening, hanging her head in shame. There is a distinct smell of burned meat.

9

Iris puts her head around the door of Ben's bedroom and contents herself that he is sleeping soundly. She has decided to let him stay in bed today, just until she's certain he's not in any danger. It appears that he was only suffering from some kind of twenty-four-hour thing but he still seems tired and washed out, turning his face away from the porridge she had made him this morning. He isn't even reading any books or watching TV but lying on his side, curled inward like a nautilus shell. When she tries to ask him what happened at the party, he merely shakes his head and says he doesn't want to talk about it.

She tiptoes into the room, careful not to disturb him, and sits on the side of the bed watching him breathe. As she runs a hand over his hair, smoothing it across his forehead – an action she is now denied when he is awake – she notes the steady rise and fall of his chest as she did when he was a newborn and then as a sickly toddler. But his cheek is cool, his breathing regular. There is no reason to fear. She thinks of all those years when she would find him hot and sticky, his pulse racing like a trapped bird in his chest. The telltale signs, when the hollows would appear beneath his ribs as he desperately tried to suck the oxygen into his lungs. Another blue-light run, as she sat in the ambulance with him, holding his hand as they hurtled through the night.

But everything is all right now, she assures herself. Ben has grown stronger in recent years. As long as he keeps his inhaler at hand and avoids certain stressful situations, the obvious foods and allergens. That's why she's determined to keep that cat out of the house, just to be on the safe side. But she is also worried about mould spores and ancient plaster. Ideally, she would have liked to strip Ben's bedroom to the bare bones and start from scratch but as usual, budget wouldn't allow. So she's had to be content with painting over the original woodchip wallpaper, which is no doubt holding the whole place together.

Leaning over, she gently opens the window; just enough to let in some fresh air but not too much to create a draught. Ben sleeps on, oblivious to her presence.

After she leaves his room, she finds herself wandering upstairs, trailing her hand along the balustrade as it spirals upwards, her thoughts winding and coiling in tandem. The previous evening at Laura's party has left her feeling bruised, the memory of events rising in her every now and then to cause fresh slices of anger, embarrassment, confusion. She had texted Steve on the way home to tell him they had left, that Ben was unwell. He had arrived home an hour later, red in the face and penitent, saying he had lost track of time taking part in Ivo's games. When he had left for work this morning she had barely returned his kiss, feeling angry with him though she's not sure why.

Iris comes to stand outside the door to the attic room on the top floor of the house. It has become a convenient storage room for junk since they moved in, filled with cardboard boxes they have yet to unpack. The light is grey and spectral up here, filtering through the small skylight, which hasn't been cleaned in many years. She had taken little notice of this room at first, directing the removals company to carry boxes up here, knowing they contained non-essentials, mainly old toys and clothes of Ben's that she can't bring herself to part with.

But as she stands here now, she contemplates the space again. The whole attic is boarded out. Exposed wooden beams, like the ribs of the house, bracket either end of the room and the walls are papered in the same ugly Anaglypta that Iris and Steve have assiduously painted over elsewhere in the house. As she picks her way through, she moves to the small window that looks down on the back garden.

The original curtains remain, now cloaked in dust and blanched by the sunlight. Iris reaches out a hand to finger the cloth, a thick damask covered in pale roses that now feels brittle with age. At the movement of the curtain, a moth falls from within the folds of the fabric and lands on the windowsill leaving a smut of silvery powder. She flicks it away to the floor in disgust and then leans closer to run her finger along the wooden casement. A graffiti of scratched markings is etched into the wood. The initials R and J, carved in varying upper and lower case iterations. The R must stand for Rosemary she thinks. But who or what does the J stand for? Did Rosemary have a special friend? Was J a lover?

Iris continues to trace her finger over these scars, mouthing the initials to herself. She turns back to the room and sees it anew, this cosy nest in the eaves of the house. In her mind's eye she can imagine it clearly, all those years ago: a small fire glowing in the grate, soft lamplight, a dressing table with a matching embroidered vanity set, a wardrobe of clothes, a narrow wooden bed with a matching coverlet, over which more roses spill and spread. Did Rosemary spend hours lying on that bed or sitting in front of her looking glass, dreaming of this person, J?

As she moves to leave, something small and luminescent catches her eye. She stoops down and runs her hand along the cracks of the ancient boards. It is a jewel, a pearl earring, lost to the dusty crevices over time. She picks it up, like a deep sea diver claiming it from the depths. It's a real one, she thinks, running the lustrous white orb through her fingers. The clasp is original too; she recognises the fine old gold. She holds it up to the light, imagining the ear from which it last hung so long ago. It must have belonged to Rosemary, she thinks. And yet again, a shiver runs through her and she must hurry to vacate the room, slamming the door behind her, as if there is a presence at her back she must outrun.

IO

The winter sun has flooded the shop today, turning the wooden floorboards to a golden gleam, illuminating the rails of clothes like jewels. Iris smiles at the customer in front of her who passes her a silk dress. It rustles and fusses under her hands as she attempts to arrange it into a neat shape but the fabric swims between her fingers, resisting capture. Finally, it is wrested between two sheets of tissue paper, folded into a parcel and secured with a small, chic sticker.

The customer thanks her as she takes the paper bag, the transaction seamless, as though she has just picked up a loaf of bread and a pint of milk from the corner shop rather than a frippery costing more than some people make in a week. Iris waves a goodbye. The boutique is empty once again. She moves around to the other side of the counter and tidies a table, rearranging a small vase of flowers, tucking a price tag discreetly out of view. The cost of things is not always a subject to be discussed in this rarified atmosphere; the clothes, the beautiful leather accessories, the finely wrought jewellery is not to be cheapened with the vulgarity of pounds and pence.

Reaching into her pocket, she steals a quick look at her phone, though mobiles are not strictly permitted on the shop floor. But she needs to be contactable at all times, in case of an emergency. Really, she has been in a state of alert ever since Ben was born, in some way or another. Perhaps it has become a part of her now, hardwired into her synapses like the tendrils of a plant that has grown into her brain. Though she would just call it common or garden maternal instinct, of course.

As she looks down, a furrow asserts itself into her brow, resting easily there among the well-worn creases of concern. She has missed a call from school. A voicemail message has been left. She jabs a finger at the screen, listening intently, ignoring the customer who has drifted into the shop. It is the head of year, asking her to come in to school this afternoon, if possible, to discuss an issue involving her son. Nothing to worry about, the voice assures her, Ben is quite safe and well. Iris listens to the message one more time and then puts the phone away. If only that were true, she thinks.

As Iris arrives at the wrought iron gates of Toppingham, she looks up at the high stone facade. She remembers reading somewhere that it was built in the Victorian era and originally intended as a hospital or an asylum, though it latterly became a boys' school in the 1920s, broadening its remit to include girls in the Fifties. Nowadays its traditional architecture is seen as charming and collegiate, the pupils all smartly dressed in the requisite blazer and scarf in the school's colours of maroon and grey. These traditions, upheld with sports like hockey and rugby and activities such as choir and debating, are tempered with the latest technology. A state of the art security system means that no one can enter or leave the grounds without a pass and Iris hovers near to an intercom system beside the school gate, waiting to be buzzed in by reception.

But once she is inside, it is like the years fall away. The same smell of rubber, sweat, pencil sharpenings, disinfectant. And she is a teenager herself; shy, awkward, walking with stooped shoulders, hiding behind her fringe. The feeling of never quite belonging, of not being good enough, engulfs her. She clutches her bag to her side as if it is the same cheap plastic one she had as a schoolgirl, unable to compete with the expensive branded rucksacks of her peers. She looks to her shoes and expects to see the scuffed brogues in need of repair. Her mouth even feels acrid at the thought of all the lunchtimes eating her packed lunch locked in a toilet cubicle, until someone would invariably bang on the door or throw something over the side.

She looks up to see the head of year, a Mrs Khan, is waiting for her in the vestibule and instantly feels the flush of panic, as if she is in trouble or has done something wrong. But the teacher flashes a broad smile of straight white teeth and ushers Iris to a nearby office.

'Sit down.' She signals to a chair opposite her desk. 'It's good to meet you finally. I know we haven't really had chance to talk since Ben started with us.'

'Yes, sorry, my husband works away a lot and …'

Mrs Khan smiles and shakes her head. Her thick black hair, threaded with grey, falls back into a neat bob.

'Really. Not a problem. Some parents need more input than others. Some feel that no news is good news. My door's always open though.' She gestures with her hands wide. 'Metaphorically speaking,' she qualifies.

'Does that mean this is bad news then?' asks Iris.

'No, no, not bad.' The teacher smiles, although she gives a little sigh as she says this. 'It's just that Ben seems to have had a difficult day.'

'Difficult?' Iris sits up straighter. 'In what way?'

'Nothing to worry about,' says Mrs Khan, holding up a creased palm in assurance. 'Apparently, he didn't have the correct equipment for his PE lesson. There was some altercation between himself and another boy. Ben accused him of hiding, or possibly stealing, his rugby boots. A misunderstanding, I'm sure. But when some spare boots were produced for Ben to use, he point-blank refused to wear them and became quite distressed about the idea of continuing with the lesson.'

'He's never been keen on outdoor pursuits,' explains Iris.

'Sure, and we are aware of his health issues. But we have many asthmatics at the school who are able to participate fully in the range of activities we offer.'

'I think it's a bit more complicated than that,' begins Iris, before wishing she hadn't said anything. She hates anyone to think of Ben as just an issue to be managed.

'How so?' asks the teacher, inclining her head.

'Well, I mean that it's not just about his asthma.'

'Go on.'

Iris is losing patience with this conversation. Shouldn't it be the teacher who is informing her, giving her answers? She asked for this meeting, after all.

'Ben's a bit of a loner, prefers doing things on his own rather than taking part in team sports.'

Mrs Khan nods her head vigorously. 'Absolutely, not everyone is a joiner-inner although we do expect all students to contribute in some way.' She casts a glance over a computer screen in front of her. 'I understand Ben has been doing quite well in some of his subjects; English, art for example. But it's been noted that he hasn't made many new friends.'

'Well, there's Freddie Peters. They've been friends since they were both at primary school together.'

'And yet they don't seem to be as close any more.'

Iris frowns at this and then remembers the Halloween party. Perhaps it is true that Freddie and her son have been drifting apart lately.

'Does Ben have anyone else he can confide in?' asks Mrs. Khan.

'Well, myself and his dad. He knows he can always talk to us,' says Iris defensively.

'And has he? Confided in you recently, I mean?'

Iris crosses her arms and leans back in her chair. This woman is really annoying her now. But perhaps she has a point. Ben doesn't talk to her as much as he used to do, she admits.

'I only ask because Ben became quite upset with me today. I brought him in for a private chat after his PE lesson and he admitted that he hasn't been sleeping well, suffering from bad dreams, nightmares even. I understand that you moved house earlier this year? Perhaps Ben has found it more unsettling than you realised. It's common for parents to underestimate the emotional upheaval in amongst all the physical admin that comes with such a big life event.'

'I'm fully aware of all that, thank you,' says Iris.

'Good, good. I imagined you would be but I just thought I'd raise it with you. Such things can be an indication of other underlying problems. Could anything else be worrying or troubling Ben?'

'I don't think so. He seems very happy with the new house, is enjoying having a new, larger bedroom.'

'Right. Of course from a purely practical point of view, young people need their sleep. We always advise parents to ensure pupils are getting eight hours a night.'

'I'll speak to Ben. Thanks for letting me know,' says Iris, gathering her coat and bag, bringing the meeting to an end.

Mrs Khan opens her office door and Iris steps out, wishing to absent herself from the place as soon as possible. This school may be a good one, but underneath it they all look and sound, smell and feel the same way. The glass cabinet stuffed with shiny silver trophies. The photographs on the wall, from which the smug faces of a head girl and boy beam. She knows this woman is trying to be nice, to do her job, but she clearly doesn't know or understand Ben at all. No one does. Not like her. How could they?

She watches as a caretaker, an older man with snowy white hair, pushes a large broom along the polished floor. He looks up briefly as Iris and the teacher stand out in the corridor.

'Thanks again for coming in,' says Mrs Khan holding out her hand. 'Did you move far, by the way?'

Iris turns her gaze back to the woman's face and the outstretched hand. 'No, not really. Over from the other side of town. We're just around the corner now, so it's much handier for school.'

'Yes, that's right; Riddleston Road. I thought I remembered as much from Ben's file. Lovely street. You must have taken the old house that needed fixing up. It's looking so much better already.'

'Yes,' says Iris, wrong-footed. She never feels very comfortable talking about this. 'Thanks,' she adds. 'We like a project.'

'Well, I'm sure you'll be very happy there. Do get in touch if you'd like to discuss anything at all with me. And we'll keep an eye out for those missing boots.'

'Oh right, yes, thanks again.'

Mrs Khan releases her hand finally and Iris walks down the corridor, remembering to leave her temporary ID pass on the reception desk, though all of the staff have disappeared. It is so dark, now that the clocks have gone back, and she pulls her jacket tighter around her before she steps through the automatic doors.

'Goodnight,' she hears a low voice call to her.

Turning round, Iris looks for Mrs Khan but the corridor is empty. Only the old caretaker remains and he looks up at her now, holding her gaze for what seems like just a beat too long before he looks back down at the floor he is cleaning.

'Goodnight,' says Iris and walks out into the early evening.

11

Laura sits at the breakfast bar, her laptop open in front of her. She is editing the photos from a previous job, spooling through image after image of a happy-looking young couple from an engagement shoot. She pauses on one that pictures the two figures turned to each other, their eyes locked, their smiles fond. Fine details jump out as though through a magnifying glass; the bright hard sparkle of a diamond ring, the delicate drops of rain trimming the umbrella, brought forward in sharp relief against the blurred fuzz of foliage in the background.

She gives a low moan of satisfaction.

'You sound pleased with yourself.' Ivo is leaning against the kitchen counter, drinking coffee. 'Want one?' he adds, indicating the coffee machine beside him; all shiny chrome and levers.

Laura frowns. 'Actually, no, thanks. I won't. I'm trying to cut back on the caffeine.' She lifts her eyes from the laptop. 'A herbal tea would be nice though?'

Ivo rolls his muscular shoulders into an appropriation of a shrug.

'Suit yourself. But you know that stuff is full of crap too. Sweepings from the factory floor, no doubt.'

'Yeah, but it doesn't make my heart race.'

He scalds a teabag from the instant hot water tap and places the mug next to her, kissing the top of her head.

'I could do something about that, you know,' he murmurs suggestively.

'Sorry, busy. I need to finish this before tonight. The clients are coming round for a quick look-see after work this evening. Speaking of which, could you get dinner on the go for me while I'm tied up?'

He gives an exaggerated swing of his head. 'No can do. Rugby tonight with the lads, remember? Anyway, can't you just email it over to them? Isn't that the whole point of modern technology?'

'It's all about the personal touch, Ivo. I want to talk them through the final selection, see their reactions. Besides, this is my favourite bit.'

'Hah! You just like showing off.' He circles his index finger in mid-air and taps the end of her nose. 'I know your game, little Miss Fancy Pants.'

'Bugger off if you're not going to be any use,' she says, more harshly than she intends.

Ivo takes a brisk look at his watch and downs the last of his coffee. 'I'd better head. See you later on tonight.' He plants another kiss on the side of her head, the smell of his coffee breath too close to her nose.

'Bye,' she calls without looking up and then immediately feels bad once he's gone.

Focusing on her work, her eyes are drawn again to the images of the engaged couple; the tenderness in their faces, that look she so often sees in the eyes of young people at the start of their lives together. She zooms in further. What is it that she sees? Love? Lust? She used to mistake it as such and think it must be so. But now she thinks differently. Instead she sees a misplaced certainty in life and each other. The assuredness that everything will always be wonderful.

Two hours later and Laura leans back in her chair, stretches her arms above her head and blinks to rest her eyes for a moment. She stands up and reaches for the table to steady herself, her vision suddenly blurring and swimming. What she needs is some fresh air, a walk to clear her head. She can get so easily lost in an edit when she's in the zone, ignoring the clock, her stomach empty. She shoulders on her puffa coat – a walking duvet that insulates her from the windswept streets – and pockets her mobile and keys. A quick look in the hall mirror makes her recoil. She looks tired, drawn, her skin parched from central heating and too many beige carbs. She's been missing meals recently, snacking on toast when she remembers. Perhaps a facial appointment might be in order soon, and a spa day. She makes a mental note to add spinach or some other leafy greens to the regular grocery order.

Walking through town, the cold making her cheeks and chest burn, Laura feels better. She decides to take a detour past the boutique where Iris works. They haven't seen each other since the Halloween party, the flurry of texts she had sent to her friend since had been curtly rebuffed with confirmation that yes, she is okay, Ben is okay, everything is okay. But clearly, things are far from it. And she can't help thinking that it's her fault.

Was she wrong to encourage them to try for Toppingham? Perhaps Ben just isn't cut out for a place like that. Whereas Freddie is flourishing. Could she do more to encourage them to spend time together? And she still feels terrible for what happened at the party. She should have been downstairs with Iris or checking on the boys but she was upstairs, otherwise engaged. She pushes this thought to one side, swallowing as though she needs to rid herself of a nasty taste in her mouth.

The boutique glows with a yellow luminosity on this dour day as the afternoon gives way to the gloom of evening. A festive display of fir tree branches and dried orange pomanders is arranged artfully in the window, illuminated with strings of tiny firefly lights, which reflect back at Laura as she presses her nose to the glass. Inside, she smells the rich scent of aromatic candles, filling the space with cardamom and cloves.

'Hi, is Iris working today?' she asks as a shop assistant looks up.

'Sorry, no. She's already finished for the day,' comes the reply.

Laura chides herself for forgetting. Iris has told her enough times, but then it can often change at the last minute due to sickness or holiday absences (something her friend has often bemoaned) and Laura reminds herself yet again how lucky she is to be her own boss. Oh well, she might as well have a look around while she's here.

She turns her attention to the clothing rails. It is sweater weather, after all. She takes a couple of items into the changing room. She has time. And anyway, it will save Ivo the trouble of trying to find her a Christmas present this year, only for her to return it after Boxing Day for something more suitable. She unsheathes herself from her polo neck and flings it onto the wooden stool.

She still looks a little wan and pasty in the mirror but she puts this down to the harsh overhead lighting. Why is it always so unflattering, even in an expensive place like this? Probably been designed by a bloke. But as she pulls the jumper on over her head it clings to her chest, tight around her back and under her armpits. She feels straitjacketed suddenly, in the confines of this flimsy square space with its cream linen curtain and woven matting. The size must be coming up small, she thinks. Discarding it on the stool, she stands to consider herself in the mirror again. Something has changed. Her breasts have a curve to them that wasn't there before, they tingle with a new sense of themselves. She's never been particularly blessed in that department – Ivo has always reassured her that 'more than a handful's a waste' – but still, they've never been the same since she had Freddie.

She turns to the side and cups herself, shocked by the feeling of tenderness. For a moment she revels in this new quality. She feels inexplicably excited but doesn't understand why. She picks up her clothes, begins to pull them back on. It's just that time of the month, she reasons, the result of the last few weeks. Too much bread and sugar. But then she turns again, looks herself directly in the eye; a shiver of a secret she whispers with her second self staring back at her. There is an unspoken truth, shared with her reflective twin, who looks knowingly before the other turns away, hauling back the curtain.

'Sorry, they're not quite right for me,' she calls loftily to the shop assistant who eyes her expectantly. 'I've just left them in there.'

'That's fine, we can take care of that for you.'

Laura looks back to the mirror, the cubicle, the sweater she has shed like an unwanted skin and she smiles, though the words feel strangely like a taunt. She hurries out of the shop; the glittering trinkets have lost their allure, the musky festive smell of Christmas threatening to pull a headache to the front of her temples.

12

At the dinner table, Iris sits opposite Ben and studies him. His hair, the colour of dirty straw, stands up in small tufts, his soft brown eyes directed towards his plate. He shovels food in at speed and she smiles at his ravenous appetite. It is impossible to fill him up at the moment. Yet he always looks so thin. She considers his gracile frame, delicate wrists, the long fingers she always imagined would make him a gifted pianist. But when she tries to pose a question to him, his mouth is full and he answers only with a muted nod or a shake of the head.

'Leave him alone, will you?' says Steve. 'Always with the third degree.'

Ben pushes his chair back, plate cleared. 'I'm going to finish my homework,' he mumbles.

Iris turns round in her chair, watches him leave. 'Ben, love,' she calls. 'Why don't you ask Freddie round for tea tomorrow? I haven't seen him in such a long time.' Her son pauses on the threshold. The hunch of his shoulders, the way he lifts his chin, alerts her. She knows something is wrong. 'You two haven't had a falling-out, have you?'

'Just leave it, Mum,' he calls as he bounds up the stairs, two at a time.

She turns back towards Steve who gives her a 'told you so' look.

'I heard from Laura the other day.'

'And?' he says, helping himself to seconds.

'Apparently, she's enrolled Freddie in some after-school clubs.'

Steve raises his eyebrows but says nothing.

'Do you think Ben—'

'No.' Steve cuts her off with a sigh.

'She mentioned some other mums,' Iris continues regardless. 'You know, parents from school. They all go to a yoga class together.' She leans over and picks up a piece of lettuce from the salad bowl, chews on it ruminatively. 'This is the start. They won't want to know us soon.'

Steve slams his cutlery together with finality and stands, gathering up the plates to take them to the sink.

'Do you have any idea how mad you sound sometimes?'

Later, Iris decides to clean the hallway. It is one of her favourite household chores because she gets to admire the original Victorian tiling; its colours and patterns becoming kaleidoscopic beneath her feet as she moves the mop from place to place. At least she can still take pleasure in this house, a bubble of pride popping in her when she walks down the street now.

She and Steve have always rented. Their landlords were pretty hands-off, especially when there was a leak or a patch of damp to sort out. She dreads to think how much money they've wasted over the years, and that's just on rent. They've also decorated from top to bottom, replaced kitchen units and even had new carpets put down – the alternative was just too depressing. She couldn't possibly live with the idea of other people's dirt. But more than that, it was the temporary feeling that always bothered her. The knowledge that they were just lodgers, passing through, no matter how long they stayed. When a house doesn't belong to you, how can you ever feel like you truly belong to it? But this time it's different, she thinks. This house is theirs. No one can take it away from them.

She comes to a halt outside the door to the lounge. They call it the lounge but she can't help thinking of it still as Rosemary's front room. When all of their stuff was moved across, she'd asked the removals company to put the sofa in here along with the TV and a few other pieces of furniture. But they rarely sit together as a family.

Ben prefers to do his homework or game in his room, using a proliferation of devices. Steve mainly comes in here to watch some sport or catch the news. Iris finds herself keeping to the kitchen; by far the warmer, cosier room, where she cooks, cleans, listens to the radio or sits scrolling through her phone. As a result, they haven't got around to decorating this room yet and it still has more than a whiff of Rosemary about it, not just in the carpet (which Iris keeps threatening to rip up when she has a spare weekend) but also in the wallpaper, the very air which permeates the room.

Loitering on the threshold, she tells herself that she is being silly and opens the door as though she is barging in like an unwelcome guest. But the room is empty. There are no ghosts in here, she tells herself. Only those that she will allow and she stands in front of the fireplace, hands on hips, her feet firmly planted in a defiant stance.

But then she thinks back to that day, finding Rosemary in the street. The sequence of events that spun out afterwards like a skein of wool unravelling beyond her grasp. She looks down, picturing the scene again in her mind's eye, how Rosemary died in this very room. Though she has arranged their furniture in a different configuration, the indentations from Rosemary's arm-chair can still be seen in the carpet. The floral wallpaper still envelops the room, bearing witness.

'Have you seen my holdall?'

Steve stands silhouetted in the doorway, fresh from the shower. His skin is pink, his tattoos standing out like livid brands on his stocky frame. She looks up, caught off guard, holding the mop like a weapon. Frowning, she brushes the hair from her face with a rubber-gloved hand.

'In the wardrobe.'

She waits to see if there is any further response but he merely nods and tracks back upstairs towards the bedroom. He is always quiet, grumpy even, before a trip. He will be away next week, driving a heavy goods vehicle the length and breadth of the country. It's a solitary job, hard on him. He hates to be away from his family, she thinks. Otherwise he wouldn't be like this.

When they first got together, they must have been one of the last couples to meet the old-fashioned way; bumping into each other in a bar rather than through online dating. She shudders to think how she would ever find another partner these days (not that she wants anyone but him).

Steve was away so often, it might as well have been a long-distance relationship, though they lived in the same town. But she liked the way they would talk for hours on the phone in the evenings as she kept him company on his long journeys.

And their reunions were particularly febrile, the absence adding to the intensity when he returned home. By the time they moved in with each other, Ben was already on the way and they married one rainy Saturday afternoon in a registry office, with a couple of random strangers for witnesses.

It wasn't until they had been living together a few months that Iris had realised the full extent of Steve's debts; a weakness for gambling online to pass the time when away, a couple of bad investments in cars that had turned out to be write-offs. But it was just about manageable. Like her credit card bills. She has always used them to plug the gaps in her finances, so that she can buy those little extras to make the place look nice. And she had needed to buy a lot of new stuff when she was expecting. Kids are so expensive. Besides, she couldn't stomach the idea of second-hand or eBay. But they're no different to most people. And it's all under control. Just about.

Iris looks about the front room again, brought back to the moment, her eyes raking the floral wallpaper. She thinks of Rosemary in her chair; unresponsive, dead. Did that really happen? Did she actually do those things? Bury a body in the garden and take the house for herself? It had all seemed so clear, so rational to her during those brief, dark hours of night. But here she is, living in Rosemary's house, faced with the reality of what she did, day after day. And now she can't tell anyone without incriminating herself or others. What would the police say, if she tried to explain? No one would ever understand.

So she stays silent. But the thought makes her scrub harder, to shine the kitchen taps brighter, turning the argument over in her head. Sooner or later, Rosemary would have been discovered. The house would have been sold. To whom? A wealthy middle-class couple like Laura and Ivo? Or a landlord, who would have developed it and charged a small fortune. The thought makes her grit her teeth as she wrestles with the hoover, vacuuming over and over the same patch of carpet that never seems to come clean, no matter how hard she tries.

She loves this house, she tells herself. She has anointed these walls, these floors with her own blood, sweat and tears. She deserves this. And she's prepared to do anything for her family. Besides, it's not like the place could have been passed on to anyone else. Rosemary had no other relatives. There is no one.

13

Laura sits on the edge of the toilet seat and quietly contemplates the gleam of the metro tiling around her, the feel of the Persian rug beneath her bare feet. In place of the usual one-size-fits-all bathroom suite, the space is furnished with foxed vintage mirrors and antique furniture ingeniously upcycled into a wash-basin stand. A chalky navy blue paint adorns the walls and a dressing gown made from recycled Indian saris hangs on the back of the door.

Laura allows herself a moment of silent congratulation as she surveys all this but it is no use, she can't be distracted for long. She has to look. The suspense is killing her. She snatches up the plastic stick she has just peed on and studies it. It has been so long since she last did this she can hardly remember how and has to read the instructions on the pack through twice. In the past she had been disappointed so many times until at last she just stopped hoping, expecting or trying. And Ivo seemed to readily accept this fate too. They had Freddie, they had each other. They were lucky, they were happy. Best not to rock the boat or want for more when they were already so fortunate. But there is no denying the incontrovertible truth. She is pregnant.

She stands and zips up her jeans, washes her hands at the sink. She considers herself in the mirror: could this be the face of a new mother? Really? At her age? Can she actually do this? She reaches for her phone and dials. She can't hold it in, she has to tell someone.

'Hi, it's me,' she says. 'Can you talk?'

'Sure, hang on,' comes the reply. 'Let me go somewhere quieter. Everything all right?'

'Not sure, depends how you look at it.' She laughs but she can hear the nervous energy in her own voice, unable to tell if it is excitement or fear.

'What's up?' he demands.

She takes a breath. 'I'm pregnant. I've just done a test. I've been feeling odd for a while and thought I'd just rule it out but ...'

'What? How? I mean, I thought ...' His voice trails off.

'That I was well past all that? Yeah, me too.'

There is a shocked silence that draws out so long she has to fill it.

'Look, I'm sorry to spring this on you when you're working. We can talk about it another time. I just wanted to give you a heads-up.'

'Right, okay. Yeah. Don't worry. We'll figure it out.'

She rings off and pushes the phone into her back pocket. She takes another breath and unlocks the bathroom door. As she descends the stairs, her hand grips the banister more tightly, as though her life depends upon it. She places her feet mindfully on each tread. With her other hand she feels under her sweater for the small round of her belly, still taut and honed from all the yoga and Pilates sessions. Her fingers long to sense the trace of a heartbeat, the flutter of a moth's wings under the surface. She is pregnant. She is having a baby.

Downstairs, there are the usual signs of life in the kitchen. The radio has been left on, having segued from news and politics to weather and now a programme about sheep farming. The dishwasher is churning and thumping and sloshing away to itself, reaching the end of its cycle.

And as she walks into the kitchen, she sees Ivo and Freddie sitting at the dining table playing a game of battleships, heads down, focused on blowing each other to smithereens. It is a slow, lazy Saturday after all. Where else would they all be? Ivo looks up, distracted from the game.

'Any idea what's for lunch? We're famished.'

Laura looks from her husband to her son. The two loves of her life. How could she have done this to them? To her perfect little family?

14

When the knock at the door comes, Iris has a load of fish fingers under the grill and is stirring a pan of baked beans on the stove; their sticky gloop rendered silky by a knob of added butter. Today's tea is sponsored by the colour orange. She looks at the clock on the wall. Who would be banging on the door at half past six on a Monday night? Ben has been home from school for ages and it's unlikely to be any friends calling for him. Even Steve is home in good time tonight, having worked most of the weekend.

These are all the things that flit across her mind as she listens to the sizzle of the grill, stirs the beans in a mesmeric figure of eight. Perhaps if she just ignores it, the person will go away. It's probably some time-waster anyway, canvassing or leafletting. But a louder knock reverberates through the house, echoing in the cavernous tiled hallway.

'Are you going to get that?' Steve shouts from the upstairs bathroom. Great, she thinks. Now whoever it is will definitely know there's someone in. She turns off the grill and moves the pan of beans to the back of the hob. Switching on the light in the hallway, wiping her hands on a snatched tea towel, she moves slowly to open the front door, hoping to delay further.

When she peers around the door she sees an elderly man standing on the step. He is wearing an anorak zipped up against the cold, his grey slacks billowing in the wind. His cheeks are pink and he has a small drip on the end of his nose. He rocks back and forth as if to encourage himself and when he sees Iris he claps his gloved hands together in a dull thump.

'Hello. I thought I had the right house,' he says.

Iris feels a small shiver run through the length of her but puts it down to the biting chill that is licking around her ankles. She does not open the door wide, ostensibly not to let in a draught, but she feels safer keeping the bulk of the wood between herself and this stranger, like a shield.

'Can I help?' she asks. There's still every chance this could be some kind of cold-caller or door-to-door salesman. Although, to look at him, he doesn't seem the type. Perhaps he's raising money for a local cause; a hospice, church roof, Xmas lights; it's amazing how many handouts everyone expects these days. As if she and Steve have the spare cash to donate to every sob story. But then Iris looks closer. There's something about his face, his white hair, the cadence of his voice that seems familiar. Where has she seen him before? And just like a coin that spirals down through the runnels of her brain before slotting into place, she remembers.

'I'm the caretaker at Toppingham,' says the man. 'Apologies for the unsociable call. I just thought I'd drop these round on my way home.' He lifts a plastic bag by his feet and hands it over to Iris. She hesitates a fraction and then takes the bag. Inside is a pair of brand-new rugby boots, albeit a little muddy.

'I found them behind one of the hedges in the car park. Don't know how they ended up there. Still, I thought your son, Ben, might be keen to get them back.'

'How do you know my son's name?'

The old man's expression turns from one of bonhomie to a slight frown.

'It's written inside his boots, Mrs Simmonds.'

Iris looks inside the shoes to verify this before staring back at the caretaker.

'How do you know where we live?'

'Well, school records, of course. And besides, you were discussing it with Mrs Khan, the same day she asked me to keep an eye out for the missing boots.'

Iris wavers for a moment. She knows she can often seem rude to people, a little prone to paranoia at times. Perhaps this man is just old-school and is genuinely trying to be helpful.

'That's kind of you, thanks. But couldn't you have just put them in the lost property department or left them with Ben's form tutor? Surely, that's the normal way of things.'

The man squares his shoulders, takes a swipe at the drip on his nose and sniffs.

'Well, I just thought Ben might need them for his next PE lesson. Don't want him getting a detention now, do we? We wouldn't want anyone getting into trouble now.'

Iris catches his eye when he says this and he holds her gaze for a moment longer than is necessary. It is the exact same way he looked at her that evening at the school. It gives her the same unsettling feeling now as it did then.

'Please,' she says. 'Stop using my son's name like that. You don't know him. You don't know anything about us. I could report this to the school.'

The man shoots her a surprised look and Iris feels herself shrink further back behind the door. He begins to rock back and forth on his heels again, a faint smile playing around his lips. His gaze travels up above the porch to take in the rest of the house.

'I used to know the previous owner of this house, as it happens. The one before you and your family moved in,' he says, as if to clarify. There is something about the way he lingers on the words 'moved in'. Iris feels herself tense, gripping the door frame to steady herself.

'Oh really?' she enquires. 'We didn't really have any—'

'Rosemary,' he cuts her off. 'Rosemary Parker.'

Iris nods, smiling, her eyebrows raised in mock interest.

'She was here for donkey's years, the whole family had lived here for a long time. We all grew up together. I went to school with her, back in the day. 'Course we all knew the Parkers, especially after what happened with her older sister, June. Quite the scandal. The family never really got over it.'

Iris feels a strange buzzing in her ears, as though she has been temporarily deafened by a loud bang or a high-pitched squeal. Her mind veers, trying to keep up with the man's laborious, chatty voice.

'Did you say a sister?' she asks in a small voice now, finding it difficult to speak.

'Yes. An unmarried mother. Nobody knew who the father was and she wouldn't say.' He holds up a hand and laughs. 'Oh, I know it doesn't seem like much nowadays, happens all the time and no one bats an eyelid. But it was the talk of the town back then. The Parkers were a very well-to-do family, you see. Turned poor June out on her ear. Cut her off without a penny.'

Iris nods her head automatically, frames her face into one of concerned sympathy when a thought occurs to her.

'Do you know what happened to them? June and her baby?'

He pauses for a moment, as though weighing something up. A cloud crosses his face and he frowns.

'No. And her sister, Rosie, wasn't for telling anyone either. She closed herself off from everyone after that.'

Iris tries to smile but her face freezes, her jaw contracting. So Rosemary lied to her. She did have family, after all. A sibling, as well as a niece or a nephew, both of whom could still be alive today.

'Anyway, I must be going,' he says. 'I've to get home for my tea. It's bitter tonight. Take care, Mrs Simmonds, and tell your boy to look after his boots in future.' He turns to leave before Iris can make any further reply but as he latches the gate, he holds her gaze once more and gives her a knowing nod.

She closes the door and leans her body against the other side, feeling the hard wooden grooves through her palms, her spine, her skull.

'Fuck!' she says under her breath and the sound escapes her lips like a long low moan.

She stays like this for a moment longer, thinking about fish fingers and sisters, the smell of baked beans, sweet and sickly. She runs an imagined calendar through her head, trying to estimate the birth dates of Rosemary, June, her offspring. What became of them? How old would they be now?

She pushes herself away from the door, grasping at the bag containing the rugby boots, and runs upstairs. She doesn't pause to knock or wait for a response but walks directly into her son's bedroom. Ben is hunched at his desk in the corner of the room, a gaming headset wrapped around his face while his hands move instinctively on a joystick as though it is an extension of his body.

At first he doesn't seem to be aware of her presence, he is so immersed in the virtual world he inhabits. She stands behind him, speaking his name without acknowledgement, until she must touch a hand softly to his shoulder. He jerks around, yanking the headset away as though he has been branded.

'I'm in the middle of a game,' he says.

'I know,' she replies reasonably, 'but I need to speak to you.'

He looks at her with reproach as though she has done something disgusting; fouled on the carpet, say, or removed her clothes.

'I can't just break off in the middle of a game. You know that. I'll be penalised.'

Iris looks at her son. At the pouchy shadows under his eyes. Her hand moves instinctively to stroke his cheek, to smooth his hair, but she stops herself as she must always do nowadays.

'You look tired,' she says. 'Are you getting enough sleep?'

'I'm fine,' he answers.

But you're not, she thinks. Your teacher told me you're having nightmares. Why could you tell her that and not me? 'Is something wrong? At school,' she blurts out instead. 'I mean, something we should know about?'

Ben looks at her astonished; fury and confusion waging a war across his face.

'What are you talking about?'

'It's just the other night, you were talking in your sleep …'

He looks back towards his computer screen in desperation and then, resigned to the loss of the game, his shoulders slump.

'Mum, what are you going on about?'

'Please, you would tell me if …'

'Why were you nosing around my room while I was asleep?'

'Never mind, it doesn't matter,' she says. 'Tea will be ready in ten minutes or so.' And then as an afterthought, she dumps the plastic bag by his feet. 'Rugby boots.'

An expression of guilt passes over Ben's face briefly before it is replaced with anger again and he turns back to his computer.

15

Pulling her scarf closer to her neck, Iris shrinks into the depths of her coat. The footpaths are glittery with frost this morning where the weak December sunshine hasn't yet reached them. She feels her feet skitter on the icy surface, her world tilting for a moment. She reaches a hand out, wishing for something stable to anchor herself against. If only she was wearing her hiking boots with their thick lugs instead of these thin-soled court shoes which are deemed appropriate for the shop.

Gripping her insulated coffee mug for warmth, she tries to walk as fast as she can without falling. She doesn't want to be late for work. Her manager has had to warn her about timekeeping recently and there was also an uncomfortable discussion about her general disposition. Apparently, she isn't as cheerful and smiley with customers as she should be.

She enters the warm, perfumed atmosphere of the shop. The sound of choral music plays in the background, adding to the beatific nature of the store. She says hello to a fellow colleague and makes her way downstairs. It always amuses Iris, the difference between the public and private face of things, the fantasy versus the reality. It is like turning over a beautiful tapestry and finding a chaos of messy knots.

In the staff room, dirty mugs sit in the washing-up bowl and the sink looks blocked again. She resists the urge to clean. This is not her problem. She has enough of her own to sort out. Studying the staff noticeboard, she sees the rotas have been updated and she notes that she has been put down to work Christmas Eve and

Boxing Day again, even though she has reiterated many times that she would prefer to be at home with her son. But then as Steve keeps pointing out to her, he's not a baby any more.

There is also a message on the board announcing this year's Christmas party, which will be held at a local restaurant, with an accompanying menu tacked beside it. Iris runs her eyes down the prices and winces. Oh and look, some bright spark has also suggested Secret Santa again. Why oh why must she waste £10 on buying something pointless and crap for someone she doesn't really know, only to receive something equally rubbish in return? She heaves a sigh and takes off her coat. Iris would much prefer to stay downstairs out of sight in the stockroom, where she can methodically fold and hang clothes in silence. Instead, she walks upstairs and rearranges her face into a smile.

'Oh, Iris. You're here, great,' says her colleague over by the till. Iris is not sure of her name. So many members of staff wash in and out of this place like flotsam. 'Can you watch the shop floor,' asks the woman, 'while I sort out an order downstairs?'

Iris nods in agreement. She casts a look at her wristwatch and calculates the hours that need to elapse before she can leave again, the credit card bill she can pay off when the wages land in her account.

The bell over the door tinkles. An elderly woman has entered the shop. She is smartly dressed and carries herself well, in spite of her rounded shoulders and shuffling gait. Iris watches her as she takes a cursory glance around the store and then begins to move towards her.

'Beautiful things,' says the woman and smiles.

'Yes,' agrees Iris and then forces herself to ask, 'Are you interested in anything in particular?'

The woman's face brightens.

'I wonder if you could give me some advice, my dear. I'm looking for something smart, not too bright. A dress, perhaps.

And it needs to be warm, long sleeves.' She gestures up and down the length of her arm.

'Right,' says Iris. 'I'm sure I can find you a few things to try. Would you like to take a seat in the changing room and I can bring you a selection?'

'Wonderful.' The woman smiles and looks relieved at the thought of sitting down.

Iris busies herself sifting through the rails, picking out a range of muted dresses, warm woollen plaids or rich velvety silks, and a couple of longer skirts with matching jackets. Discreetly, she passes the clothes into the cubicle and the woman thanks her.

'Let me know if you need anything else,' says Iris and picks up a dusting cloth again. After a small amount of shuffling and sighing from beyond the curtain, Iris hears the woman call out.

'Are you there, dear?' the voice warbles.

Iris hovers by the cubicle. 'Can I help?'

When there is no answer, Iris draws back the curtain and finds the woman with her arms in the air, head covered, caught within the restrictive binds of a dress bodice.

'Oh,' she says. 'I think there's a zip somewhere. Let me try.' After a little pulling and pushing the dress is removed. The woman sits in her nylon slip, her neatly styled hair now in disarray. Her shoulders slope in resignation. Iris sees that her legs are swollen and embroidered with spider veins.

'I hate shopping,' says the woman with a wobble in her voice, 'And it used to be such a pleasure when I was a young slim thing like you.'

Iris doesn't know what to say. To agree would seem unfeeling and yet there is something used up and spent about this woman. But Iris watches as the woman dips into her handbag and pulls a comb through her hair, squares her shoulders as she looks in the mirror. Iris wishes she would cover herself up. She takes a cashmere scarf from the shelf behind her and arranges it around the woman's shoulders.

'Thank you, my dear. You are kind,' says the woman who looks at the pile of clothes around her and sighs. 'I can't give up. I must find something. The funeral's on Friday and I can't let her down. She was my oldest friend.'

Iris sees with alarm that the old woman's eyes are filling with tears.

'Who was?' Iris says with suspicion, her voice rising to an accusatory level. 'Who are you referring to?' The old woman looks bewildered, her eyes still glassy with unshed tears. 'What exactly are you trying to say?' Iris demands to know.

The woman's mouth opens in shock as she tries to formulate a response but Iris finds she cannot hear the answer. Perhaps it is the close confines of the cubicle, her proximity to this stranger or the fact she had rushed to work this morning without having any breakfast, but all she can hear is a persistent ringing in her ears again. That same feeling of the ground shifting beneath her feet. She puts a hand out towards the wall but grasps at thin air. Her fingers find a length of thick cloth; the changing room curtain. Iris feels herself falling, her weight bearing down as the curtain rings strain and pop, one by one, from their fastenings.

16

Laura steps out of the house engulfed in her duvet coat. Her feet are snug in her sheepskin-lined boots and her head is insulated against the cold by a pair of plush earmuffs. She is impervious to the weather, the sounds of the market traders as they shout and bang, erecting this year's Christmas stalls. She will not think about the mini catastrophe that is swirling within her. Just for now, she wants to enjoy the feeling of being pregnant. Besides, guilt and regret are wasted emotions as far as she's concerned.

And as she strides along, she feels the pulsing of her blood, imagines the opening and closing of her ventricles as her heart struggles to process all of this extra stuff. She thinks of the other heart inside her, its small but perfectly formed muscle pushing and pulling beside her own. If indeed it is beating. It is impossible to know how far gone she is, if she is truly pregnant.

After taking the test, she had booked an appointment to see her usual doctor. He knows her medical background, her fertility problems. There was no way she was doing this on the NHS. The last time she had been to her local GP, the experience had been nightmarish, waiting weeks for an appointment, delays, harried staff.

So instead she's gone private, as much for the comfort factor as the confidentiality. She wants to keep this to herself for now, until she's worked out what she's dealing with and how to proceed. As she checks her watch, she notes she has plenty of time so she slows her pace a little and tries to breathe steadily. She is calm. She is in control.

She thinks back to the shoot she has been editing, the way she had stared at her computer screen, lingering on certain details more than usual. The wispy hair on the baby's head. The dimples in her pudgy hands like fingerprints left in a freshly made pie. How could she forget how miraculous a baby's eyelashes could be?

Laura's hand moves to her midriff again as she continues to walk. She told herself she wouldn't think this way. Not until she had decided what to do. There are significant risks at her age, after all. Or what if it's a phantom pregnancy? Some strange, bizarre symptom of perimenopause? Her cycle has always been so unpredictable, so unfathomable. What if the baby doesn't make it? And that's before she even allows herself to contemplate other issues like paternity. She closes her eyes briefly, bites down on this thought. Deep down, she already knows who the father is. She and Ivo haven't had sex for quite some time now. But still she continues, walking with purpose. She will not allow anything to pierce this bubble of happiness.

She sits down in the consulting room and the doctor asks her to confirm her name, date of birth, first line of address. She rattles them off with ease as though it is an exam for which she's revised. She wants to get all the answers right today.

'And when was the date of your last menstruation?'

She falters, her smile fading. She's never been very good at plotting her cycle. Her period had always been so infrequent when she was younger, something for which she felt grateful when all her friends were moaning about the curse and not being able to go swimming on holiday.

'But how can you not know,' a friend had asked her once, incredulously, as though such information should be indelibly printed on a person's mind, like a telephone number or a horoscope. And once a boyfriend had been shocked at its sudden arrival one Saturday morning, his barely concealed disgust at the browning stains on the bedsheets.

Conceiving Freddie had felt like a happy accident but when she failed to fall pregnant again, she had become a rapt student, reading every book on ovulation and fertility, marking her digital calendar with a red balloon emoji. Yet, in recent years, sightings of her period had become even rarer.

'Well, that's the thing, I'm not exactly sure,' she replies.

The doctor nods at her, before checking her age briefly on his computer screen.

'Can you say roughly, approximately?'

Laura casts her mind back, which has promptly gone blank under the scrutiny.

'I think it must have been a few months ago. Maybe longer?' she guesses. 'I'm sorry, I didn't make a note of it.'

The doctor writes something down then. 'So, forgive me, Mrs Peters, but what makes you think you could be pregnant now, given your age and fertility issues in the past?'

Patiently, she explains her symptoms and the positive pregnancy test.

'And you weren't using any form of contraception?'

Laura colours at this, despite herself. 'I, we, didn't think I could get pregnant any more.'

The doctor raises his eyebrows at this but says nothing, tapping out more notes into his computer. 'Well,' he says eventually. 'Most at-home pregnancy tests are very accurate these days so we must assume this result is correct. But in your case, your age and situation—'

'What do you mean. My situation?' she asks.

The doctor looks away, back to the screen. 'I only meant that at your age, you are technically viewed as a geriatric mother and with that comes other possible difficulties.'

Laura is stung. The word 'geriatric' is like a physical slap. Her mind automatically turns to images of grey hair, walking frames, wrinkles. It suggests her womb is wizened with age, her eggs are past their best before date. She feels actual tears lance her eyes but blinks them back furiously while the doctor looks suitably abashed.

'Look, you're an otherwise fit and healthy woman. There's no reason to think you're not capable of having a perfectly normal pregnancy. But I think it might be a good idea to book in a dating scan as soon as possible. Perhaps run some tests. Work out where we are, so to speak.'

'Yes,' she says, swallowing. 'So, I'm really pregnant then? I still can't believe it after all the failed attempts over the years.'

'It is unusual,' agrees the doctor, 'but not impossible. Whatever problems you and your husband have had in the past, it is plausible that some factor has changed. It only takes one,' he says with a grin.

Laura returns the doctor's well-meaning smile but cannot hold his gaze for long.

'I'm just very nervous about it all,' she says truthfully.

'That's understandable.' He nods. 'Why don't you jump up,' he says, patting the nearby examination couch. 'Let's see if we can hear baby's heartbeat.'

Laura lies down, her feet tearing the thin white paper. She pulls up her sweater and shivers. The doctor busies himself with a machine that looks ludicrously arcane. Slowly, he moves the pestle-shaped device around Laura's abdomen, at first gently and then more insistently, staring into the middle distance, at the wall, above Laura's head. An eerie static hiss issues from the microphone. Time seems to stretch out like an elastic spool as they both listen and wait.

Together, she and this stranger search. They plumb a deep dark ocean. They drift through space, listening for signs of life.

The doctor presses down harder, prospecting. He trawls Laura's body, before moving to another area. Nothing. The machine is mute, it refuses to talk.

Laura realises she has been holding her breath for too long. Her jaw, clamped tightly, is beginning to ache. She feels herself flush with embarrassment. She has got it all wrong. How stupid of her. She has failed again. An involuntary prickle stings her eyes. A membrane of tears is beginning to form and must not be allowed to break. She swallows once and then again. Then the doctor moves to the other side, the machine deployed once more with renewed stoicism.

It pitches briefly across the planes of her flesh before it stops, sensing something. At first shallow and indeterminate, it is an echo across space and time, becoming stronger, more insistent. It is surprisingly fast and yet reassuringly steady; a tattoo beaten out against taut skin. Laura gasps; the surface tension is finally pierced, the tears come, and with them the knowledge that she wants this baby. She wants it more than anything.

17

Iris forces herself to remain still, to drink her tea, even though it is heavily sugared. She left work early after her 'funny turn'. That's what she's calling it, anyway. Her manager explained that she had fainted and banged her head and to be fair, there is a bruise emerging on her right cheekbone which aches if she tries to smile. Not that she's smiling, of course.

It had been such a shock, so embarrassing to wake up on the shop floor of all places, with so many faces staring at her. The old woman in the changing room looked appalled. Another member of staff brought her a glass of water and asked her several stupid questions, like what did she have for breakfast, whether she was ready for Christmas, what was Steve's telephone number. She realises now they were trying to ascertain whether she was concussed rather than making conversation.

She had promised to get a check-up at the GP or pop down to A & E to have a once-over, but she knows she won't bother. She's fine. Besides, she'll only have to wait hours just to be told what she already knows. She is perfectly okay. Just a little hypoglycaemic. Perhaps a bit stressed. Maybe it's her age, her hormones playing up. She's read somewhere that there's a long list of symptoms to look forward to from dizzy spells to panic attacks, night sweats, anger and tearfulness. Which pretty much encapsulates her emotional and physical state for as long as she can remember now. So whatever it is, she guesses it's just normal.

Finishing her tea, Iris stands and does what she always does in situations such as this. She cleans. Dragging the hoover around like a ball and chain, she starts on the ground floor and works her way upwards. She only did it yesterday but it won't hurt to give the floors another going-over. What's the point of having a beautiful house if she can't make every nook sparkle, every surface shine?

She is on the stairs when she first notices it. Cat hair, she's certain of it. Small tufts, gossamer-light. It rises up, escaping her fingers like smoke when she reaches out to grasp at it. She fingers the stray hairs in her palm, examining them; the same brindle colour of Rosemary's cat, she's sure. She scrambles up the stairs on her hands and knees looking in every tread, in every corner. She runs her hand between the banisters and finds more of the same colour.

How is this possible? She has cleaned this house from top to bottom ever since they moved in, having blocked up the cat flap immediately. She was so careful to try and eliminate any dander that might have been left behind, deep cleaning the carpets, sucking up any residue. In truth, Ben hasn't shown any signs of an allergic reaction. She would be the first to notice if his eyes were red and swollen or his breathing strained.

She swears softly under her breath. How has that bloody cat got inside the house? The windows are never left wide enough to allow an animal to gain entrance, especially in winter. And Steve and Ben are just as vigilant as she is. They would never let it in. She continues to prowl around the house, eyes alert, nose trained for any unusual smells or signs of life. Finally, she reaches the top landing and the attic. Iris hasn't set foot inside this room for some time. She even had a mind to ask Steve to put a lock on the door but she knows he would have questioned her reasons.

Taking a breath, she reaches for the handle and turns it, sensing resistance. But then she is inside. Again, it feels like she is intruding. Bursting in on the fading strains of a conversation cut off in mid flow. The room seems to expand and contract for a moment, as if it is inhaling and exhaling or perhaps merely sighing at the interruption.

On first appearance, it all looks the same as ever; the spare furniture covered in dust sheets, rendering the shapes indistinguishable in the half-light of midwinter. One piece is left uncovered though; an old sofa bed which has a broken slat and a stained cushion. Iris had kept hold of it but then decided it looked out of place in the grandeur of Riddleston Road. And so it was shoved up here until they decided what to do with it. Its dust sheet has been flung aside, she sees, and not replaced. As though whoever used it last had been in a rush, hastily vacating the room. Iris moves to lift the paint-speckled sheet from the floor, holding it up, searching it for clues and then she hugs it to her chest.

She puts a hand up to her temple and presses the tender skin there, works her jaw a little to test the pain. Closing her eyes, she tries to block out everything for a moment, feels herself sway slightly as she reaches out a hand to steady herself. When she opens her eyes again they come to rest on a small saucer tucked away beside the sofa.

Kneeling down, she puts her face towards the dish and sniffs. There is a thin puddle of white liquid in its centre; milk. She dips a finger, hesitating and then tastes it to confirm. Fresh milk. She stands, still staring at the saucer, compelling her brain to make sense of it all when a sound, several floors below, catches her attention.

She lifts her head, responding to the call, and moves to the door. At the top of the house, on the uppermost stair, she pauses, nerves straining, listening and then it comes again. It is a shiver of a sound, a whispering tinkle that carries up every flight to reach her; a bell. The kind of bell that hangs from a cat's collar, to alert innocent birds that danger is present.

Iris launches herself down the stairs, stumbling, tripping, hanging on to the banister like it's a rope thrown to her across a roiling sea. She follows the tinkling notes of the bell until she is on the ground floor. The sound of it is louder and then quieter, evading her senses as she turns her head left and right, trying to orient herself. Breath coming hard now in shallow pants, her limbs convulsing with contained adrenaline, she stands in the hallway. It can't be in the house. She's just hearing things, surely.

She looks to the front door and yanks it open, hoping to find the moggy stalking the garden. But instead, she sees a man standing at the gate, looking up at the house, as though he is inspecting the brickwork, trying to understand what has changed. He is wearing a white shirt and chinos underneath his dark mac and carries a leather briefcase in his hand.

Before she can slam the door closed, he catches her eye and raises a hand in a gesture of acknowledgement. Iris can't avoid it now. Still, she backs away into the hall.

'Hello?' she hears the man's friendly tone call to her.

She moves to close the door but she can see him walking up the front path now.

'Hello there? Could I have a word?'

Iris feels herself shrink. Why can't people just leave her alone? She peers around the door.

'Hi, I hope you don't mind. I was just wondering …' He smiles but he appears confused, nervous even. 'The old lady, who used to live here. Rosemary. Is she around?'

Iris takes in the conventional dress, the lanyard hanging around the man's neck, the briefcase he has set down by his feet and her stomach lurches. This guy looks worryingly offi-cious. The type who would investigate a missing person, an unreported death.

'Why?' she asks and immediately hears the defensive note in her voice.

'I'm just checking in really,' he says. 'Haven't seen Rosemary for a while and, well, I thought she lived alone actually.'

'I'm a relative,' says Iris, the words bubbling up and out of her before she can stop them.

The man frowns, a cloud of doubt crossing his face as he studies the ground and then looks back to Iris. He continues to smile but she can see he is wary.

'Really?' He glances at his briefcase, perhaps considering some case file or other in there. 'That's not ... I didn't think she had ... a relative, you say?' he asks.

'Yes, she's my mother-in-law,' mumbles Iris, wincing inwardly. She wishes she could just get rid of him.

'Right,' he says, drawing out the word in a way that suggests he is unsure. 'And, I'm sorry, have you moved in with Rosemary? Are you living here now?'

Iris swallows, nodding, unable to trust her voice.

The man turns his blue eyes to her again, runs a hand through his hair which is flecked with grey. Iris tries to read his lanyard but it is concealed beneath the lapels of his coat.

'Would it be possible to have a quick word with Rosemary?'

'Oh, no, sorry. She's asleep. She's not been feeling well recently.'

'Is that right?' the man asks, his eyebrows raised in enquiry.

'Nothing to worry about. We can take care of her now.'

At this, the gate clangs behind them and both Iris and the man turn to look as Ben walks up the path, shifting his school bag on his shoulder.

'Hello, sweetheart,' calls Iris, elated by the distraction. 'My son,' she adds to the man.

'I see. So you've moved in as a family,' he says, clarifying.

Iris purses her lips before answering, ushering Ben into the house. She would prefer for him not to be a party to this conversation. 'That's correct,' she says eventually. 'Look, I really need to go now. I have things to be getting on with.'

'Tricky age,' he says, nodding towards Ben. 'I see he goes to the local school. Toppingham, is it?'

Iris refuses to confirm or deny this. She would really like this stranger to stop asking questions now. But the man merely nods to himself in confirmation, as though he has already come to some conclusion of his own.

'Well, thanks for the update,' he says briskly. 'I, er, hope Rosemary is feeling better soon.'

'Thanks,' says Iris, already manoeuvring herself into the house and closing the door in his face as he is still mouthing the words 'goodbye, then'.

She slumps down onto the bottom stair, her knees weak. She holds her head in her hands, chanting softly to herself.

'Shit, shit, shit, shit, shit.'

Bloody social services, she thinks, poking their noses in. Why can't they catch some real criminals? Sort out some real problems. She sighs. Maybe he'll just update his files and the paperwork will get forgotten about. It takes ages for any of these things to filter through anyway. They're all so stretched and underfunded. Rosemary is just a needle in a haystack to them. But then, if that's true, why was he calling round? And more importantly, when will he be back? She rakes her fingers through her hair, scratching furiously at her scalp, which is beginning to flake and bleed. She turns to see Ben standing in the hallway. He looks at her, shoulders sagging. She recognises that look in his eyes, the same one she has seen present in Steve's face. It is worry, pity, a question; what the hell is wrong with you now?

18

Laura watches through the bay window as Ivo brings the large fir tree up the garden path. He carries the thickest part of the trunk on his shoulder, all burly lumberjack in his checked shirt and jeans, thick gloves and fur trapper hat. Behind him, Freddie has hold of the other end, taking up the strain. They have done this since their son was little and it is one of Laura's favourite things about the time of year. Although, Freddie seems less and less inclined, as though the activity has become deeply uncool nowadays.

She whips out her phone and snaps away. There is a carousel of similar images, stored in iCloud, one from each year, when she has captured this scene for posterity. Every time, Freddie gets a little taller and Ivo looks a bit more dishevelled. She runs to open the front door for them and flings it wide.

The boys tramp inside like victorious hunter-gatherers, although really they have just driven a few miles to the nearest Christmas tree farm, pointed to the largest, bushiest specimen and loaded it into the back of the Range Rover. To see their red-cheeked faces, you'd think they had spent the morning hacking it down by hand. But Laura claps her hands together with glee as they squeeze the tree through the front door, dropping pine needles through the house.

'Oh, it's beautiful,' she says as Ivo plants it like a flag in the centre of the room. 'Smell that,' she adds, and inhales deeply. 'Gets me every time.'

Once the tree is secured in place, Laura sets about unboxing her extensive collection of ornaments while Ivo untangles the tree lights. He curses softly to himself.

'Why do we always leave this job to the following year?'

'Because we are disorganised people,' she says with a laugh. 'And because life's too short to worry about these things.'

'That's because it's never you who has to do it.'

'I decorate. I style. I prettify,' she says, lifting an elaborate crystal bauble from its tissue-paper nest and placing it on an upper branch.

'Wait, don't start until I've got the bloody lights on. For God's sake, woman. Always jumping the gun!'

'I can't help it, I'm sorry.'

Ivo curses again, running a hand through his black curls. They are threaded with more steel each year, Laura notices, sticking up in tufts like wire wool.

'Think of it as a mindfulness exercise,' she teases. 'Try to be a bit more Zen. Who was it that said you can tell a lot about a person by the way they handle a rainy day, lost luggage and tangled fairy lights?'

'I don't mind the rain, actually.'

'Nor me,' she replies with a smile. 'Of course I'd be fucking furious if anyone lost my luggage.'

She turns to open another box. 'Oh, look. Freddie's first Christmas bauble,' she says wistfully. 'And look, remember this one he made at nursery?'

'He'd be mortified by that stuff now.'

Ivo stands, holding aloft a string of white lights. 'Plug that in, would you?' he says, nodding towards the end of the wire.

Laura remains sitting on the floor, reaching for one tree decoration after another, as though each one were a happy memory that falls into her head, swiftly to be replaced by another and another.

'Babe,' prompts Ivo.

She looks up and stares into his face.

'Do you ever wish we'd had another baby?' she blurts, the question coming out of nowhere.

He returns her gaze, his shoulders dropping.

'Of course I do,' he answers softly, his voice wary somehow. 'But it wasn't to be.' He blows out a huff of air. 'Besides, can't you remember how hard it was in those early days? All that crying, the sleep deprivation. No bloody fear!' He nods again towards the end of the lights and Laura crawls on hands and knees to plug them into the socket. Ivo's arms are instantly illuminated as though he is a shop sign, switched from off to on.

'Hey, hey,' he says with a grin. 'I think we're in business.'

She looks at him and smiles, bringing her hands to her face in delight. As her fingers graze her ears, she softly strokes her empty lobes and frowns. A while ago now she had discovered that one of her earrings was missing, having fallen out at some point. It was a precious pair as well, an heirloom. Antique pearls passed down to her from her grandmother. She had tried to retrace her steps, think back to who she was with, what she was doing, but to no avail. And in that moment, once again, she is reminded that she has lost something that can never be replaced.

19

'Would you mind going up to the attic and bringing down the tree?' Iris loiters on the bottom step calling up the stairs, hoping her voice will carry.

'Did you say something?' replies Steve sticking his head over the banister.

'The tree. Could you bring it down when you're next going up to the attic? I thought it was about time we dragged this place into Christmas!'

'Sure,' he says from the upper landing.

'Oh and by the way,' she adds as an afterthought. 'Do you know if Ben has been using the attic recently?'

'Using it?' parrots Steve.

She hates it when he does this; answering every question with a question.

'You know, going up there, hanging out. I can't think why, but I noticed that someone had moved the dust sheet off the sofa bed and not replaced it. I thought maybe he'd gone up there to look for something?'

There is a pause as Steve, still leaning over the banister, seems to search the wall for an answer.

'What would he be looking for?'

Iris sighs. Sometimes she could happily strangle her husband. 'I don't know, do I? That's why I'm asking you.'

He pauses again, eyes moving from side to side as though the conversation has completely lost him. 'Have you tried asking him?'

'No, I don't want him to think I'm checking up on him. He's already so prickly with me these days.'

Another silence.

'So, do you want me to go and get the tree then?'

'Yes,' she hisses with emphasis. 'Please.'

Steve's head bobs back around the banister and she can hear him sigh as he trudges away but then he stops as though something has just occurred to him and he calls back down to her one last time.

'By the way, I like the flowers. Very festive!'

'Sorry?' she replies, tired of straining her voice now. 'Look, why don't you just come downstairs?'

Steve returns to the top of the landing. 'You just asked me to go up,' he says in exasperation.

'What flowers are you talking about then?'

'The ones on the front step. I thought it was a wreath for the door. I can put it up if you like? When I've finished bringing down the tree.'

Iris frowns at him and gives her head a little shake that suggests she has finally reached the end of her patience.

'Suit yourself,' he says under his breath and begins to climb again.

Iris looks back towards the front of the house and after a moment's hesitation she opens the door. There in the porch, just as Steve said, is a wreath of twisted greenery and red berries. White roses are threaded through the arrangement too; Christmas roses, although the overall effect feels a little funereal to her. She stoops to lift it off the ground, turns it over in her hands to examine it front and back. There is no florist's card or hand-written note; nothing to suggest who has sent it or even who it is for. Perhaps there has been some mistake and this has been delivered to the wrong house. Iris bends her head to inhale the fresh, tangy smell of fir, pine and yes, looking more closely, she can identify it now; rosemary.

As she stands on the porch, Iris looks out, craning her neck for any sign of a delivery van or person. She takes a few steps down the front path towards the gate. Leaning out onto the pavement, she checks up one length of the street and back down the other. Finally, she catches herself, suddenly aware that someone could be, at this very moment, watching her, safely disguised in a near-by car or in an upper window, behind the slats of a closed blind. Perhaps they are waiting now, to see her reaction, to watch her as she frowns in puzzlement at the wreath in her hands. She turns and walks back down the pathway, ready to toss the flow-ers into the nearby wheelie bin when she checks herself again. She is overreacting.

Instead, she retraces her steps to the pavement and turning, walks back up the path leading to the house next door. She has not seen her Italian neighbour since the debacle with the tree in the back garden some weeks ago. Knocking on the door, she stands back appraising the same brick facade as her own and the surrounding borders and shrubs. The garden is tastefully kempt despite the owner's habit of being overseas half the year. It must be nice to be able to afford gardeners, she muses, and steps forward ready to knock again when the door opens.

The Italian neighbour – what was his name? Mario? Luigi? No, those are names from one of Ben's computer games – stands before her. His glasses are perched on the end of his nose, a bi-focal tint to them visible as he chews some food. Iris has obviously disturbed him while he is eating but he doesn't seem annoyed. She gets the impression he is always in the process of starting or finishing some kind of meal. He rubs a few flaky crumbs from his sweater-clad belly and opens the door wider when recognition floods his face.

'Ciao, Irees!'

He says her name with an inflection she can't help enjoying. His eyes alight on the wreath in her hands.

'Ah, *bellissima*.' He points, nodding with obvious delight.
'*Buon Natale*.'

Iris smiles and tries to repeat the phrase back to him in a
faltering Italian accent.

'You got my gift?' he asks.

'The flowers? Right, yes, I was wondering if they were
from you?'

He frowns.

'There was no card, you see.' She raises the wreath slightly by
way of example. 'But they are lovely, thank you. Very bellissima,'
she adds.

The man shakes his head, bewildered. He repositions his
glasses further up his nose and leans closer to look at the wreath.
'These are for me, no?' he asks, and gives a nervous laugh. He
waves a hand around, turning his palm up and then down and
then up again.

'Oh, are they? Yes, I think they might be. But I couldn't be
sure. Sorry. There's no name on them. Were you expecting
them?'

He frowns again, a crease indenting itself into his leathery
forehead. 'In my country,' he places a hand to his heart, his face
a little hurt, 'it is the custom to give our neighbours gifts at this
time of year. But it is not necessary.'

'Yes, I see. Well, in that case, I think you had better take
them,' she says, thrusting the flowers into his hands as she turns
to leave.

She is halfway back down his path when he calls to her.

'I put a panettone here.' He gestures across the fence towards
her doorstep. 'The other day. For you and your family.'

'Oh, a what?'

'Cake, sweet bread!' he says with added emphasis.

He looks cross now, taking his glasses off his nose so that he
can give her the full force of his gaze. The glasses rest on the
shelf of his belly, suspended by a leather cord.

'Right. Okay. Thank you, once again.' She nods. As she moves away, she can hear him grumbling under his breath in an angry-sounding foreign tongue, throwing his hands up in disgust as he disappears inside.

Iris pauses at the front step to her own house to unravel the confusion as it twists around her brain. She walks into the kitchen, looks into one or two cupboards and sure enough, she finds a glossy square beribboned box in festive colours, with pictures of a domed cake on the side. A present from her neighbour. So, if he didn't send the wreath, who did?

She is mulling this over, trying to quell the growing feeling of unease, when Steve wanders into the kitchen.

'Where have the flowers gone? I thought they were quite nice.'

She turns to look at his stupid, enquiring face. Thinks how blithely he moves through life, leaving her to shoulder every stress, every worry.

'Oh, shut up, Steve.'

20

'Ooh, look at that sky,' exclaims Laura as they step outside the house. It is golden hour, that time before sunset, and she and Ivo are on their way round to Iris and Steve's house for pre-Christmas drinks and nibbles. The sky is full of colour; the blue turning a hard, flinty shade while the clouds are yellowing and pinking like the inside of a shell.

'Don't even think about stopping to take photos,' says Ivo. 'We'll be late.'

'I wasn't,' laughs Laura. 'I was just appreciating it. I can be in the moment, you know.'

'How long's this thing going to last?' he asks.

'Not long. An hour. Maybe two?'

It's the first time she will have seen Iris since the Halloween party so she's keen to smooth things over and catch up.

'I hope she's not going to be a pain in the arse again.'

'Why would she be?' Laura nudges him. 'Don't be mean. They don't have it easy.'

Ivo shrugs, thrusting his hands into his pockets. 'Some people make life more difficult for themselves, if you ask me.'

'Ivo!' she remonstrates a little louder. 'You forget how lucky we are that Freddie's always been fit and well. I can't imagine what it must be like having a child with health issues.'

She stops, stock still, the thought suddenly coming up to meet her head on.

'Okay?' calls Ivo who has continued walking a few paces further on. 'What's up?'

Laura registers a wash of nausea sluice through her. That vertiginous feeling as she looks down upon her life and sees it for what it really is, in micro detail. What is she doing? What risks has she taken? She takes a breath and nods her head vigorously.

'Yep, fine. For a second I thought I'd forgotten something.'

He holds his arm out to her and she jogs the couple of steps towards him, taking up his hand like a proffered baton. It is warm and large, enclosing her small, cold one. As they reach the end of Riddleston Road, Ivo sets eyes on Iris and Steve's house.

'Bloody hell,' he says. 'This place has changed a bit.'

Flashing blue and white lights have been strung around the door and bay window, pulsing at various intervals while a wreath of red, green and gold ribbons adorns the front door. Ivo tries to find the door knocker behind the decorations and lets it fall with a couple of resounding thuds.

As Steve opens the door, he smiles his usual shambolic grin as if to say 'here we go again'.

'Hey, mate,' calls Ivo thrusting out his hand and slapping Steve on the back with the other.

'Merry Christmas,' Laura says and leans in for a peck, which doesn't quite make it to his cheek, before she sidesteps into the hallway. She makes her way along to the kitchen where she finds Iris bent double, lifting mince pies out of the oven. As she turns around, Laura sees that one side of her friend's cheek is bruised.

'Hey, you. Gosh, what have you done to your face?'

Iris puts a self-conscious hand up to the side of her head.

'Oh, nothing. Just had a bit of a funny turn at work. It looks worse than it is.'

'Are you sure? We can come back another time if you're not well.'

She waves Laura's concerned expression away with an oven-gloved hand. 'Honestly, it's nothing. It'll have gone in a couple of days. Drink?'

Laura looks about the kitchen, at the selection of bottles and cans lined up at one end of the work surface, which she has just added to with her own contribution.

'Glass of fizz going?' shouts Ivo as he comes into the kitchen. He whistles softly. 'Aye-aye! What's with the shiner? Old Steve's not been knocking you about, has he?'

'Not now, Ivo,' Laura mutters under her breath.

'Prosecco all right?' asks Iris, ignoring his comment.

'Sure, perfect.'

Iris turns towards Laura. 'One for you too?'

'Oh, er, no, I erm …' She puts out a wavering hand.

'What's wrong? Not like you to turn down a glass of fizz,' says Ivo. 'You know, at uni she was known as Miss Popov on account of her dexterity with champagne corks. Although I always wondered whether it didn't allude to something else.' He raises his eyebrows at her provocatively.

'Bugger off, Ivo. In any case, Miss Popov was so-called because of her hay fever allergy. Didn't she teleport or something every time she got a whiff of a flower and sneezed?'

'That's the one,' roars Ivo and laughs heartily.

Iris looks between them both with the bottle in her hands.

'Hilarious!' she says without smiling. 'So, do you want a glass or not?'

Laura feels herself admonished and straightens up.

'Thanks. I'm not feeling … my stomach feels a bit acidic at the moment.'

'How about some mulled wine?' says Steve from where he is standing behind her in the doorway. 'I can just put some on to warm. I might join you, actually,' he adds.

A look of surprise passes over Iris's face as Steve reaches for a pan and puts it on the stove. It is clear she has never known him to drink such a thing before.

'Well, if it's really no trouble?' asks Laura.

Steve pours wine into the pan, reaches for an orange to slice it, and all three of them watch him for a moment, as though they are observing a monkey at the zoo performing some unaccountable feat.

'No trouble at all,' comes his low reply as they all continue to stare for a moment longer.

'So,' Ivo says finally, rapping his knuckles on the worktop. 'Enjoying the new gaff?'

On the way home, Ivo is a bit more than tipsy, weaving his way along the pavement as Laura tries to prop him up.

'So much for not wanting to stay long,' says Laura. She is carrying a large panettone that Iris foisted onto her, which feels suspiciously like a regift.

'Well, you know, good will to all men,' he drawls. 'And I will say one thing for old Steve. He keeps a decent beer cellar.'

'Did you go down into the basement then? I've always wondered what it was like down there.'

'Oh, it's a godawful mess, don't get me wrong,' replies Ivo, hiccupping. 'They'd have to spend a ton of money on making it habitable. But there's room for a washing machine, couple of bikes. Place to store furniture I suppose. Crying shame when you think about the potential. Perfect space for a home cinema or gym.'

'Wow, and they've got the attic room at the top as well, which would make a fabulous master bedroom with en suite bathroom. So much potential,' muses Laura.

'Shouldn't think they'll ever have the capital to do it out properly though, do you?' says Ivo. He is zig-zagging along the street, readjusting his course at various intervals, so that it is taking them twice as long as it should to walk the short distance home.

'No, and besides, why spend all that money when they're only renting? It doesn't make any sense.'

Ivo shakes his head. 'Madness. Whoever's letting that place to them needs their head looked at. They should just sell up. Make a killing.'

Laura nods, and then sighs as Ivo veers into a nearby hedge.

'Maybe they just want to keep it in the family or something. You know how some inheritance works; comes with all sorts of clauses,' she replies. 'Right, come on sailor, let's get you home. Before you start singing.'

Ivo turns to her suddenly and leans forward. 'You know I love you, Laura,' he says in a voice thick with drunken affection.

Laura turns her head to one side, trying to steer him back in the right direction. Ivo stumbles against her, squeezing her into a bear hug, his head hanging heavy on her shoulder.

'No but I do. I really do.'

He is nuzzling into her hair now, planting clumsy kisses into her neck. His voice ricochets into her ear canal and she reels back but his grasp on her only tightens.

'I know, I know. Let's get you into bed,' she cajoles. 'Not much further.'

She is worried that he is going to fall and take her down with him. They teeter for a moment together like this as she tries to counter-balance him. His hand reaches round and gives her breast a firm grope and she recoils from the painful tenderness.

'Whatsamatterwithyou?' he says, leaning back and leering at her.

'I'm just tired and I want to get home,' she says, irritated now. 'Please, Ivo. Can we just go home?'

He looks at her, screwing his eyes up further as he sways unsteadily. He points a wavering finger at her, accusingly. 'There's something going on with you,' he slurs, prodding the finger into her chest. 'Something you're not telling me.'

'For God's sake, Ivo,' she says. 'I hate it when you get like this.' She disentangles herself from his grasp and starts to walk on. 'See you back at the house. I'll leave the door on the latch.'

'Wait,' he calls forlornly. 'Hold up!'

She can hear him swearing to himself as his feet trudge and scrape along the pavement behind her. Perhaps she should stop and help him home, make sure he crosses the road safely. Bugger it, she thinks to herself. He can get himself home. He used to manage perfectly well before they were married. She hugs her arms closely around her middle, holding herself. She's sick of worrying about everyone else. Thinking of their needs before her own. After all, there is something far more important to consider now.

21

Laura opens the front door and switches on a couple of lights, trying to make herself feel a little less despondent. She is about to call out to Freddie before remembering that he is staying at a friend's tonight. She considers going through to the lounge to watch something mindless on TV in an effort to distract herself. But she finds she hasn't the heart for it. Instead, she reaches down to the nearby plug socket and flicks on the Christmas tree lights. They shimmer in the darkness casting their own shadows into the room, each light spangling the walls in the gloom.

Any moment now she is expecting Ivo to come stumbling loudly into the house and she can't stand the thought of another beery confrontation. She needs to think, to work out how to tell him what he is already beginning to suspect. So she turns and climbs the stairs. She will have a bath. She can absent herself, relax, wallow. Lock the door if necessary. Fitting the plug, she runs the water into the roll-top bath, testing it until it has achieved the perfect temperature, pouring in a long drop of lavender-infused oil.

Above the roar of the tap, she thinks she can hear the front door. Ivo must be back. She strips hastily. He is less likely to disturb her once she's submerged. Peeling herself out of her jeans, flinging her sweater to the other side of the room, her pedicured toes pad about beside the claw feet of the tub. She is naked now aside from her pants which she shimmies out of, pushing them to one side with a desultory foot. Reaching a speculative hand into the water, she trawls her fingers through, marbling the oily slick on its surface, breathing in the floral fragrance.

She is about to step into the bath when she senses there is someone standing on the landing, their breathing slightly laboured, having climbed the stairs. The door stands ajar and as Laura looks up she can see that a hand is gently pushing it open.

'Ivo, I'm just getting in the bath.' She straddles one leg over the side, making good on her promise and it is like this – naked, half in, half out – when she realises there is a man standing in her bathroom. A man who is not her husband.

'Bloody hell,' she cries, staggering out of the bath and lunging for a towel hanging on the rail.

Steve is fully clothed, dressed for the outdoors and still wearing his trainers. It is incongruous in the sanctity of her perfect bathroom. This is the thought that occurs to her first when he reaches out towards her across the room, clutching at her skin, his mouth seeking hers. He is shushing her, a smile on his face, a finger held to his lips.

'What the hell are you doing?' she says hoarsely. 'Ivo will be back any minute.'

Steve shakes his head. 'I followed you both,' he says, 'after you left. I saw you arguing. He's headed into town,' he adds with a tilt of his head. He looks at her, eyes ranging over her hungrily as she tries to cover herself with the towel. 'You're so beautiful.' He reaches a hand up to touch her hair, to run a finger along her temple. She looks down, moves her feet back a fraction so that he doesn't stand on her toes.

'Won't Iris wonder where you are?' she says, turning her head away from him.

'No. I said I needed some air and anyway, I'm returning this.' She sees he is holding her pashmina in his hand. 'Clever of you to leave it like that.'

'What? I didn't. Not on purpose.'

'Oh.' His face falls a little but then brightens. 'Still, we've got a few moments. If we're quick.' He leans towards her again, placing a gentle kiss on her shoulder as his hands graze her back.

Laura allows herself to be kissed. He feels so different, it is always a surprise. It still makes her feel good but then she manoeuvres herself out of his reach.

'I can't. Everything's changed. We need to talk about … what's happened.'

Steve looks crestfallen again. 'Does that have to change anything?' he asks. 'I mean I thought it was pretty obvious what we need to do.'

Laura wraps the towel tighter around her, securing it toga-style, and sits down on the toilet seat.

'Obvious? In what way?'

He stands before her, looking even more of an unlikely presence in his bomber jacket and jeans. The steamy atmosphere of the room has added a sheen to his forehead and he looks hotly uncomfortable. He passes the pashmina back and forth between his hands, like a supplicant standing before a deity, his feet shuffling on the earthenware tiles.

'Well, because of the situation and …' His voice trails off.

'And what?'

Steve swallows, his eyes wandering around the room before he sighs, opening his arms wide in appeal.

'Your age, Laura. Our age. We've both got kids at secondary school. You've got a husband, I've got a wife. Homes, families. There's too much at stake here. Anyway, I thought you said you couldn't get pregnant any more.'

'I didn't think I could,' she spits out. 'This is as much of a shock to me too. But, Steve, this could be my last chance.' She puts a hand to her stomach protectively.

'Fuck's sake. You're not serious,' he says, taking a step backwards. He has dropped the pashmina to the floor now and she sees that his right foot is standing on it. 'I thought we agreed, we were going to take care of this. Sort it out.'

'I need to think,' she says, closing her eyes, shutting out the sight of him, his dirty trainers, the crumpled pashmina, his appalled face.

'What is there to think about?' he asks, raising his voice, forcing her to clench her eyelids shut tighter.

She reaches for her phone over on the cabinet, scanning the screen and tapping into an app. With a sharp intake of breath, she stands up.

'You've got to go. Ivo has been at the kebab shop but he's heading back now.'

She moves to usher him out of the room, to buffet him down the stairs, out of the house, out of her sight.

'Wait a second. So what are you going to say to Ivo? About all of this?' He gestures in the region of her stomach, the invisible connection that still binds them.

'I don't know,' she says, running her fingers through her hair in desperation before pushing him away, propelling him from her. He takes another step back, hesitates.

'You're not going to tell him, are you? Not the truth, anyway.'

It is an accusation rather than a request. Steve looks at turns both angry and devastated. Is he a lover spurned or a retreating cad? Is she his friend or his enemy? He doesn't seem to know any more. They cannot decide what roles they are meant to be playing yet in this unscripted scene, this drama unfolding between them, which neither anticipated. They have moved so swiftly from illicit sensuality, the bond of shared secrecy and pleasure, to warring factions. She can't quite recalibrate what her emotions, her responses should be.

'Please, just go. Now!' she shouts. And dutifully he hurls his burly figure out of the room, down the stairs and out the front door, while Laura continues to breathe slowly in and out. In. Out.

22

Lying in bed, Iris considers whether to stay there a little while longer. She is not due in to work until 11 a.m. as she's doing a lunchtime shift today. She stretches out her legs, her feet finding cold corners of the bed, her toes flinching as she reflexively curls back up into a foetal position. Why is it called so, she wonders? Surely we were all upside down and back to front in the womb. Perhaps it is because this is the only position in which she could be comfortable towards the end of her pregnancy with Ben.

She often asks herself why her son is the way he is. Why he was born that way. Or came to be so. Was it something she ate too much of while pregnant, or too little? Something harmful she imbibed without her knowledge. Or is it genetics? Though no such allergies run in either her or Steve's side of the family. Her husband is an omnivore with the constitution of an elephant. He doesn't even really get man-flu. And she has never reacted to anything.

So why? She curls in on herself a little tighter. What did she do wrong? What didn't she do? Sometimes she thinks about the really scary stories that make the news headlines. That poor boy on a flight to Europe suffering a fatal attack, having mistakenly eaten a snack with seeds in it. Caught in the air like an ill-fated acrobat, having left the safety of one airport but not able to reach the security of another in time.

Iris closes her eyes. She mustn't think like this. It was a million to one chance. An awful, tragic, isolated case. Things have changed since then. People are more careful. But, what if she's not there one day? To make sure. Who will check the lists of ingredients or remind Ben to avoid certain places, scenarios? He won't even let her rub in his eczema creams now, recoiling from her touch, shooing her from the room.

She turns onto her back, flinging her arms wide crucifixion-style, taking up the whole of the bed. Steve left for work early this morning, unusually quiet and gruff. And she'd heard Ben's bedroom door bang shut in a hurry before his feet thundered down the stairs, late for school. She is alone.

And that's when she smells it. Perfume. Roses. She's sure of it. She sits up in bed, sniffs the air. It is a sweet, floral smell but heavy, sickly. Where is it coming from? Neither Ben or Steve would use a deodorant or wear aftershave that smelled even remotely like that. She doesn't wear perfume herself. Has never seen the point of it. She winds her legs out of the sheets, pushing them back with her feet, reaching for her dressing gown. She lifts her head again, trying to catch a trace of the scent. It seems to come and go, wafting through the air, travelling along some unseen vapour, weaving like smoke. She finds herself wanting to follow it greedily like a child in a Bisto ad from her youth. And yet the smell is repellent; cloying, artificial, headache-inducing.

When Iris steps out on to the landing, the smell dissipates. She walks to the bathroom, but it is weaker yet. Still, she opens the window to flush it out, dilute it further. Downstairs, she flicks on the kettle, counsels herself to have a good breakfast. She can't be having any more dizzy spells at work. The bruise on the side of her face has almost faded now and is easily concealed with make-up but her cheekbone is still tender when she brushes her teeth.

She puts two slices of bread into the toaster, selects a jar of apricot jam from the fridge, along with butter and milk. She sticks out a foot towards the kitchen door and checks that the cat flap is definitely closed up securely. Nothing can get in or out.

Every time she makes herself a cup of tea in this kitchen, takes a teabag and a mug from the cupboard, she thinks back to the day she first met Rosemary. The same view of the garden reaching her now through the window as she takes her first tentative sip of the morning.

The stump of the felled laburnum tree looks like a headstone now, a monument to the past. Iris misses its leafy branches that would have been coming into bud in the next few months. She lifts onto the balls of her feet, peers a little closer through the distorted glass. There is something on the raised patch of turf near the tree stump. It looks like someone has scattered something – breadcrumbs, perhaps for the birds? She strains her eyes, trying to make sense of it. Has someone been putting food out for that bloody cat? But then she registers a darker green, the first early shoots pushing up through hard ground.

The timer on the toaster elapses, ejecting the contents rudely; the anticipated jack-in-the-box that still surprises, causing Iris to jump. Dragging herself away from the sight of the garden, she begins to butter toast, slather jam. She will just ask Steve to put down some weedkiller. But then she reconsiders. No, she will do it. She doesn't want anything to draw attention to that part of the garden. It's too risky.

She stares straight ahead at the dull grain of the kitchen cabinet, chewing mechanically. She thinks of the caretaker, his mention of Rosemary's sister. June, that was her name. And she had a baby. Where are they both now? Why haven't they come looking for Rosemary? And what claim do they have on this house?

Iris walks back to the window and contemplates the patch of grass again. If only she hadn't been in such a hurry to bury those letters along with Rosemary's body. There might have been a clue, an address, some information on their whereabouts.

The thought steals upon her quietly then. She moves her head to one side, as if to dismiss such an idea. It is terrible, awful. She cannot, will not consider it. But then it taps her on the shoulder again. What if she were to dig down into the grave, take up the box and letters? What if she were to remove the body entirely? And destroy any lasting evidence of Rosemary. She imagines the old woman's remains. They have been in the ground for six months. No, she can't. She isn't capable of that. Is she? Her chewing slows. The piece of toast in her mouth balling up into dry, claggy dough so that she must pivot towards the pedal bin and spit it out.

Iris commands her thoughts, focuses her mind. Back to the here and now. This is where she must always be. There are a million and one things she needs to organise if they are to be ready for Christmas next week. The food shop must be done. Most of the presents are bought but not wrapped. The tree and decorations are up in the lounge but she hates the way it all looks, even though she doesn't spend much time in there.

At this, Iris marches down the hallway and opens the door to the lounge. It is incongruous; her tree, her ornaments, her furniture all surrounded by Rosemary's wallpaper. She wishes again that they had got around to redecorating this room sooner. It should have been the first thing she tackled as soon as they moved in. Spontaneously, she reaches down to a dog-eared corner of the wallpaper by the skirting board and lifts it. The paper comes away easily, like a book opening, offering its pages to her obligingly.

Emboldened, she continues to pull at the paper, tearing a gash through the patterned surface, cleaving through the roses until a long, tapering strip falls to the floor revealing an expanse of bare plaster beneath. Iris inhales. The smell is the damp must of crumbling powder, blackened in places with mould and spores. She hooks a fingernail underneath the nearest flap and picks at it. More paper comes away. She knows she shouldn't. As they suspected, the walls are in a terrible state and will certainly need skimming if not completely replastering; a job that is beyond even Steve's handyman skills. Where would they get a tradesman this close to Christmas and how would they even be able to afford it? She's already maxed out her credit cards on buying gifts for Ben.

But still she keeps pulling and soon one entire wall of the lounge is stripped. With each scrap she feels as if she is flaying the memory of Rosemary, peeling away the skin of the house and its previous inhabitants finally. She is galvanised, feverish now as she continues around the room; the mottled, dusty remnants of paper piling up by her feet. She reaches to pull at another strip and as it is released she sees some markings on the wall beneath.

Thick, graphite pencil still legible despite the age of the place. It is the looping, curlicued handwriting of a teenage girl. Iris rips more paper away, carefully, forensically this time, excavating the past, piece by piece. The writing is innocent, ebullient, the way it sprawls across the wall with no heed or care. The lower seraphs lunge and swoop before returning to join up with their fellow ciphers. The letter i is dotted with a heart. An abundance of crosses spill out, emphasising each heartfelt kiss. Whoever wrote these words was not worried about ever being discovered. They were happy in the knowledge that their secrets would be kept beneath the paper roses, secured in place. Iris reads them out aloud, each one, smiling in spite of herself, reminded of her own girlish crushes. Nothing really changes. The heart wants what the heart wants.

> June was here. I love Billy Maddox.
> JP 4 BM.
> Roses are red, violets are blue.
> Sugar is sweet and so are you.

23

As she tramps across the frost-encrusted sports field, Iris feels her toes growing numb with each step. Why does she never seem to have the right footwear? As she stations herself along the painted white boundary of the rugby pitch, she casts a furtive look left and right at the other parents, who are dotted together in clumps. They huddle at various intervals in their full-length coats, heads drawn together in Russian-style hats, thermal headbands or cashmere beanies. They stamp their feet, clad in thick-soled hiking boots with shearling and fur linings. Their hands clasp expensive insulated mugs and flasks. She's seen Laura with one similar while out walking in the park. When Iris had returned home, she'd looked it up on the internet and found it cost over £200. How could someone spend so much just to keep their coffee warm?

She turns away and shuffles her feet together, drawing her coat tighter around herself, her arms crossed in a defensive stance. Her mother always used to say to her as a child 'uncross your arms, make an effort' or 'smile, don't look so miserable'. She was always willing Iris to make new friends, to be open and sociable, amenable. 'You catch more flies with honey than vinegar' she would say.

Perhaps she should try to go over and introduce herself, she thinks. If only Laura was here – she would know everyone. Iris looks around again, steeling herself to approach someone, any-one, a face she recalls from the Halloween party. But then a whistle blows, the players on the pitch launch into action and everyone on the sidelines begins to shout and cheer.

Iris strains her eyes to follow the match. It's the last game before Christmas and it's supposed to be a friendly but it all still appears very rough, in her view. She sees Freddie is playing, charging to the fore having gained possession of the ball already, but she doesn't know any of the other boys. Ben is in reserve and she can see him standing at the other side of the pitch looking cold and forlorn. She's not surprised. The wind is biting, the temperature barely above freezing and he is standing in shorts and a rugby shirt, throwing bear hugs around himself to keep warm and jogging up and down on the spot.

'Come on, Rory!' shouts one mum, her hands drawn to her mouth, mimicking a megaphone. She is particularly tanned, notices Iris, as are most of the parents. She's overheard some of them discussing half-term breaks. One woman talked of their house in Palma de Majorca, another mentioned the 'perfect temperatures' in Marrakech in October. Iris looks down at her own pale hands – she has stupidly forgotten her gloves and must stand with her fists plunged into her pockets or under her armpits. When did everyone stop being pasty in winter? She muses. Even in summer, she only turns a flushed pink. But these people have the even, all-over gleam of a fresh golden pastry. Not the orange gravy-browning stain she's seen on some young girls but a natural tan, nut-brown, layered on year after year until it seems baked into their skin on a cellular level.

'Get him, Bruno!' shouts another mother. 'Bring him down!' she adds, her voice hoarse with exertion.

Iris looks over to where Ben is standing, trying to catch his eye. Eventually he notices, his eyes sliding over her face, recognition blooming momentarily in his features before he frowns and his eyes slide away again. She tries a little wave, but resists a thumbs-up gesture. His gaze remains determinedly averted. Only the grim set of his mouth, the furious look in his eyes, tells her that he knows she is there.

Instead, Iris focuses her attention back on the match. She is unsure of the rules of the game but she tries to follow the action. A couple of tries have been scored by the other team and the field is looking churned and filthy despite the crisp coldness of the air. Plumes of steam issue from the boys' mouths like dragons, their cheeks red, their skin pinking and raw. Suddenly, a tide appears to turn and a boy has claimed the ball from a particularly ferocious-looking scrum and is now tearing down one side of the pitch.

'Go, Freddie,' bellows a man's voice.

As Iris cranes her neck to see, she recognises Ivo's broad-shouldered stance as he whoops and hollers, throwing his hands up in the air to clap. He is standing amongst another group of dads, a tight-knit pack of waterproofed individuals who look like they are dressed for an expedition to the North Pole.

Ivo turns his head, aware of Iris's gaze, lifting his chin in acknowledgement and she smiles back, hoping to infer enthusiasm. Freddie has thrown himself to the ground in triumph, the ball clutched to his body like a newborn babe as he skids along the wet, icy turf. He is soon surrounded by his team members, who hug him to them, mashing his hair with a fist while holding him in an affectionate headlock. Iris still finds these displays of machismo amusing, even among young lads. To think Ben won't let her kiss him goodnight any more or even embrace him and yet in a sports arena they are so tactile, aggressively loving. She imagines it is the same in warfare.

The game continues until mercifully another whistle is blown, signalling half-time. Trays of orange segments are brought out (an archaic tradition the school apparently likes to preserve) while most of the boys suck vigorously on fortified energy drinks and water bottles. Iris makes her way over to the other side of the pitch. She has a specially selected, allergen-free nutrition bar for Ben, which he takes from her wordlessly, his eyes darting from left to right. He stands several paces away from her, chewing miserably, and responds to her questions and comments monosyllabically.

'Is it really necessary for you to stand out here in the cold? When are they going to bring you on?'

'I don't know, do I? Maybe if there's an injury. It's fine. Just leave it, Mum.'

'But you're freezing! Look at you, you're shaking.' Iris reaches up and pulls the woolly hat she is wearing from her head. 'Here, take this. I would give you some gloves but I've forgotten mine.'

'No, Mum. I'm not wearing that.'

She stands with her arm outstretched, proffering the hat as he turns and begins to walk away.

'Ben. Wait. I'll see you at the end of the game then?'

He turns briefly and looks over his shoulder before giving his head a shake. 'No. Please don't. I can walk home by myself. It's not far.'

Iris sighs, resigned, and then moves away, covering her head and ears against the wind. It is a rather lurid bobble hat she thinks, on reflection. As she finds herself back in position at the side of the pitch, she wonders what is the point. Steve would be better at this. At least he's actually interested in sport. He would probably have inveigled himself amongst Ivo and his mates by now, a shared love of traditional male sport providing the enduring social glue of ages.

When she looks across in the direction of the other dads, she catches Ivo's eye again and, to her surprise, this time he breaks away from the pack and makes his way over to her.

'All right,' she calls, cheered by the presence of one other person who seems to want to know her.

'Hello, Iris,' he says, in his usual 'hail-fellow-well-met' voice. 'Didn't have you down as a rugger fan.'

'Guilty.' She smiles. 'We're supporting the greens, right?'

He pauses, a look of consternation on his face.

'Just kidding,' she says. 'I do know that much.'

Ivo laughs with relief, nodding. 'You do look a bit out of your comfort zone,' he admits.

'Is it that obvious? It's bloody baltic, as well!'

Ivo makes a strange noise, somewhere between a groan and a cheer. 'Oh, character-building stuff, Iris. At least they don't make the boys endure cold showers. Not like my schooldays.'

Iris smiles but makes no comment. She's heard Laura talk about Ivo's strict boarding school upbringing, being sent away from home when he was seven years old. His brutally competitive father and emotionally absent mother.

'Here, take my gloves,' says Ivo into the silence that has fallen between them. 'You look like you could do with them more than me.' He laughs again. He is given to laughing often, Iris notes, even when nothing is funny. She always thought it a little false, even dim-witted of him but now she realises it is borne of nerves.

'Freddie's doing well,' she says, nodding her head towards the pitch as she gratefully pulls on the thickly wadded climbing gloves. They are far too big for her but the relief is instant.

'Yes,' says Ivo enthusiastically, back on safe ground. 'Chip off the old block. He's going for the national try-outs in the new year, did Laura tell you?'

'No,' answers Iris. 'We haven't had the chance for a proper catch-up in a while actually. You know how mad this time of year is,' she adds by way of excuse.

'Really?' he asks, latching on to this piece of information. He looks away, seeming to sift over his thoughts for a moment before he turns back towards her and says, 'Iris, can I ask?' He laughs, dipping his head. 'Look, this may sound like an odd thing to mention. Just ignore me if I'm barking up the wrong tree. But have you noticed, I mean, do you think Laura …? Well, she seems to be acting a bit out of character recently. I'm worried something might be wrong, or bothering her.' He laughs yet again. 'I know how you girls like to get together and gossip.' He nudges her arm convivially at this but when Iris doesn't answer, his face grows serious again. 'Well, has she?'

'Has she what?'

'Said anything to you, I mean.'

'About?'

A raucous cheer goes up around the pitch and Ivo claps his hands along with the rest of the crowd before he turns back to Iris.

'Anything. Work problems? Or … health issues? Perhaps she finds it easier to talk to other people these days,' he adds a little wistfully.

'I don't know, Ivo,' says Iris. 'She always seems on top form to me. Always looks amazing. You know Laura!'

'Yes.' He grins wryly. 'Yes, I know. But then she wasn't really drinking the other day at your place and she's been so quiet lately, a bit you know, withdrawn. Am I being an idiot?'

'Don't worry,' says Iris. 'I'm sure it's nothing. Too much pre-Christmas stress? A dicky tummy, possibly?'

'Probably, probably,' he agrees, staring at his feet as though trying to convince himself. 'Well, I'd better get back to the lads.'

'Oh, okay then,' says Iris. And then as an afterthought she calls out. 'Ivo, would you mind if Ben caught a lift home with you and Freddie? I need to be getting off.'

'Sure, no problem.'

As Iris turns away from the pitch and faces into the wind, she continues to mull over Ivo's words, his concerns about Laura. Iris hadn't noticed anything strange or out of character about her friend, although she has had her own stuff going on lately. But now that Ivo mentions it, she does see how Laura is changed. It is a subtle, almost imperceptible thing. The way Laura seems to float about in her own world, as though she is only half there, half-listening to the conversation instead of dominating it as she normally would be.

The way she seemed preoccupied the other day but not troubled or worried, rather serene, smiling a secret smile. Iris had mistaken it for her friend's usual carefree confidence, a touch of the smugness and self-satisfaction that has always ground her gears a little. But now she thinks how Laura seemed to be hugging something to herself; she glowed with it as though nurturing a small flame.

Iris recognises that feeling suddenly. The only time she has ever experienced it herself was when she first found out she was pregnant. Before she told Steve. Before she'd had the chance to share it with friends and family. She had preserved it for a few hours, moving through the day, walking amongst strangers, knowing that a new life was growing inside her and, just for a short while, she and only she knew about it.

Iris stops short. Surely Laura can't be pregnant, can she? She and Ivo have always seemed content to have an only child. Just like herself and Steve. They themselves had made a conscious decision to stop at Ben – partly for financial reasons but also because he'd had so many health issues. And yet she could always see Laura and Ivo having a large brood of poster-worthy children, all of them in rude health. She'd even envied the way Freddie had been so robust, so easy as a child.

But then she remembers a conversation a few years ago when Laura had confirmed she'd 'shut up shop' gynaecologically speaking. She'd said it with her usual light-hearted chutzpah but Iris had been surprised at the time. 'What about Ivo?' she'd blurted out thoughtlessly. In the early years of their friendship, he'd always been so vocal about wanting a whole rugby team. The idea of not fathering several more kids in his image akin to letting the side down. But Laura had just shaken her head and shrugged her shoulders, before moving the conversation on.

Iris looks down at her hands. Too late, she realises that she is still wearing Ivo's gloves. Turning to call over her shoulder, to wave and catch his eye, she sees he is thick in the throng, his attention glued to the game, his voice one of the loudest as it carries across the cold afternoon air.

Iris takes a few steps forward and thinks. Well, he certainly hasn't got a clue about the baby. She takes a few steps further, shaking her head in mystification at Laura's behaviour. Why would she act like that, be so secretive? Is it because of her age or the presumably unplanned nature of the pregnancy? She takes a few more steps before casting one final look over her shoulder. Ivo is jumping up and down, cheering, his arms flung around the other dads as they celebrate an equalising try. She imagines him as a young man, at university, his hair dark and full, his sweaty body in a mosh pit with his friends at a concert. He is still that over-eager puppy, his enthusiasm guileless, innocent.

She stumbles on through the field and onto the tarmac of the school grounds. Weaving her way around the perimeter of the school building, she is almost at the car park when she bumps into someone half concealed in the shadows of the shrubbery. Looking up, brought short, she mutters an apology before registering it is the caretaker, the one who came to her house the other week. His eyes have the same blue twinkle, like chips of ice in a cragged rock face.

'Beg your pardon,' he says quietly, touching his hat with a hint of deference.

'Oh, it's you,' Iris says, surprise making her rude.

He smiles at her, that same knowing smile he had given her that evening. It feels like a draught of cold water pouring down the back of her neck.

'Have a good Christmas,' he says, touching his head once more, and makes to move off in the direction of the playground.

Iris opens her mouth to say something but she is not sure what the words might be if she were able to formulate them. But then an authoritative voice carries across the car park towards them, commanding their attention.

'Mr Maddox,' calls the head teacher. 'Would you be so kind as to empty these bins please. They appear to be full.'

The man bows his head and responds 'will do,' as he lopes away.

24

Laura piles the Christmas decorations onto the floor, ready to be packed up and put back into the loft. Lengths of tinsel snake around her ankles like shimmering feather boas. The fairy lights are twisted in a knotty pile once more, each individual bulb now blank, its brightness extinguished for another year. It is a dreary job that she hates, only matched by the weather, which is suitably rainy, lashing against the window. As she carefully wraps each glass bauble in tissue paper, she thinks of the precious form inside her, perhaps the size of a plum or an apricot. The fruit of her womb, she thinks with a smile. *But not of Ivo's loins*, says a small voice in her head. Laura silences these voices when they whisper to her, drowning them out over the last couple of weeks with constant rounds of food, celebration, board games, films.

She had done her best to be on form. Although her appetite had disappeared and the cooking would often make her gag, forcing her to run to the French windows and throw them wide, filling her lungs with fresh air to quell the nausea. She had managed to make it through Christmas Day by playing the hostess, serving canapés, topping up everyone else's glasses before retreating back to the refuge of the kitchen. A small bite from a plate of blini here, a little dry toast, a cocktail sausage or two, sustained her. And naps, of course. Many naps. On the worst days, she feigned illness and asked Ivo to take Freddie out on festive adventures; ice skating, a trip to see the latest blockbuster at the cinema, father and son hikes in the woods.

Of course, she'd had to screen a few texts from Steve, though she had been wondering what he was doing, how he and Iris were passing the time. As her thumb had hovered over various composed messages, she realised how dangerous it was, and resisted pressing send before finally deleting each one to cover the traces.

This affair with Steve was never planned. He had discovered her in tears one day having dropped Freddie back home. She can't even remember why she was upset any more. But suddenly Steve had felt interesting, responsive, different. No doubt there had been an attraction all along, simmering under the surface. She's a bit of a flirt, she admits. Can't seem to help herself. And Steve had always seemed so laconic, distant. The epitome of the strong, silent type. Perhaps he was a tough nut she'd always wanted to crack, somehow. Whatever, it had only really been a physical thing, for her. Reconnecting some part of herself that had been lost along the way. But it was a mistake, she realises now. She should never have let it continue, brief though it was.

The Christmas tree stands denuded of its finery, pine needles littering the space. It strikes a desolate figure next to her honey-coloured floors and Persian rugs. Now that all the decorations are down and the lounge is restored to normality, the tree looks even more incongruous. She opens the front door and drags it out, unceremoniously pulling it down the front path and depositing it out on the pavement. The bin men should collect it soon. Laura feels another jolt of sadness as she looks up the street and sees that it is joining all the other half-dead pines and firs abandoned outside everyone else's houses. It is a trail of devastation, a forest of death. The idea brings tears to her eyes, unaccountable emotion spilling over. It must be her hormones, she thinks, and turns back towards the house, running to avoid the rain, eager for distraction.

Inside, the house looks barren, bereft. Not for the first time, she thinks how it would make far more sense to keep the decorations up for longer than Twelfth Night. If any month needed a bit of twinkle and sparkle, it is the dark days of January. She contents herself with the thought that she will double down on candles this week. It will be a nice excuse to treat herself to some really luxe ones when she's next in town. Taking a look at her watch, she gathers up her camera bag, phone and keys. She will also need her indoor lighting equipment. She has arranged to visit one of the mums she knows from the primary school days. Apparently, she is in need of some portrait shots for her daughter – a budding actress – and they have agreed to set up the shoot at their house.

Laura is not really in the mood for this assignment but it will be good to keep herself busy, she decides. Later on that afternoon, she has an appointment with her doctor. She is to be scanned, to be screened for possible complications, birth defects. She doesn't even shape the names of these tests in her mind because she doesn't want to think about them, the results and what they might mean. If only the doctor hadn't been quite so doom-mongering. Instead, she shoulders her bag, tucks her lighting kit, reflector and tripod under her arms while she slams the door behind her. Everything will be fine, she tells herself. It always is.

When she arrives at Tanya's house, she is reminded of how large and grand it is; easily twice as big as hers and Ivo's. And to be honest, this woman is a bit up herself, even for Laura's taste. The place is like something you'd see gracing the cover of *House & Garden* magazine and Tanya never lets anyone forget it. That and the fact that she has sent her kids to St Olave's; in her opinion, a far superior school even to Toppingham.

Laura climbs out of the car, bracing herself for an hour or so of one-upmanship, remembering the conversation they'd had the previous year. Tanya had cornered her in the playground one day at school pick-up, asking where she and Ivo were intending to send Freddie. Thankfully, they had already moved and been able to put Toppingham down as their first choice.

Tanya had scoffed at this, suggesting they were mad to move into catchment, when they themselves had decided to go down the faith school route.

'St Olave's actually does way better than Topps on GCSE and A level results,' she had pointed out.

'I know,' Laura had replied. 'But we're just not religious and I'm not sure I could take all that Bible bashing.'

'Oh, totally. Neither are we to be honest,' Tanya said. 'But we just got James and Lilly a quickie baptism and luckily my parents agreed to take them to church on Sundays, so we could still have a lie-in. Once you get their school place confirmed, you can just knock it all on the head, obviously.'

Laura had nodded, unconvinced, trying to disguise her feelings of distaste.

'Look, it's as simple as this,' Tanya had continued. 'You do what's necessary to get your kids into the right school. Everyone else is at it. It's just the way of the world.'

As she climbs up the steps to the elaborate porch, Laura turns this conversation over in her mind. Either side of her, two bushes emerge from carved stone urns in a Cornetto whip of foliage. She lifts the brass knocker, held between the jaws of an enormous, gaudy lion, and lets it fall. She thinks of Tanya's words again.

'You'd do anything for your kids.'

And something about it makes her think of Iris. The way she dotes on Ben, her love almost ferocious at times. And the way she had managed to secure him a place at Toppingham, against all odds. The thought lodges somewhere within her, uncomfortably, though she's not sure why. But then the large door is opening and Tanya is standing before her, regaling her with commands to 'come in, come in. It's been too long'.

Laura smiles, arms full of kit, as she tries to focus her mind on the task in hand. Yet still the thought tugs at her as she moves into the wide, marbled hallway. What exactly would Iris do for her son?

25

Iris is late for work. There was nothing clean to put on this morning. None of the specific garments she is required to wear in the shop anyway. She lifts a dress out of the washing pile and gives it a tentative sniff but it is crumpled and stale and she doesn't have time to get out the ironing board. Perhaps if she wore a sweater or cardigan buttoned up, it might hide the worst of it.

This lack of organisation is unlike her. She's usually on top of the laundry. Ensuring Steve has clean clothes for his trips and Ben's uniform is washed and dried by Monday morning. But things seem to have got away from her a bit in the last week. The return to work and school schedules has caught her by surprise this January. More than most years, she has yearned to stay in bed, at home, hibernating.

As an introvert, she finds winter a struggle and Christmas even harder. Coaxing herself out into the cold weather and forced jollity. She imagines Laura laughing at her, shaking her head. She once called her 'a bit of an Eeyore' when she had admitted as much during the early days of their friendship. Her thick wavy hair had bounced and her eyes had shone with mirth. It was obvious even back then that she was very much the Tigger in this scenario, her irrepressible energy and joie de vivre what had drawn Iris (and most other people, it must be assumed) to her. They had seemed a good match though, a yin to the other's yang. Although, in retrospect, Iris has often wondered if the sparkly, charismatic people are also attracted to the quiet, withdrawn type for a reason. Perhaps everyone needs a foil, a counterpoint. And doesn't something shiny seem all the more appealing aside something dull?

But what does she think of her friend now? She could be wrong, of course, but she's pretty sure her hunch about Laura, and the unplanned pregnancy, is right. She's been very quiet over the Christmas break. Normally, Iris would have received a text by now inviting them over. Laura is the sort of person who revels in the festive season. Twixtmas – as she and everyone else will insist on calling it these days – is not an opportunity to down tools and rest up in front of the box like most people, but a chance for more outings, more expense. It had made Iris's head spin when she first met her but she was happily carried away on the social wave of it all, back when they still moved in similar circles.

Yet no invitation for a New Year's Eve bash landed in her WhatsApp. Even Steve had mentioned it and he usually can't stand going around to Laura's. Instead, he'd sat comatose in front of the TV, watching Christmas specials with a bottle of beer permanently affixed to his right hand. When she'd suggested a short walk he'd immediately refused before looking up from the screen to ask 'have you arranged to go with anyone else?'. When she'd answered 'no, just us' he'd made a face, looking out the window and citing the bad weather.

Surprisingly, Ben has been the more upbeat of the two this time. He has been making an effort to come down more and socialise, to help her make a couple of meals, tidying his room (on the condition that she no longer goes in there) and once or twice she has eavesdropped on him in conversation, presumably on his phone. Rather than the short monotone exchanges she has overheard in the past, his voice sounds chatty, engaged, breaking into sporadic laughter. Who is he talking to, she wonders.

Iris looks at the clock and curses. She is running late. Oh well, they will just have to take her as she is, even if her attire isn't exactly immaculate today. Better there and scruffy than not at all. She is just getting into her coat, making sure she's remembered her packed lunch, when the post drops through the letter box. There is something about the arrival of the mail in this house that still makes her hold her breath, her stomach tightening reflexively. She has given out this address to so few people. No change of address cards were sent. They have no friends save Laura and Ivo, and little family.

Perhaps it is the memory of the utility bills that arrived in Rosemary's name when they first moved in, like a slap in the face or a punch to the gut. She had quickly swept them out of sight before Steve could see them, phoning up the energy companies and council to change the accounts over. Luckily, Rosemary's landline had been cut off a long time ago and they had decided to just rely on their mobile phones.

Of course, the internet had to be connected as soon as possible. With every new form she filled in or representative she spoke to on the phone, it felt like another piece of incriminating evidence against her, a paper trail. But it wasn't like they weren't paying their bills like other respectable citizens, she reasoned with herself. They were just doing it in a house that didn't belong to them (or anyone else, she might add). Or so she had thought when she first moved in. Rosemary had been so adamant the day she died. '*There is no one, Iris.*'

She stoops to pick up the post from where it has fallen onto the florid Victorian floor tiles, the ones she had so coveted when she first stepped into the house. Her heart beats a little faster, the blood pounds in her ears. It is mostly the aforementioned utility bills. Why do they arrive in January when everyone is skint and payday seems such a long way off? They will have to tighten their belts for the next couple of weeks. Though where they are to make any further savings is a mystery to her. Steve's debts suck up all their spare cash and her credit card bills are spiralling out of control.

She cycles through the envelopes in her hands, discarding the bills on the hall table, until she comes to a small square envelope, addressed just to her. It feels thick and stiff. It must be a belated Christmas card, she thinks. Someone who was even more disorganised than her and missed the last post. She opens the door and lets it close behind her, walks down the front path as she thumbs open the envelope, tearing at the paper. Reaching inside, she sees it is indeed a card; a resplendent robin redbreast is featured on the front. She opens it up, wondering who might have sent it. Her and Steve's parents had definitely got theirs to them in time. And not that many people their own age send cards any more. Was it one from work or a local church group?

Inside the card is a typed script rather than any personalised handwriting in the customary biro. Iris runs her hand along the sticker, onto which a message has been printed and then stuck down onto the card. How impersonal? Maybe it's from the school, she thinks, and begins to read.

I KNOW WHAT YOU DID. DON'T WORRY I'LL KEEP YOUR SECRET. FOR A PRICE. SEND £1000 TO THE PO BOX ADDRESS BELOW OR I GO TO THE POLICE.

She reads it once and then again. She is stalled in the middle of the pavement, the blood draining from her, her stomach dropping. Her legs feel weak and she must focus on taking one step after another. She is still gripping the card in her shaking hands as she reaches the end of the street before she realises and stuffs it hurriedly into her bag, out of sight. At the corner, she stops beside the lamp post at the intersection between two roads, leans her hand against the wall, bends her head and vomits into the weeds.

As Iris stumbles into work, she sees that the shop is thronged. She had forgotten that it would be busy with the January sale in full swing. She puts her head down and marches past her manager who eyes her aggressively. She should have been here twenty minutes ago. Instead she hurries downstairs and straight into the loos. Looking into the small spattered mirror over the sink she considers her wan face. It is as if all of her fears, every nightmare, each small anxiety or worry have finally come to meet her at once. What has she done? What was she thinking? How could she have been so foolish to think this crazed plan would ever work? But as each week had drifted by, it had seemed more likely that maybe, just maybe it would be okay. As Ben gained entrance to Toppingham and she and Steve began to change each part of the house, bit by bit, she had felt herself grow bolder, more assured of the fact that this was right, that she wasn't doing anything wrong, that they deserved to be there.

But now she sees how deluded she was and how much is really at stake. She has risked everything for her family, thinking that they were worth it, but now she sees that it is Ben and Steve who will suffer the most. She thinks of Ben, her brave son who has already been through so much. How he is just starting to appear happier, more relaxed. And Steve, her loyal, hardworking husband who asks for so little from her. Ben will have to transfer schools and start again, somewhere else with another group of strangers. And Steve will never understand or forgive her for what she has done. Their marriage will be over. Laura and Ivo will disown them. No one will want to know them now. It will be in the papers, perhaps on the news. The police will be involved. She'll be arrested, questioned. She might even go to prison.

Iris stares at herself in the mirror, her eyes wide with fear, filling with tears, her mouth quivering as a strangled cry reaches up out of her throat. She vomits again into the sink, trying to avoid splattering her outfit. Her hands shake uncontrollably as she washes them over and over again until the water is so hot, it is burning her skin. She doesn't care. It is a cleansing fire, a distracting pain, the only sensation that is keeping her tethered to the here and now. There is a sharp rap on the door which makes her start.

'Iris, are you nearly done in there? There are customers who need serving. We're run off our feet upstairs.'

It is Diana, her manager, speaking to her through the door in her usual high-handed tone. Iris mops at her mouth, splashes water on her face and dries it with a paper towel which is coarse and scratchy against her cheeks.

'Just coming,' she calls.

When she opens the door feeling weak, insubstantial, Diana is waiting for her outside, standing imperiously, hands on hips. Her features soften slightly as she takes in Iris's haggard face and damp dress.

'Sorry,' Iris manages to say. 'I've not been feeling well.'

Diana raises an eyebrow at her, looking her up and down, assessing her dishevelled appearance.

'You know full well that any reason for sickness or absence should be reported to a member of staff as soon as possible.' She sighs with displeasure. 'Are you able to join us upstairs?'

Iris nods mutely. She needs to keep busy. If she can just get through her shift today, she will think things through tonight. Besides, they need the money. She can't afford to lose this job.

'Very well, kindly do so please.'

Iris runs up the stairs. She can feel the weight of the Christmas card in her pocket. She had put it there for safekeeping and she reaches for it now. Her hands smart from the blisteringly hot water, her throat is scorched from the acidic bile. As she reaches the shop floor, she makes her way to the till where a long line of customers is queuing, their impatience palpable.

As she reaches across to take a garment from a customer, Iris attempts a smile. She is an automaton. A cog that will fit seamlessly back into the machine. She will repeat the same actions over and over today. Smile, scan, tap, fold, wrap, clean, steam, hang, dust, hoover. Until the day is done.

26

Finding a vacant bay in the clinic car park, Laura shuts off the engine. She is aware of a tingling feeling in her solar plexus, caught on the cusp as she is between excitement and fear. She has been looking forward to this appointment for a couple of weeks and yet dreading it at the same time. For so many years she has longed to feel a new life growing inside her, to feel those butterflies in her belly. But there is a small part of her that also feels like the shame-faced teenager, the irresponsible woman who should have insisted on using a condom, who has thrown caution to the wind with a passionate roll of the dice. Played Russian roulette with life itself.

She swings open the car door, grabbing her bag from the seat beside her. She takes a quick look at herself in the overhead mirror. Her eyes are bright, her skin looking fresher than it has in weeks. She applies a slick of lip balm and another roll of essential oil. Nothing bad can happen today, she consoles herself. She is going to meet her perfect baby for the first time and she smiles to herself like a child who is about to open a much anticipated present.

The sonographer is quiet yet professional. A younger woman with short, neat hair and glasses. Laura feels in safe hands but she wishes there might be a bit more chit-chat. She is suddenly nervous and conscious she is alone with no one else to hold her sweaty palm or share this moment with her. But she relishes the cold gel on her stomach, tissue paper tucked into the waistband of her jeans. Lying back on the examination couch, her neck turned to the side. The screen is angled away from her while she is scanned until a heartbeat, quick and strong, is detected. Laura smiles, craning her neck, wanting to see.

'Just taking a few more measurements,' says the woman in her low, considered tone. Laura wishes she would warm up a bit. This is a show for which she's been waiting a lifetime seemingly and it is all she can do not to sit up, reach out and yank the screen towards herself.

'Everything all right?' she ventures. 'Remember, I don't want to know the sex.'

The sonographer nods but says nothing as her hand roves around the small mound of Laura's belly, checking and checking again. Laura tries to breathe steadily although she is feeling a little discomfort. She wishes she'd drunk more now. Perhaps her bladder isn't full enough and it's proving difficult to get an accurate picture of the baby. Yet she feels fit to burst and tries to ignore the sudden urge to pee.

Finally, the monitor is moved towards her and Laura raises herself up onto her elbows, eager to get a closer look.

'Here's your baby,' says the woman, continuing in her monotone voice. 'The head here, and the spine.' She traces a finger along the outline of a shrimp floating in the murky waters of Laura's womb.

'Oh wow,' says Laura and she instinctively wants to share it, like she did with Ivo all those years ago. But he is not here. She peers closer, eyes hungrily feeding on the fuzzy black and white images. 'It's quite hard to see, is that the heart?' she asks instead, pointing to the small, dark pulsing sac.

'Yes, you're a little on the small side. Still very early days,' says the woman.

'Oh, really? Is that a problem?'

She shakes her head noncommittally. 'I'm going to print out all the information and pass it on to Dr Wilson. He'll be able to discuss everything with you in more detail. I've taken lots of screen grabs so you'll have plenty of photos. If you want them,' she adds.

There is something unsettling about this woman, thinks Laura. How can she be so mechanical when she has such an amazing, miraculous job? Has she really done this so many times that it has become commonplace?

'Right, thanks,' says Laura as she wipes the gel away from her tummy and repositions her clothes. 'I'd like as many as possible, please.'

When Dr Wilson calls her through to his consultation room, Laura feels heartened by his familiar face and kindly smile. She starts up a continuous stream of small talk, compensating for the lack of conversation during the scan. She finds herself prattling on about the weather, how it is hard to believe that it is still January, the most interminable month, asking him with a self-conscious laugh if it is too late to wish him a happy new year. He listens to all of this good-naturedly as he closes the door, gestures for her to sit, takes his position behind his desk and proceeds to bring up information on his computer.

'We've now got a fuller picture of what's going on following your nuchal translucency ultrasound scan,' he begins. 'The main thing to remember, Mrs Peters, is that you're still very early on in your pregnancy and you have plenty of options. It's important to have all the information available to us so that you can make the right decision for you and your family.'

'The right decision?' asks Laura.

The doctor nods and continues.

'Taken together with the blood tests, we can confirm that there is a higher chance of Down's syndrome. The scan picked up some abnormalities in the foetus, I'm afraid, as is the case sometimes with pregnancies at this stage of a woman's life.'

Laura sits very still. She is struggling to find the right response, her words having run on earlier are now like a tap that has dried up. Then a thought comes into her head and without pausing she blurts it out.

'But lots of women my age and older have babies. Perfectly healthy ones. You read about them all the time. That actress,' she says, her hand scrabbling in mid-air for a name. 'You know, the one married to James Bond, um …'

The doctor looks momentarily flummoxed and then responds: 'Daniel Craig's wife?'

'Yes.' She pounces on this. 'Rachel Weisz. She had a baby at forty-eight, for goodness' sake.'

The doctor nods and smiles as though this is exactly the reaction he was expecting and Laura is behaving in a totally appropriate way.

'I'm healthy, I'm fit,' she goes on. 'I look after myself. My body, my eggs – they're not the same as my actual age, surely?'

The doctor looks at her quizzically. 'I'm sorry is that a question or a statement?'

Laura sighs in exasperation. If only Ivo was here. He is always so confident, so forthright when it comes to doctors, medical staff. He would never have put up with this nonsense.

'Look, I'm just saying there's no reason why my baby might not be fine. And I would really take care of myself during the pregnancy. I already have been. I've cut out all caffeine and alcohol and I've been taking the right supplements.'

The doctor smiles again. He is trying to be nice, she's sure, but right now she would like to slap that condescending smile clean off his face.

'You're quite right,' he says. 'There is a chance the foetus might be healthy and normal and there are further diagnostic tests, though not without risk, that you could elect to have if—'

Laura puts up a hand to stop his words.

'Okay, please will you stop referring to my baby as a foetus, thanks.'

The doctor pauses. 'I'm just using the correct medical term, Mrs Peters. It would be remiss of me not to make sure you were completely aware of the full facts and their implications. Should you wish to continue with the pregnancy, then—'

'Should I wish?'

'Yes, there are things to consider. Take some time to think it over, discuss it with your husband. It's an important decision that you'll want to make together so that you can plan for the future. I have some literature for you here.' He pushes several leaflets across his desk towards Laura, which she automatically picks up and then puts back down again as though they are too hot to handle.

'Depending on your decision, I can book you in for further tests including an amniocentesis that will determine for certain whether the foetus, er, I mean your baby, has Down's but there is a small chance of miscarriage with this procedure. Or ...'

Laura leans forward, looks him directly in the eye.

'Or?'

'You may wish to have a termination and we can of course arrange that for you as well.'

She leans back in her chair, resting her hands on her stomach protectively.

'Look, I know it's a lot to take in,' says the doctor. 'Give yourself some time. Arm yourself with all the information. It's not an easy decision.'

'Oh it is,' she says, standing up. 'It is for me.'

The doctor looks at her, his face a mask of concern, his mouth opening, as if to offer further advice.

'And thank you but I don't want any further tests.'

Back in the car, Laura sits for a while before starting the engine. After she left the doctor's office she had marched straight to the toilet to relieve herself and then immediately left the building, despite the receptionist trying to attract her attention from behind her little booth.

Now she concentrates on her breathing, trying to centre herself (or whatever the hell Keith the bloody yogi calls it). She remembers reading somewhere, in one of the many pregnancy books she bought when expecting Freddie, that stress is not good for an unborn child, that it can transmit from the mother via the womb. After a few moments more of deep breathing, which has actually resulted in her feeling a little dizzy and lightheaded, she pulls herself together and inserts the key in the ignition.

She's about to start the engine when her phone begins to vibrate and ring. She would like to be alone with her thoughts or the radio, but then reaches into the bag and sees that it is Steve calling. She sighs. His timing is incredible. She considers screening the call but then relents. Perhaps this is a conversation they need to have. They have unfinished business to discuss.

'Hi,' she says. 'All right?'

He doesn't answer at first. There is a slight pause and when he does speak, his voice sounds breathy, nervous, surprised at his good fortune. 'Laura. You picked up. How are you? How did the appointment go?'

At first she is blindsided. Where is he? How does he know that she's at the private clinic, has he followed her here?

'Erm, okay, thanks,' she replies haltingly. 'Have you been checking up on me?' She tries to say this with a casual air to her voice but for the first time she is disquieted.

'Don't be daft.' He laughs. 'It's been tough. Not being able to see you, speak to you, since the last time. You stopped answering my texts.'

'Yes, well I think you made it pretty clear where you stood …'

Steve laughs again, more uncertainly this time.

'That night was a bit crazy, wasn't it? I think we were both caught off-guard.'

Laura listens in silence. She would like this conversation to be short-lived, to bring Steve up to date and to agree to just leave things there.

'So have you sorted everything out at the doctor's?' he asks.

'Well, I've had a scan and some tests ...' She trails off. She's not sure how much she really wants to share with him any more. Everything feels so different between them. It is sour, like milk that has turned overnight. It is making her stomach feel queasy and she registers the urge to turn her face away from it all, to throw it in the bin where it belongs.

'And?' he asks, with a note of impatience.

'It's not straightforward. There's a chance the baby could be born with Down's syndrome, some possible birth defects.' She's not sure why she's even telling him this. 'But nothing is certain,' she adds. 'And, my feelings haven't changed.'

'You mean you're going through with it? Even after this?'

'Of course. Steve, I want this baby. I thought I made that clear.'

There is a beat of silence as he takes this in. When he speaks, his tone has shifted.

'Right. And what Laura wants, Laura gets. You really are the spoilt bitch I had you for, right from the beginning. Have you given any thought to what I want? How I might feel about the idea of bringing a sick child into this world? After everything I've been through with Ben?'

Laura sighs. 'You wouldn't be expected to pay for anything, Steve. If that's what you're worrying about. I'll take care of all that.'

'Ha! You mean, Ivo will.'

She continues, ignoring him. 'Look, I don't want anything from you. I'm merely informing you, out of courtesy.'

'Oh, I see. But it would still be my child, Laura, my responsi-bility. The thought of another person, walking around with my flesh and blood ... don't you get it, you callous bitch? This is not just your fucking decision to make!'

Laura moves the phone away from her ear. Why had she ever thought someone like him could behave with the decency and decorum she expects of everyone else in her life? He is behaving like a Neanderthal, embarrassing himself. She quickly looks about the car park to make sure no one is around in case they can hear him barking at her. She takes a breath, tries to deal with the situation calmly. It's not a good idea to provoke him, she realises.

'Steve, I'm sorry you feel that way. But, simply put: my body, my rules. I get to decide, not you. As I said, there's no need for you to have any further involvement.'

'And what are you going to tell Ivo? When he notices you're showing. How do you even know it's definitely mine?'

'Because, since my last period, I've only had sex with you,' she answers through gritted teeth.

'And you're going to pass it off as Ivo's? God, the poor sod, I almost feel sorry for him. Come on, Laura, the man's not a complete idiot, he'll figure it out, you know.'

Laura takes another deep breath and lets it out through her nose. She will not allow him to upset her.

'Ivo and I have had problems conceiving since Freddie. You know that, Steve.' She tries to keep the wobble out of her voice. 'But, the doctors never ruled anything out. I'm sure Ivo will be happy that we're having another baby, regardless.'

She hears Steve grunt at the end of the line. 'Well, I guess you got what you wanted. A willing sperm donor. Your little bit of rough on the side. You'd better hope the baby looks like you, Laura,' he adds.

'How many more times, Steve? I didn't think I could get pregnant any more. And Ivo's never taken much interest in my cycle or that sort of thing. Besides, the baby is small, the dates are uncertain ...' She trails off, trying to convince herself. She hangs her head, willing Steve to end the call. She can hear him pacing up and down, wherever he is, sounding agitated.

'So, then,' he says finally, the sound of resignation in his voice. 'You've got it all worked out, haven't you? All decided.'

'Yes,' she answers after a stuttering breath. 'Yes, I have. I'm sorry, Steve. This is what I have to do. It's for the best, I think. I didn't mean for any of this to happen. But now that it has, I've got to deal with it and this is what I've decided to do. For everyone's sake, I'd be grateful if you could accept that.'

She looks up and out of the windscreen, focuses on a bird that is sitting on a telegraph wire before launching itself off into the sky. Bending her head, she inhales some more of the calming lavender and eucalyptus oil on her wrist.

'Oh fuck off, Laura,' says Steve and the call is ended.

27

Iris pauses as she winds herself into her dressing gown on the way to the shower. She stands before Ben's door. She had solemnly vowed that she wouldn't go into his bedroom any more, to respect his privacy. But she feels the thread of connection with her son growing longer and thinner. Instead, she is reduced to eavesdropping, as she is now.

She leans her ear closer to the door. There is the sound of murmured conversation and Ben laughing in response to something said. It is conspiratorial, clandestine. She fights an urge to barge in. To demand to know what he is doing, with whom he is talking, what is it they are planning. This is her house, after all. He is her son.

Raising a hand, she is about to knock politely on the thickly painted door, when she notices something lower down, near her feet. Dropping to her knees, she runs her finger along the coarse indentations in the paint, scratches gouged here and there, that reach all the way up one panel of the door, up towards the handle and along the architrave. As though someone or something has been trying to get in. Spinning around, her eyes rake each surface around her. She searches the staircase, the walls, the other doors to see if there are signs of any more scratches, of any other similar markings, but there are none. They are only on Ben's door. Whatever made these marks, only seems to be interested in her son. And with that knowledge, her quiet fury turns to a cold realisation. She and her family are not alone. They are sharing this house with others.

Iris backs away from the door and hurries into her own bedroom. She sits on the edge of the mattress and grabs at handfuls of the duvet either side of her; a safe mooring. The idea of climbing in, sinking down beneath the covers, pulling them over her head, feels so appealing right now. She would like to close her eyes, drift off into the longest, deepest sleep and only wake to find that everything is well again. As it was. Even to be in their old rented place next to the constant grind of traffic on the road, the windows always smutty with polluted dust. But then she remembers how it used to exacerbate Ben's asthma. How she would worry about his chest. She lifts her head from the bed. She can hear the sound of her son's bedroom door opening, his feet thundering down the stairs as he calls out a goodbye from the hallway. It is too late, she has missed him again.

Instead, she finds Steve in the kitchen. He is opening cupboards, staring into them sightlessly and then banging them closed. Whatever it is he is looking for, he cannot seem to find it. She can tell by the hulking curve of his back, the tension in his neck and shoulders, that he is upset. Angry.

She reaches for the kettle, fills it at the sink, takes a cup and then another, places teabags in them. They dance around each other like this in silence for a few minutes, weaving in between one another, as Steve continues to slam doors and sigh with barely controlled frustration.

'Why don't you tell me what you're looking for and maybe I can help you find it,' she says eventually.

'Why is there never anything decent to eat in this house?' he says.

Iris laughs. 'Oh my God, Steve. Don't be such a baby. You sound like Ben.'

'Don't fucking laugh at me,' he says and bangs a final door shut for added emphasis.

'I'm making tea,' she says in answer.

'I don't want bloody tea. Where have all my beers gone?'

She looks into the cupboard where all the soft drinks and alcohol are usually stored. 'There were a couple of cans here yesterday,' she says.

'Well I haven't drunk them,' says Steve.

'Are you sure?' she says without thinking.

He gives her a cold, hard look from the other side of the room. She hadn't realised how livid he was; he looks close to tears.

'You think I can't remember how much I've had to drink?' he says.

'No, no ...' she backtracks.

'You'll never let me forget, will you?' he says, quietly, crossing his arms in defence.

Iris draws in a sharp breath. They both know what he is referring to, though they never speak of it. A few years ago, Steve had had a near-miss in the car while under the influence. Since then she has kept a watchful eye on his drinking, though he swears he has it under control.

'Will you?' he hisses at her. She prefers it when Steve shouts. This slow, low whisper is far worse.

'Steve, I didn't mean anything by it. It's fine. I'll get more.'

'Always watching me, checking up on me, counting every sip I take from every fucking bottle.'

'I don't. I've never said a word about your drinking.'

'You think I'd run the risk of getting a driving ban? When our whole livelihood depends on my job?'

'Well, no. But I earn too, you know. You're not the only one who works.'

He makes an ugly noise, halfway between a grunt and a snort. 'A few shifts in that stupid, jumped-up little shop is hardly going to keep the wolf from the door, is it now? But you've always been happy to leave it to me. Put all the burden on me. Let me take all the strain.'

'I seem to remember you were happy for me to give up my career so I could stay at home and look after Ben, too. Wasn't that the deal?'

They stare at each other across the kitchen.

'Listen to us,' he says finally. 'How can you call this a life?' To Iris's surprise, she hears him begin to laugh; a hollow, bitter sound. 'And now, I've got to spend my weekend bloody decorating, since you went crazy in the lounge, ripping off all the wallpaper, you mad fuck. Didn't even discuss it with me first. But then when have my feelings, my opinions ever come into any of this?' He puts his hands in the air to indicate the kitchen, the surrounding walls and floors of the house. 'I was happy where we were.'

She watches the resigned slump of his shoulders as he slopes off down the hall and into the lounge, hears him switch on the TV, and the sound of a commentator's voice emerges over the dull roar of a football match. Iris sighs. She had forgotten about the state of the lounge. She has avoided going in there since Christmas. The walls are flaking, crumbling. Patches of the original paper still cling on in places. It looks diseased. And, of course, there are still the graffitied messages. Another trace of Rosemary's family that can't be fully erased. She knows who June is now. A sister. Her words those of an infatuated young girl declaring her love for a local boy: Billy Maddox. She visualises the pencil strokes, revisits the name over and over again in her mind's eye. Where has she heard that name mentioned before?

28

Stepping into the shower, Iris closes her eyes as the water covers her head and cascades over her face, her shoulders, her body. She hates this bathroom; its mildewed tiles, its cracked lino, its clanking pipes. But the water is hot and the pressure is strong, which is all she needs right now.

If only she could block it all out, everything. Swaying, she places a hand against the wall to steady herself as she tries to think clearly. To weigh up each piece of knowledge she has, to make sense of it all. Rosemary said she had no family. There was no one, she insisted. But then there were the markings carved into the attic window sill, the graffiti on the living room wall. A sister, rejected by them all. Perhaps June has remained embittered all these years and is now seeking revenge. Did she send the wreath? Is she the blackmailer?

She allows the shower to continue, beating down on her. Iris is normally so frugal with the hot water, limiting herself to short, cool showers, never allowing the central heating to come on until the coldest months and only for a few hours each day. But now she lets the water run on and on as the steam billows into the cold air of the bathroom and condensation builds on the windows in the poorly ventilated space. She doesn't mind about the cost any more, she no longer cares about the water rates, the bills that will pile up on the mantelpiece. When you are this much in debt, what difference does it make?

Her mind winds back to the blackmail note. It already feels like a figment of her imagination, a bad dream. But one look in her handbag will remind her of its reality. How can anyone know what she's done? Nobody could have seen her. Who would be so sick as to blackmail her and how is she to pay them off? As the water swirls and eddies around her feet, she stares into the plug hole, willing the answer to come to her. There must be some way out of this. She thinks of the possible suspects, people who might have guessed her secret. She counts them off on her shrivelled fingers, her skin turning prune-like now.

There is the man from social services, who called recently. Well, she presumed that's where he was from anyway. Perhaps she had got it wrong. Maybe he's just some nosy neighbour – sorry, public-minded citizen – taking a bit too much of an eager interest. Whatever, it's only a matter of time before he comes sniffing round again. She could tell at the time that he didn't quite buy her story. How long before he does some research and smells a rat? But dangerous though he is, Iris doesn't believe the card is from him. It's someone closer to home. What about Laura or Ivo? Surely not. They are both way too wrapped up in their own lives and it's not like they need the money. The Italian next-door neighbour, Gianni? Perhaps. He had taken a keen interest in the improvements they had made to the house. But he is hardly ever here, in this country. He couldn't even remember Rosemary's name.

What about the school? Hadn't Ben's head of year, Mrs Khan, been rather inquisitive about the house? Her comments to Iris at the time felt a little too personal for a teacher to be making to a pupil's parent. And then, of course, there was the caretaker himself. He must be about the same age as Rosemary was and like he said, he's lived here all his life and knew the family. There is something so peculiar about him as well. If anyone looked the type to try and make a bit of money on the sly, it would be him. Why else would he still be working at his age, if he isn't desperate? And as Iris only knows too well herself, desperate people are capable of desperate things.

Finally the tears come, mixing with the water that runs down her face and onto her chest. Huge, stuttering sobs shake her body as she cries, safe in the knowledge that no one can hear her as the shower drums away. All the stress, all the anxiety, all the guilt, all the worry comes forth and empties out of her. For Ben, for Steve, for herself. And she thinks of all the years of struggle, not just recently but as a young woman, a child. Wrong clothes, wrong face, wrong accent. The name-calling, the shaming. How in her twenties she had moved away and tried to start again in another town, another city; different name, better clothes and finally a husband, friends, a child of her own. A child she wishes to protect from any hurt or harm. A child whom she knows, one day, she might not be able to save from danger.

As always, the thought of her son is what finally galvanises her. And with that she turns off the water, wringing the excess from her hair. She steps out of the shower and reaches for a towel to dry herself. As she presses it to her face, she briefly registers the faint smell of roses. But then it is gone. She reaches over to clean the mirror. The ghost of a hand-written message, the residue of a finger some time before tracing letters on the glass, is wiped away with the steam. Instead she focuses on the woman in the mirror, the directness of her gaze, the jut of her jaw.

She knows what she must do. It's simple, really. Either they leave or Rosemary does. They can't both stay here. The thought of moving, disrupting her family once again, is not an option. She will not countenance it. This house is theirs now. So, the old woman must go. The face that looks back at her in the glass hardens, her eyes darken with resolve.

This night is very different to the one when she first buried Rosemary. For a start, her husband and son are in the house, upstairs, asleep. Secondly, it is a bright, clear winter night. A smuggler's moon, they would call it. Illuminating the night sky like a floodlight. And it is cold. So cold, the breath billows out from her in clouds as she treads softly into the garden. Tonight she is wearing a thick anorak but it seems to rustle with every movement. Her hood falls back with each gust of wind. Her hands are numb and clumsy when she picks up the spade to dig, unable to get a firm, strong grip.

The ground is like stone. It glints and twinkles with frost, in contempt of her. She looks all around. Yet again, she mourns the loss of the laburnum tree, whose large, long-reaching branches provided such a welcome disguise. But there is still plenty of cover. Clouds briefly pass over the face of the moon. The exterior fence is still high, the long-established shrubs and bushes both private and secretive.

You can do this, Iris thinks. With her back to the next door garden, she considers the stump of the tree, the position of the trench she dug all those months ago. She tries to remember which end she placed the strong box with Rosemary's effects, the letters tied with ribbon. And which end, Rosemary's body. Will the pink bed sheets – the hastily chosen shroud in which she wrapped her – still be intact? How difficult will it be to move her? She has brought an extra-large rubbish sack, a thick, durable one intended for garden waste disposal, and a pair of Marigolds. She intends to contribute the body to the general mulch and compost at the recycling centre.

But as the spade makes contact with the frozen earth it glances off the hardened surface. Each attempt to penetrate it is rebuffed. Iris grows hot and sweaty within her thick woollen layers. She pushes the coat's hood back to feel the coolness on her cheeks, to let the air circulate around her damp neck.

She stabs and hacks at the ground repeatedly, swearing under her breath. But the spade is making little impact. With another effort, she hears the splintering of the shaft before she feels the pain in her hand. Crying out, in spite of herself, she realises a vicious sliver of wood is embedded in her palm. Falling back onto the grass, she stares in shock at her hand before easing the splinter out, dark blood pumping from the wound.

The injury is enough to shock her into her senses. She thinks of the sound she made; a scream that could have been a stray cat or an urban fox. Was it enough to wake her sleeping son and husband? She looks back towards the shallow grave, which refuses to give up its prize, now that it has been claimed. It feels like Rosemary is always having the last laugh, always confounding her in this nightmarish game of tit for tat. And as she sits prone on the ground, clasping her bleeding hand, she thinks of the bones and matter beneath her, only a few feet down. How the old woman's face will have fallen in on itself, her beatific smile receding now into a horrific rictus grin.

The vomit rises in her, unbidden and she coughs and splutters into the nearby bushes. Heaving once more, she then straightens up, reaching for the broken tool, the plastic sack and gloves. She is beaten. You win again, she thinks.

As she turns to stumble back down the garden and into the house, her eyes snag on a small movement at an upper window in the house next door. It is so brief, she could almost be mistaken. Her eyes are glazed with tears from the retching, her head dizzied, but she is sure of what she saw. Someone at the window, watching her.

29

Laura lies on her back, staring at the ceiling. She watches as the morning sunshine filters through the curtains, how it strikes the glass of the chandelier suspended from an ornate ceiling rose in the centre of the room. How the light splinters into a fragmented rainbow across the wall that plays and dances for a few minutes.

Turning over with a contented sigh, she wraps an arm around Ivo's waist, leans her face into his broad, muscular back, tanned against the crisp whiteness of the sheets. He makes a sleepy moan of pleasure, manoeuvring his arm so that he can join his hand with hers. Laura breathes in his reliable, comforting smell of soap and cologne; wood and musk and laundry. She kisses his skin, planting her lips gently against the curve of his spine, between his shoulder blades until she recognises a responding ripple of desire, a shiver.

With a giggle, she blows on his skin and watches the goose-flesh rise. He is still pretending to be asleep but she knows he will be growing hard, down below the duvet, and before long he can no longer resist. She laughs again as he turns, rolling over suddenly to lie on top of her, twisting himself between her legs, kissing her lips. She closes her eyes, the view of the sun-dappled ceiling, the translucent drapery, disappearing from sight as she sinks down lower into the soft sheets.

Afterwards, Ivo stays inside her for a while and she cradles his head against her chest, threads her fingers through his springy curls, strokes his back as though comforting a child who is tired or upset.

'I thought I'd lost you for a while there,' he whispers into her breasts, so quietly that she can hardly hear him. She is unsure how to interpret this statement. Ivo so rarely talks about his feelings, always being the type to put on a brave face and carry on. Weakness, sadness, feeling sorry for oneself, is what other people do.

'Why ever would you think that?' she asks cautiously, as she continues to stroke his back.

'Just that we'd lost connection somehow, become distant. It doesn't matter, babe. Ignore me.'

'I've had a lot on my mind,' she says. 'Not been feeling myself lately but I'm better now, much better.'

Ivo pushes himself up onto his arms, his biceps tensing into a ripe curl, so that he can look at her properly. He smiles, his eyes exploring her face as they always do, as if he still can't quite believe his luck that she is his.

'You seem better. Like something has shifted, whatever it is.'

Laura smiles back at him, her face breaking into a grin. She can't keep it in any longer; this bubble of a secret, this child-like glee.

'Ivo, I'm pregnant,' she whispers into the quiet morning air, a shaft of sunlight beaming through the curtains, sanctifying this moment, these words.

His face doesn't exactly fall, but the smile evaporates from his lips. There is a look of bemusement, disbelief, quickly succeeded by something else that Laura can't quite read. He looks as if someone has winded him in the side. His arms sag, no longer able to bear the weight of his body, deflated. He climbs off her and repositions himself on his side of the bed.

'Aren't you going to say anything?' says Laura, her voice betraying fear for the first time.

Ivo thumps his pillow a few times, sits further up against the headboard as Laura watches him in profile, trying to translate his actions.

'Wow,' he says finally.

'I know it's a shock. Trust me, I know,' she says, latching on to his one word response. 'But it's okay. It will all be okay. We can do this. And Ivo, I'm so happy.'

He turns his head towards her then and she registers the tears welling in his eyes. She smiles at him, moved by the rawness of his emotion.

'We're going to have another baby,' she whispers again, so quietly, because she still doesn't want to frighten away this reality.

Ivo studies her for a few seconds. He reaches up and stops a teardrop with his thumb, and then clasps her cheek with his large, capable hand. Laura turns her face to kiss the inside of his palm, over and over, her lips grateful for his touch.

'That's amazing,' he says eventually, exhaling a long-held breath. 'I don't know what to say, Laura. That's incredible news.'

'I know, but don't be scared, Ivo.'

He shakes his head. 'I just can't believe … I mean, I didn't think it was possible. Didn't think this would ever happen …'

'I know, I know.' She laughs. 'Me neither. But it has. It finally has.'

She squeezes his hand and he turns to look at her again. He smiles but it is as if he has commanded his face to hoist itself upwards, the smile not quite reaching his eyes, which are sad somehow.

'What's wrong?' she asks.

'Nothing, nothing.' He gives a hearty laugh then, pulls her into one of his trademark bear hugs and she feels herself encompassed again within his strong arms and chest, his expensive smell, the soft bristle of his chin. 'It's just a bit of a bloody shock, woman.'

And she laughs along with him, pressing herself closer into his skin, breathing him in as his arms tighten around her.

The light of Sunday morning grows brighter outside the window and with a sigh Ivo eventually disentangles himself from

Laura and the duvet. She watches as he reaches for fresh boxer shorts, pulls on yesterday's jeans and shirt over his long, strong limbs.

'I need to get Freddie to rugby practice,' he says, running a hand through his hair to straighten it and rendering it more unkempt in the process.

Laura nods. 'I'll go and rake him out of bed,' she says. 'Will you make breakfast?'

Wrapping herself into her dressing gown, she makes sure she's covered herself appropriately. Her son seems to grow ever more prudish about the thought of his parents' naked bodies or, God forbid, that they might actually still desire one another. All this despite the fact she's sure she found him looking at some dodgy photos on his phone the other day.

She wonders what Freddie will say when she breaks the news of the pregnancy to him. No doubt he will be mortified. The knowledge that your parents still have sex, let alone the physical evidence of that in bump form, will be the equivalent of social death. She's not looking forward to that chat. But he'll have a few months to get used to it. And at least she doesn't have to do the twice-daily school run now, standing in the playground exchanging gossip. She will be the gossip instead, she realises, wincing at the thought. Hopefully she can disguise this pregnancy for as long as possible. She had such a nice, neat little bump with Freddie almost all the way through, she remembers, smiling to herself with pride.

'Freddie,' she calls outside his bedroom door.

There is no answer so she walks straight in. The room is a soup and really starting to acquire that fetid, pubescent boy smell; a combination of sweaty armpits, humming trainers, sticky glasses and rotten apple cores left in an overflowing bin. She's been so ashamed of his bedroom for months now that she doesn't even let the cleaners come in here (which is part of the problem, obviously).

Striding to the curtains, she wrenches them open and light floods the room, illuminating further the scene of devastation.

'Oh, Fred. What a state you've let this place get in,' she wails, picking up cups and plates and chocolate bar wrappers. She lifts a few more garments from the floor, sniffs them tentatively, and tucks them under her arm, to be taken to the laundry basket.

Freddie groans and turns his face away from the window, pulling the pillow over his head.

'Get out, Mum. I've told you. You can't just come barging in here any more.'

Laura stands at the side of the bed. Is it her imagination or was he trying to cover up his crotch? The thought makes her nose curl as much as the dirty socks but then she relents.

'All right, all right, I'm going. Get up though. You'll be late for rugby practice. I'll get some cereal out for you.'

Freddie gives another moan of complaint and she backs away, not before casting a cursory glance over his desk which is strewn with exercise books, pens, chargers, a games console and some chewing gum. She crouches down to throw some of the litter she's collected into his bin. She sighs at the amount of dust bunnies that have accumulated by the skirting board. She really must get the Hoover in here soon, it's disgusting. More detritus litters the floor; broken stationery, scrunched-up paper next to the digital printer he keeps stored beneath his desk. Then her eye is caught by a colourful plastic shape which at first she thinks is a lighter, but turns out to be a discarded vape, smelling suspiciously of artificial strawberry. With another sigh, she secretes this in her dressing gown pocket. That is a whole other conversation she and Ivo will have to broach at some point in the future. Straightening up, she gathers the bin under her other arm and makes her way out of the room.

'Downstairs, Freddie. Five minutes,' she shouts before she catches the door with her foot and slams it closed behind her.

As Laura sits up at the kitchen island, she is the only still point in the room. Ivo moves about, fixing his morning coffee, fastidiously tinkering with his favourite toy. It does fill the house with the most lovely smell in the mornings, especially when combined with toast and Radio 4 burbling away in the background.

She watches Freddie, his face inscrutable, as he shovels in milk and cereal, head down, hardly allowing himself to chew before the next mouthful. Ivo leans against the work surface and sips his espresso. He looks distracted, his eyes averted as he stares at his feet. But then he looks up and attempts a smile.

There is something about this morning's revelations, the unscheduled sex, so urgent and tender, her feelings of fear swiftly replaced by gratitude and reassurance, that have made her feel a little giddy, untethered. And presumably it is the same for Ivo. He looks at his watch and knocks back his coffee.

'Come on, buddy,' he says to Freddie. 'We'd better make tracks.'

Laura accepts a kiss from Ivo as he leaves, much to Freddie's distaste and he makes a kind of gagging sound. She lunges at him, proffering her face for another kiss, but her son veers away in disgust and she listens to both of them bang and clatter on their way out.

Sliding off the bar stool, she takes up Freddie's bowl and rinses away the milk and leftover cereal before putting it into the dishwasher. She leans over and turns up the radio a fraction. Her mint tea has gone cold so she tops up the teapot from the instant hot water tap. Settling herself back on the stool, she allows herself to feel a moment of contentment when there is a knock at the door.

For a second, she considers ignoring it. Whoever it is, should know better than to disturb anyone on a Sunday morning. And then with a curdle in her stomach, it occurs to her that it could be Steve. Has he been outside, casing the house, waiting for Ivo and Freddie to leave? She wouldn't put it past him. His behaviour of late has been distinctly worrying and she doubles down on her resolution to freeze him out of her life. There is another sharp rap at the door, more insistent this time.

Tightening her dressing gown, pulling it across her chest and up to her neck, she opens the door a crack. She has taken the precaution of putting the security chain on the door and she peers through the gap. But it is only Iris. Laura lets out a relieved noise.

'Oh, it's you,' she says, closing the door so she can undo the chain, and then opening it again wider to her friend.

'What's with the chain?' asks Iris. 'Expecting trouble?'

Laura laughs. 'No. Just being extra careful. Come through.' She leads Iris down along to the kitchen and switches off the radio.

'What's up?' she says, turning round. She has a clean mug in her hand, which she raises slightly as an offer of a drink. Iris looks at her intently, apparently taking in the dressing gown, the hand-thrown terracotta pottery. This is not unusual. Laura has become accustomed to Iris's laser-like focus, always assessing every item she is wearing, every object she uses, everything she owns.

'Tea? Coffee?'

Iris leans forward on the island, her eyes resting on Laura's midriff where her robe has pulled apart a little.

'When were you going to tell me about the pregnancy?' she says with a slow smile.

Laura is dumbstruck. Her arm hovers in the air, the mug clasped loosely in her hand before she replaces it on the work surface. How much does Iris know? Her mind darts but then she sees her friend's soft, indulgent expression. The pleasure of a shared confidence. There is no anger in her face, no accusation in her voice.

'How did you guess?' she asks.

Iris shrugs, clearly pleased with herself. 'Woman's intuition. Takes one to know one,' she says. 'Besides, I've never seen you without a washboard stomach,' she adds, nodding towards Laura's tummy.

'It's still really early days,' she says, placing a hand there. 'I've only just told Ivo.'

Iris nods and then turns her face away with a raised eyebrow. There is something about this cocky, knowing reaction that Laura doesn't like but she brushes it away.

'We haven't shared this with anyone else yet, not even Freddie, so please keep it under your hat.'

'Sure, of course,' says Iris.

She's enjoying this, Laura can tell. It must be the first time Iris has ever had the upper hand in their relationship, she acknowledges with displeasure.

'I, we, didn't think we could even get pregnant any more,' she continues shakily. Why is she disclosing all this? Iris has caught her off guard. Nerves are making her too candid. This morning is taking its toll on her and the unsettled sensation spreads over her. 'But we're both thrilled,' she says in a voice that sounds more confident than she feels.

Iris continues to regard her from her perch on the stool and merely nods. 'Well, that's great,' she says. 'Really great. Good for you.'

Laura looks about the kitchen, her eyes falling on the pot of mint tea she refreshed, running her hand over the marble island, thinking of the radio programme she has had to forego.

'Was there something else, Iris?' she asks with an awkward laugh. 'Only I was about to run myself a bath. Take advantage of a quiet house while the lads are at rugby.' She decides not to repeat her offer of a drink. A small triumph, but one she will savour. Hopefully Iris will get the hint soon and go. 'Everything okay with you and Steve?' she asks with mock interest.

At this, Iris's face changes. A hint of sourness or regret passes over her features. Ah, so that's it, thinks Laura with satisfaction. Trouble at the mill. She's not surprised but all the same, she should be careful. She's still not sure how much of a loose cannon Steve might be. What he is capable of doing or saying.

'Oh it's fine, really,' says Iris. 'Just a row. Nothing out of the ordinary.'

This is typical. Iris never admits to the fact that her and Steve's marriage has clearly been floundering for years, that they've been papering over the cracks when it was clear to Laura – even before the affair – that all was not well.

'And the house?' prompts Laura, moving on to safer territory. 'Still coming along nicely? It was looking fab at Christmas. And those houses must have really big attics too. Such a great space, should you ever wish to go up into it. I can put you in touch with some wonderful builders, you know. Not cheap, but an amazing finish. Might be worth getting on their waiting list now.'

Again, Iris's face seems to fall at the mention of these things, as though she has been reminded of a bad memory.

'Maybe,' she answers noncommittally. 'I think we'll have to save up a bit before then.'

Laura nods vigorously. 'Sure, sure, of course.'

'I just needed to get out of the house, to be honest,' says Iris, looking about herself as if she is surprised to find herself here, in Laura's kitchen, on a Sunday morning, without invitation. She collects herself, scrambling off the stool. 'I should be getting back actually. Need to get the roast on soon. The boys will be expecting the usual, you know.'

'Ben all right?' asks Laura, as an afterthought.

'Yes, good. Really good,' says Iris. 'I think he's really starting to settle in at school now.'

'Oh, I'm so glad. So it was worth it all in the end?'

Iris blanches. She looks like a rabbit caught in the headlights.

'Worth it? How do you mean?'

'To get Ben in to Toppingham,' she prompts.

'Yes,' Iris replies eventually. 'Yes, I suppose it was.'

Laura allows the conversation to peter out and a silence stretches between them.

'Congratulations on the baby,' says Iris as she turns to leave. And then she adds: 'It's just what you've always wanted.'

Laura leads her back down the hall contemplating this last statement, turning it over in her mind like a stone. She opens the door and then a thought occurs to her.

'By the way, you didn't happen to come across an earring at yours, did you? I lost one of mine a little while ago. Antique, pearl. Quite valuable actually.'

Iris falters for a second before answering.

'Oh, that was yours? I thought ...' A frown crosses her brow. 'Never mind.'

'Great, well, let me have it back when you can. You know how it is when you lose something precious.'

Iris nods thoughtfully and then steps over the threshold. Laura watches her friend as she walks away, only now just realising that Iris isn't even wearing a coat, in February. That and the fact that her right hand is covered in a thick bandage. She wonders why Iris really called round. What is it that she's not saying? She hesitates for a moment, considers whether she should be more worried before she remembers her mint tea, her bubble bath, the radio programme she wants to catch.

30

Iris walks briskly down the road, away from Laura and Ivo's house. How stupid of her to think that she might be able to confide, to offload. She must be more careful. For a moment then she almost cracked. She folds her arms against the cold, head down into the wind. There is no one who could possibly understand what she has done. She knows that. So she must keep this secret. Find a way to keep going.

Continuing along, she crosses the road, making her way back towards the high street. She left Ben in bed this morning and Steve decorating the lounge; thumping and banging his tools around, swearing audibly. He has already relined the walls but they haven't even conferred about the paint. What colour the walls should be. She just wants them covered, restored, smoothed over.

'I don't care,' she'd muttered to him when he'd asked. 'Anything pale. Grey, beige. Whatever.'

'I thought this was important to you. Why else have you been chewing my fucking ear off about DIY all these months if you don't even care?' he'd said.

'Fine. I'll do it myself.'

But then he had shouldered her out of the room, setting up his usual dust sheets and ladders in a silent sulk.

As she walks along now, Iris reaches into the pocket of her jeans, her fingers enclosing the plastic bank card. She had spotted her chance when she saw Steve's wallet and keys on the worktop. He was busy in the lounge, the radio turned up, involved in his task.

And as she'd taken the card from his wallet, like a thief in the night, she had run from the house. She had continued to run, until she realised her feet had found their way to her friend's house. What had she been hoping to find? A sympathetic ear? A shoulder to cry on? Laura will never, ever understand how it feels to be her, to live a single day in her shoes. To look back on the years of struggle, the scrimping, the saving, only to see it all disappear each and every month into a landlord's pocket or the black hole of interest rates or loan arrears. To look back on a life that has always felt like an uphill struggle from the very start; parents whose meagre savings were swallowed up by inflation, relatives whose property was sold to pay for medical care and nursing home fees. Being sent to a sink school where the best you could hope for was to emerge physically unscathed and with a handful of GCSEs.

When Iris decided to leave school – her parents had never been to university and couldn't understand why she herself would want to – the careers advisor had suggested hairdresser or estate agent to her, because she enjoyed reading glossy magazines and had been good at art and design. They didn't seem to be aware of Iris's quiet, shy disposition, her tendency to be a loner, her inability to socialise like other girls at school. At no point had they considered Iris's personality traits or behaviour at all, merely asking her to fill in a simple questionnaire. If they had, they might have realised that either of these roles would be completely unsuitable.

However, Iris had managed to pass her driving test not long after leaving school – something her parents felt was worth paying for if it meant she could chauffeur them around, do the supermarket shopping or pick them up from the pub. So she joined the team at her local branch of Coleridge & Brown estate agents. To her surprise, she found that she was quite adept at driving to appointments in the company's liveried Renault Clio in order to open up for viewings, mutely watching couples wander around flats and houses, answering by rote their questions about council tax and school catchment areas. It's no wonder really that these things have come to obsess her, to dog her heels.

Iris has reached the cash machine now and she takes a shifty look up both sides of the high street. It is filled with the usual Sunday morning dog walkers and leisurely strollers. Sauntering in their goose down-filled jackets and limited-edition trainers, they cradle takeaway coffees, which they sip at like a caffeinated teat; a thirst which they never seem quite able to sate. Kids in brightly coloured outfits commandeer the pavement with scooters. A tiny trio of girls in frou-frou tutus and wellies skip along excitedly with balloons suspended from their hands. Their mothers follow on; older, elongated versions of their daughters, heads drawn together like gossiping hens in the wake of their downy chicks. She turns inward as a man approaches from the other direction, shouting into his mobile phone.

'Yeah, we're all meeting up at the Lord Admiral for lunch. Roast beef and beers followed by the Six Nations on the big screen, mate. Everyone will be there. Lara, Suki, Teddy and Frazer. Wanna come with?'

Iris curves her body around the ATM, hiding the screen from onlookers though nobody is paying her any attention. She knows Steve's PIN, always has. He uses it for everything; gym locker, Sky TV, phone screen lock. Quickly, she keys it in and tries not to look at the summary of his bank balance as it flashes across the screen in neon green. There should be enough funds. He's only just been paid and he has the usual overdraft, which they've never been able to pay off no matter how hard they try.

With a sharp breath she presses the button for £250. She will have to withdraw another £250 from another machine, and another and another. The story she will stick to, is that she needed to pay off the Christmas credit cards. She took his bank card because she didn't want to bother him while he was busy. It all comes out of the same pot anyway, in theory. They've always pooled their resources even though they kept their separate accounts. He doesn't know that she isn't paying the rent every month.

As she swiftly pockets the notes, looking about her, it crosses her mind that £1,000 isn't a very large sum for a blackmailer to request. Not in the grand scheme of things. Why wouldn't the caretaker ask for more if he really wanted to rinse her? Never mind, she thinks, turning away from the hole in the wall. She will deal with him next time she sees him. In the meantime, she needs to get the money to the PO box before there are any further repercussions. And that will be the end of it.

Monday morning rolls around far too quickly. Today, Iris is determined to start the week afresh. She leaps out of bed the moment the alarm goes off, leaving Steve fast asleep. They appear to be avoiding each other at the moment and she finds herself relieved that he has another work trip coming up soon.

She showers quickly, not pausing to condition her hair or moisturise her skin. Nothing seems to make any difference anyway. Her hair is dry and frizzy and her skin lacklustre. These subtle changes have come upon her so slowly that she hardly noticed them at first. Her nails became more ridged and brittle, like her mother's and her grandmother's before her. Her knees and back now twinge with pain at the end of the day and she finds herself elevating them at night to try and drain her swollen ankles. She has put it down to spending all day on her feet, running up and downstairs to the stockroom, not eating properly or taking the right supplements.

These days, she finds her stomach bloats more easily too. She feels sluggish. The flesh on her arms and legs no longer cleaves to her bones like it did when she was younger. Of course, she could do more exercise, eat more sensibly. Like Laura does. But when does she have the time or energy? After she's finished work and kept on top of the cleaning and done the food shop, preparing all the meals so that she can carefully monitor ingredients for Ben, there is nothing left.

Iris takes a clean blouse and skirt from the wardrobe, freshly pressed. She wants to make sure her outfit looks perfect today when she arrives early at the shop. Her packed lunch was made last night and stored in the fridge. The £1,000, in crisp twenty pound notes, is packaged up in a jiffy bag with the PO box address clearly written on the front. She hesitated over whether to include some communication and hastily scrawled a note which read:

THIS ENDS HERE. STAY AWAY FROM ME AND MY FAMILY OR I WILL BE THE ONE WHO GOES TO THE POLICE.

But then she had thought better of it. She doesn't want anything that could link back to her personally, that could make her look complicit in all of this.

Iris dresses and pulls her hair back into a severe ponytail. She applies the sparest layer of make-up; some mascara and a quick swipe of lipstick. Looking in the mirror, she tries to find the steely determination in her face, the facade she puts in place when she heads to work. But it is slipping away. Her shoulders sag and she feels the telltale quiver in her cheek as a prickle stings her eyes. Why is she always on the verge of tears these days?

She never used to cry, used to pride herself on her lack of emotion, leaving it to other, more vapid, silly women. This is not her. This is not who she is. She's always had to be so strong. For herself. For Ben. But she's not sure what the point of all this is any more. She only ever wanted to keep him safe. To give him a better chance. One she never had. To level the playing field a little. And yet, since they moved into this house everything seems to be even harder, more uphill than ever. It's since that fateful night when she had jumped one way rather than another, made an insane decision that seemed so rational, so fair at the time, that her life feels to be falling apart.

And it is the realisation that she has done this that makes her quake. She feels like the earth is shifting, tectonic plates beneath her feet. A layer of ice that is cracking underneath her. There is nothing to hold her any more. Not her parents, or her husband. Certainly not her friend. And obviously not her son. She is the one who looks after him. It always comes back to Ben in the end. She pulls her blouse down, tucks it more tightly into her skirt, straightening the seams. Her lips form an O shape in the mirror as she blows slowly out through her mouth.

'You can do this,' she says to herself.

Steve stirs in the bed beside her and not wanting to be engaged in conversation, she grabs her bag and hurries out of the bedroom. She needs to leave early so she has time to take a detour via the post box en route to work. But as she passes by the door to Ben's room, she can't help pausing. She reaches out a hand and gently pushes the door. He is still asleep, his shock of dark blonde hair resting on the pillow, eyes screwed up tight as if to shut out the reality of the world. And in that moment, she knows that she really would do anything for her child. Anything to protect him. Anything to prevent others from doing him harm.

31

Laura drinks down a juice, feeling the pulp and froth catch at the back of her throat. It is a sludgy green colour but she can feel it is doing her – and more importantly, the baby – good as it slips down into her stomach. She's a firm believer that you are what you eat. And you are also what you think. Mind over matter is one of her and Ivo's mantras. Think it, be it. A positive mental attitude is essential. She puts all of their success down to this belief system. Yes, they both came from good backgrounds, went to the best schools and universities, but only because their parents had paved the way for them, setting a good example. Positivity breeds positivity.

She slings the blender jug in the sink and takes her keys from the pot on the windowsill. She is not sure what to do with her day. She can't face sitting still, staring at a screen, editing photos.

Laura smooths a hand over her tummy. She is relishing the fact that she can stop hiding the pregnancy. Now that Ivo and Iris (not to mention Steve, of course), all know, she feels like she can cut herself a bit of slack. At the thought of Steve, she takes in a deep breath. What if he says something? Loses it in a moment of anger and admits to the affair? Or casts doubt on the paternity of her child. This new-found happiness could all come crashing down around her ears.

But she juts out her chin. It will be okay. Steve is spineless. He might not be happy with Iris but he would never do anything to rock the boat or hurt Ben. To risk losing contact with his beloved son. No, she has longed to be pregnant for so many years now.

She refuses to deny herself this pleasure, this pride. She will enjoy this and all will be well. Walking down the front path and past a few of the manicured gardens on the street, she stops to admire the delicate white perfection of snowdrops that have sprung up in clumps. The green bullet-like shoots of daffodils are nosing their way through the earth as well, ready to trumpet spring in glorious yellow.

She unlocks the car and slides into the front seat of the Range Rover. She loves its size, its bulk. The feeling of safety and security it provides, especially now she is pregnant with such precious cargo. It's like nothing bad could ever happen to her in a car like this. She steers out of the parking space and away down the middle of the road.

Driving on autopilot, Laura realises that the car seems to have found its way out of town and is travelling along country roads, far away from the smog and the enclosed environs of buildings and houses. She recalibrates, trying to rethink her route, to double back and navigate her way to the town centre. She'd like to do a bit of shopping. Just a few things for the baby. But then she finds herself pulling up in a lay-by next to a low, purpose-built building in rural surroundings. Chickens and pigs are penned close by. There is a cordoned off adventure playground, surfaced with wood chippings, where swings and a slide and a covered sand pit reside.

The sign in front of the gate reads: Green Fields Forest School. She knows this place. She recognises it now. It is an address she has remembered subconsciously from her many furtive google searches for Down's syndrome kids & babies, facilities, schools, parent support. Other suggested search terms had also included: learning impairments, health conditions, life expectancy but she had skirted over them, trying to unsee the words, let alone click on them.

So this is where she needs to be today, she realises. Perhaps the baby has guided her here intuitively and she smiles a wobbly smile, her hand shifting to her belly as she turns off the engine and stares out of the window. Laura watches as a couple of shaggy horses stand tethered nearby in a field, leaning their heads over the side of a five-bar gate. Steam curls from their nostrils as they gently snort, plumed tails tossing behind them.

Before long she is aware of voices; the low authoritarian tone of adults mixed with the louder, more high-pitched calls of younger children. She sees them now as they come running out in their primary-coloured anoraks, hats and gloves. Feet inserted into a rainbow of wellies, this higgledy-piggledy crocodile wanders over towards the field, a range of heights and ages. One child holds on resolutely to an adult's hand, never leaving her side. Another child, a boy, charges out boisterously and promptly trips, falling to his knees. But he doesn't cry, rather his face cracks into a wide grin and he laughs a loud honking laugh, looking around at his peers, inviting them to join in.

Laura winds down the window to gain a better view and as she does, she catches the excited range of sounds that travel across the wind towards her. All of the children squeal and shout, the very feeling of being outside, surrounded by nature, seeming to fill them up. Laura can sense how intoxicating this fresh air must be and she finds herself breathing it in too. The rambunctious boy child is still the loudest. His vowels are clumsy, ill-formed and yet his joy is palpable. She doesn't need to understand what he is saying, it is obvious.

She continues to watch as one of the adults stations themselves next to the gate, picking up a nearby bucket. The boy is led over to the nearest horse, encouraged to be quiet and gentle. He shushes everyone including himself and his teacher with a loud, audible sound, his finger held demonstrably to his lips. Still the excitement bubbles out of him. He can't keep it in.

The horses are incredibly tame, not tempted to shy away despite the commotion, the unpredictability of the children.

Well-trained, docile, with reserves of never-ending patience, they stand obediently, chewing grass as the boy strokes the coarse darkness of their manes. He lifts his finger and with infinite care, touches the velvety muzzle of one, shrieks with laughter when it bares its yellowed teeth. As the boy turns his head a little further now, Laura can see his face more clearly; the height of his forehead, the wispy hair like thistledown, the large, almond-shaped eyes, the snub nose. As though sensing finally that he is being observed, the boy looks over directly towards the verge where Laura is parked.

'Car,' he says clearly and points.

His supervisor looks over, following the direction of his outstretched finger. The horse tosses its head at the sound and continues to crop the grass. Laura blushes, and turns away, hurriedly fumbles to start the engine. But when she looks back again, the boy is waving at her and smiling. She is not sure what to do, how to act. Does she look suspicious, like some kind of predatory paedophile? But the boy continues to wave, repeating the word 'car' to himself and to her surprise Laura finds herself smiling too, returning the wave.

And she thinks to herself: 'It's going to be okay. Whatever happens, no matter how this turns out, it will all be okay.'

She is about to pull the car away from the lay-by when a call comes through the loudspeaker. Steve's name flashes up on the screen. Danger, it seems to say, like a hazard warning. Laura pauses and then cancels the call without answering. A second later the call comes again, its tone blaring through the sound system of the car, disturbing the peace of the bucolic scene outside. She looks over through the side window again but the boy has disappeared along with the rest of the schoolchildren. That beautiful child, this beautiful setting, the beautiful feeling that had flooded her only a moment ago has been swept away by this intrusion. Anger suffuses her. How dare he do this? What right does he have to harangue her like this?

Rifling through her bag, locating her phone, Laura begins to scroll through her address book until she finds Steve's number. Her thumb hovers over the contact name and its corresponding number and after a second's hesitation, she acts, pressing the option to block and then delete. And with that, Steve disappears from her phone. If only she could do the same in reality, she thinks. Erase him from her life. Permanently.

It's just a shame that she feels so entwined with Iris. But then friendships come and go all the time. It happens. Though something tells her that Iris and Steve will not be that easy to get rid of. And besides, she relents, flicking on the indicator and pulling out into the country lane, she can't abandon Iris. If ever there was a woman who needs a friend, it's her. Something is not right there. She knows it. And you don't kick a dog when it's down.

32

The woman stands in front of Iris, feet planted in her Veja trainers, wearing a long cream mac reaching to the floor. She clutches a leather handbag under her arm in the same way one might carry a small dog, like a dachshund. The other hand she waves around is tipped with the boiled sugar shine of a fresh manicure. Her eyes survey Iris up and down before she closes her lids dramatically and sighs.

'Scarves. I'm looking for scarves. Can you help me with that or not?' she asks, turning to look around the shop in desperation, but realising there is no one else available.

Iris swallows, feeling the heat rise in her face. There's something familiar about this woman. She has a feeling she might have been one of the school mums at Laura's Halloween party. Though, clearly, the woman has failed to recognise her.

'Like I said, we do have some in our winter range, but I've already shown you those,' Iris replies slowly, enunciating the words carefully.

The woman tuts, flinging an arm out in the general direction of the rails and the mannequins.

'No, no, they're all wrong. I can't have those. Too thick, too bulky. I have a delicate frame and those would swamp me. Besides, I'm allergic to man-made fibres. I need a hundred per cent natural materials. Silk, cotton, cashmere.'

Iris has to physically stop herself from rolling her eyes. As if, she thinks. But then she checks herself. Lots of people are allergic to even the most benign or bizarre materials, her son being one of them.

'Right, I see. Well, I can go downstairs and look in our stock-room to see if we have anything down there from our previous spring/summer range?'

'Amazing,' comes the reply, the woman's voice loaded with sarcasm.

Iris walks towards the stairs. A bloody 'please' or 'thank you' wouldn't go amiss, she thinks. She casts a look over her shoulder towards the school mum who has moved to stand by the window. She is gesticulating to a sports car parked nearby, her husband sitting impatiently in the driver's seat, pointing at his watch.

'Won't be long, darling,' she calls, shrugging her shoulders apologetically. 'Stupid staff,' she mutters by way of explanation, tilting her head in the direction of the shop.

As she stomps down the staircase, Iris feels herself seethe. These people really are the fucking limit. She locates a storage box in the back of the stockroom marked 'S/S 23 accessories' and begins to rummage, pulling out a beach bag that has lost its strap, several sun hats looking a little worse for wear and some lightweight scarves and sarongs. She gathers them together, trailing coloured silk and chiffon behind her like a magician halfway through a stage performance.

Back on the shop floor, Iris feels herself pant from the exertion. She is suddenly hot, her face growing red. The heating is on quite high in the shop. Her clothes feel too tight, too thick. A fire quickly spreads itself through her body, rising up from the soles of her feet, radiating out through her solar plexus, rendering her cheeks aflame.

Presenting the scarves to the woman as neatly as she can, she tries to exhale a breath of air, funnelling it upwards to cool her face. The woman turns to her, a frown etched on her forehead and raises her arms in alarm.

'Oh!' she exclaims, taking in the ragtag selection of items in Iris's arms. They do look a little creased, to be fair.

'I can steam them for you, if you like?' Iris hears herself offering, though the thought of using a hot vaporous device right now is the last thing she feels like doing.

'No, no, no,' says the woman tutting, appraising the scarves aghast, as though Iris has just presented her with a box of dog turds. 'These won't do at all. Really, how difficult is it to find a suitable scarf these days?' she asks, turning to the rest of the shop as though beseeching a sympathetic audience, though no one else is around. 'I'm obviously reaching for the moon,' she adds with a hollow laugh.

Iris steels herself. She resolves to bite her tongue, to rise above it. She cannot stand the way these people act as though a scarf – or lack of – is the be-all and end-all. A catastrophe. A disaster. She catches sight of one of the labels, the price tag which is well over £200. The cost of just one of these items could feed a family. Pay someone's weekly rent. Buy new shoes, a school uniform, PE kit.

'Perhaps it's not the scarves that are the problem, but you.' Iris blinks, her mouth falling open. Did she just say that out loud? Surely it was only her inner monologue, the one that runs continuously now, commentating sardonically on everyone and everything.

'I beg your pardon. What did you say?'

'Nothing,' says Iris.

The woman screws her eyes up and peers more closely.

'Don't I know you from somewhere?'

'Laura Peters' Halloween party. My son goes to Toppingham,' supplies Iris.

The woman gives Iris a long slow look that grazes her from top to bottom and back again. Recognition finally dawns on her.

'That's right. You're the witch who got her knickers in such a twist about the nuts.' She wags her finger, pleased that she has finally made the connection. 'Didn't your son wet himself?' she asks with a disgusted frown.

'That's not what happened at all,' says Iris, raising her voice. 'And I presume it was one of your nasty little brats who was picking on him that night.'

Right on cue, Iris's manager is at the top of the stairs, making her way on to the shop floor.

'Is everything all right here?' she asks as she approaches them.

The woman smirks. 'I suggest you have a word with your staff about customer service. This is what happens when you hire the wrong sort.' With that, she flounces from the shop and waves in the direction of the sports car, responding to the toot of its horn.

'What was all that about?' asks the manager, looking from Iris to the disappearing customer to the pile of scarves.

Iris considers her options. Can she stomach a dressing-down? The predictable tittle-tattle that will be whispered behind her back by the other staff members. The condescending tone that is already reserved for her, increasing ever more. She thinks about the school mum, the cloud of expensive perfume she has left in her wake, the sleek red sports car parked right outside the shop as though claiming some personalised bay all of its own. And the words 'stupid staff' echo in her ears. It doesn't matter what you do, she thinks. How hard you work, how pleasant or deferential or helpful you try to be. When you are working in a customer-facing role, in the service industry, there will always be people who think they know you. Who judge you and make assumptions about your life, your IQ, your upbringing, your worth.

'I quit,' says Iris and drops the scarves, whereupon they float luxuriously down to the floor to settle at her manager's feet.

Iris walks. She walks with no particular direction in mind, waiting for her pulse to slow. There is a fresh wind today but it is welcome. It is a delicious, cooling breeze though it is brisk and bracing. She scuffs at her face, wiping away a stray tear that has leaked from the corner of one of her watering eyes. It's just the cold, she thinks. She will not cry. She will not allow it. If she starts, she might not be able to stop.

The feeling of initial relief, the euphoria at resigning, telling her manager where to stick her job, is subsiding and the slow, creeping dread of reality is encroaching. What is she going to tell Steve? How will they survive on even less money? It's not like her to be so emotional, so reactive. She's always been a grafter, priding herself on her resilience. But something just snapped.

She finds a park bench and takes out her phone, brings up a jobs website and begins searching for local vacancies. Maybe she can get away with not saying anything for a week or two. Pretending she is heading to work while she looks for something else. She is scrolling through ads for receptionists, bar managers, call centre operators – all of them involving the requirement to be friendly, outgoing, excellent at customer service – when a call comes in from Ben's school. She immediately feels her stomach clench.

'Hello,' she answers, trying to keep her voice under control.

'Morning, is that Mrs Simmonds? It's the attendance officer here, from Toppingham School.'

Iris leans into the phone, gripping it more tightly. Again, that feeling that she is in trouble. She has done something wrong. 'Yes,' she croaks in confirmation.

'I'm calling because Ben wasn't at form registration this morning and no reason for absence has been given.'

Iris's mind races through all the various reasons for Ben to be missing: road traffic accident, anaphylactic shock, abduction.

'Oh. Really? I, er, I don't know.' She tries to keep the wobble from her voice. 'He set off for school on time I believe. Let me try and track him down,' she mumbles apologetically.

'Right, I'll mark him down as absent,' comes the terse reply.

Iris lowers the phone from her ear, letting her hand fall to rest in her lap. Her heart starts up its usual hectic hammering before she counsels herself. He's probably fine, just truanting. But why? She thought that Ben was doing better these days and yet sometimes she feels like she knows him less and less. This move, the new school; it was supposed to be the answer to all their problems. But it feels like everything is going wrong.

A thought enters her head: is she being punished? Swiftly followed by the accusations: you stole someone else's house. You hid a body. You broke the law. It is not often that she looks these facts straight in the eye. It is as though these wrongs were committed by someone else entirely and if she keeps her eyes averted, refuses to look directly, she can pretend that everything is normal. There is a name for this, she thinks. There is a term for people like you. Her hands begin to shake and she has to concentrate on her breathing. Focus on what's important: Ben. Seizing her phone again, she types out a text to her son:

Where are you? Why aren't you at school?

She hits the location app she uses to track Ben's phone but he has turned off his Wi-Fi so it's impossible to identify his where-abouts. Where could he be? Why is he missing lessons? She tries not to panic, to not think the worst, to stop her imagination spiralling out of control as it always does where Ben is concerned. But she knows there is no point going home, looking for him at the house. He wouldn't risk being caught there out of normal hours. Taking a look at her watch, she gathers her things together and heads off in the direction of the school. She needs to speak to the head of year.

33

Laura drives back towards the town centre, decides she will brave the traffic and see if she can park up somewhere near the high street. Today feels like it could be the first day of spring. March is just around the corner and the sun is shining through clear blue skies. It has brought everyone out it seems. The pavements are lined with bistro tables and chairs. Couples sit outside in their thick coats and sunglasses, turning their faces towards the thin rays like plants starved of light.

She snags a parking space big enough for the Range Rover and finds the ticket meter. As she taps in her details, she acknowledges the strange feeling of being observed somehow. She is used to being admired, to be honest. It is something inherent, which she has grown up with since she was a young girl, that first time she became aware that this face of hers, this body, were not just hers but everyone else's as well.

Laura looks one way and then the other, checking the length of the street, but there is no one from school or the yoga class who she recognises. She hasn't mounted the kerb or accidentally scratched someone's bumper. So why does she feel the telltale prickle on the back of her neck, the hairs on her arms rising like a caterpillar's fur?

She gives herself a little shake and dismisses the thought. She doesn't do paranoia or self-doubt. Instead she grabs her bag from the seat. But there it is again. For no reason, she feels nervous, as though she is about to be caught out, reprimanded.

As she closes the door, she looks briefly over the road. A shape, a shadowed face, a familiar figure stands half concealed beside the nearest tree but as Laura's eyes flick back to the same spot, it is gone. It was a man, definitely a man, she thinks. Wasn't it? Was the hair dark or just covered with a hoodie, a beanie hat? She can't be sure, but it unsettles her. The desire to be gone, out of sight, overwhelming.

As she weaves along the pavement, threading between other people, she stops in to an artisan bakery to pick up a decaf coffee. She munches on a buttery pastry still in its bag, dropping crumbs as though leaving a trail for someone to follow her. It would be nice to sit, people-watch, take photos but she hasn't been able to shake off the earlier feeling, the creeping of her flesh. She feels vulnerable, a target somehow. Trying to dismiss the sensation, she keeps moving.

She walks past the usual shops that line the high street; the wine merchant, the art gallery, the specialist cheese shop. She tries not to notice the litter that races up the gutter or the little old lady standing at the bus stop looking forlornly at the electronic timetable. Instead she turns to look at the shop windows. They are filled with floral displays; planted bulbs exploding into narcissi and hyacinth, painted eggs and pastel-coloured ribbons, bunny rabbits and woodland creatures.

She halts outside one boutique called Maman et Bébé. It is somewhere she would have avoided in recent years, turning her head away or even crossing the road, but now she can feel her mouth water as she enters the shop. She needs to be restrained, she thinks. Just one or two bits in a sensible, gender neutral colour. But then her hands fly to a floral all-in-one, in pink and blue and mauve. Is she having a girl?

Everything about this pregnancy is urging her to trust her instincts, to question less and trust more. Perhaps it is the fact that this is her last chance, her body's last hurrah and like a flower that blooms brightest before it goes over, she is the same. She will not compromise. She will have whatever her heart desires.

'I'll take this one, thanks,' she says, grasping the outfit on its little white hanger and taking it to the till.

'Lovely,' chimes the shop assistant. 'Is it a gift?'

'No,' replies Laura and she beams with pride. 'It's for my baby.'

The shop assistant checks herself, shrewd eyes flicking from Laura's face to her belly and back again.

'Wonderful. Congratulations. When are you due?'

Laura does a quick calculation but she knows the dating scan was inconclusive and she has read that the baby might need to be brought earlier by caesarean so she tilts her head, not wanting to name a month in case she jinxes it.

'In the summer,' she replies and gives another beaming smile as the shop assistant hands her a chic bag rustling with delicately scented tissue paper.

As she leaves, swinging the little bag by her side, she feels an overwhelming sense of completeness. For so long, stores like this made her feel exempt, lacking, sad. But now she is whole again. She is just contemplating this, thinking of how so much can change in a matter of months, how life really can turn on a sixpence, when she runs straight into a man standing outside the shop. Something about this guy is familiar and she wonders if it wasn't the same figure she saw standing over the road earlier, fleeting as it was.

The man stands about as tall as Ivo but his build is slighter and his steely grey hair whips about in the wind. He is wearing quite a sharp suit, she notices. She can spot good tailoring when she sees it and the gold signet ring that flashes on his little finger as he raises a hand to brush his fringe out of his eyes. Quite a silver fox, all in all.

'I'm so sorry,' she says automatically, although she's pretty sure it was his fault for getting in her way.

The man holds her gaze, his piercing blue eyes looking right into her face as though he has something much more important to say. As if he actually knows her.

'It's Laura, isn't it? Iris's friend. Iris Simmonds from Riddleston Road?'

34

As Iris approaches the gates of Toppingham, she realises that it is lunchtime. Swarms of school kids are wandering around, the older sixth formers heading into town for food, others on their way back. She feels conspicuous, hanging around, though no one seems to have noticed her. So as a large group of lads buzz themselves in through the side gate, she sneaks behind in their slipstream. They are so caught up in their raucous conversation and good-natured joshing that they are oblivious to her.

Sometimes it pays to be invisible. Iris has always felt like part of the background scenery rather than the main event but there was a time when, if she really made an effort with her hair, her clothes, make-up she could catch the eye of one or two passers-by, gain a smile and a wink from a friendly café owner or bus driver. But in recent years, people have tended to stare straight through her, like she is made of cellophane. Young people especially don't seem to register her presence; she is deemed so old, so utterly irrelevant. And as for men? Blokes stopped looking her up and down a long time ago. Even Steve no longer watches her when she undresses or comments on what's she wearing.

Laura had once joked that this was the ideal scenario. 'You can buy anything you like,' she would say, 'and he wouldn't even clock it. Take up an inappropriate hobby. Even better, take a lover,' she had said with a cackle. Iris had dismissed these crass remarks with a shake of her head. As if she has the spare cash for indulgent purchases or even the time and energy for an affair.

Besides, she just couldn't do that. To either Steve or Ben. It would feel like she was cheating on both of them.

And just as she is thanking her stars for being so anonymous, she hears someone calling her name. It is a slightly higher, more fluting voice than the deep baritone of the older boys, but recognisable somehow and she stops where she is, spinning around to locate the owner.

'Hello, Mrs Simmonds. What are you doing here?'

It is Freddie, Laura and Ivo's son. Iris is immediately struck by how tall and stocky he is now. All that rugby is really filling him out. And he appears to have even more of an arrogant swagger than before. Being the star of the rugger team and blessed with a combination of Laura's and Ivo's good looks has resulted in a confident sophistication that now radiates from him. He is bookended by a couple of other boys – Iris doesn't know them – who appear to be gilded with the same self-assured glow.

'Oh, hi, Freddie.' She is flustered, taken aback. 'I, er, I'm just here for a meeting with one of Ben's teachers.' Her mind flits back to the underlying, ever-present anxiety that her son is currently unaccounted for and therefore technically missing. 'By the way, you haven't seen Ben today have you?'

Freddie captures her in the gimlet gleam of his eyes – pure Laura, Iris thinks – as he smirks and looks away. He seems to consider something for a moment, how much to say, how truthful to be and then a look of devil-may-care comes over his features.

'Actually, I saw him bunking off with his girlfriend this morning, before the start of school.'

'What girlfriend?' asks Iris, appalled. Ironically, she realises she is more upset about the idea of another significant female in her son's life than she is about the truanting.

'Becky Jones,' confirms Freddie. 'They've been an item for a couple of months now.'

'I see,' says Iris, her voice trailing off.

'Mind how you go, Mrs Simmonds,' calls Freddie with another smirk as he joins his friends and then proceeds to share some joke with them. The group erupts into laughter before they slink off together, Freddie flanked by his two stooges.

Cocky little shit, thinks Iris. He really isn't improving with age. Freddie was always a bit precocious at primary school but there was a wholesomeness to him back then and she actually believed he was on Ben's side, would stand up for him and protect him. But now there is a cruel veneer to the boy, a callousness that wasn't there before. She wouldn't be surprised if it was him who caused Ben to be sick at the Halloween party. Him or one of his mean little friends. No wonder the poor kid is having nightmares, talking in his sleep.

She wanders over towards the school entrance hall and presses the buzzer. When she is duly admitted she goes straight up to the reception desk and asks to see Mrs Khan.

'Do you have an appointment?' comes the electronic voice through the intercom system, the receptionist sitting well behind a layer of double-thickness glass.

'No. But my son is missing from school today and I'd like to speak to his head of year urgently, if that's possible,' says Iris. 'Ben Simmonds, 1G,' she adds.

The receptionist raises an eyebrow in response but then says, 'Take a seat, please. I'll see if she's available.'

Iris ignores this request and instead paces around the large vestibule area like a caged tigress, running over her thoughts; the whereabouts of Ben, what the school is doing to help him, how she feels about this so-called girlfriend, his secretive behaviour recently. But then she becomes aware of a squeaking, the sound of a bucket on castors being dragged along the corridor and the accompanying slosh and swipe of a mop.

Casting a glance back towards the receptionist, who is now blithely spooning pasta salad into her mouth and reading a book, Iris wanders around the corner in the direction of the noise.

As predicted, she finds him. The caretaker. A powerful feeling of loathing floods her out of nowhere. This man is the cause of all her problems, after all. Striding up to him, she positions herself in his eyeline.

'You! Don't think I don't know what you're up to,' she says in a hoarse whisper. She finds she is shaking now, her throat constricting with the effort not to cry. Digging an index finger into his chest, she looks into his blue eyes. 'You've got your money, you've played your little game. Now stay away from me and my family.'

The caretaker stares at her blindly as he backs away from her, tripping into his bucket as he does so. He makes a small, strangled sound of alarm. Iris's face must be really contorted in rage for him to recoil like this but it's only now that she realises how angry she is.

'And don't think I haven't sussed out who you are.' She gives his chest another jab as the realisation dawns on her in real time. She remembers now where she heard the name Maddox, how she had read it on the walls of the lounge. JP & BM. 'I've got your number. Billy Maddox? You were the father of June's baby, weren't you?'

The caretaker's eyes widen at this. 'How do you know that?' he asks, his voice a thin quaver.

'Wouldn't you like to know?' she replies.

He continues to stare at her, searching her face. Fear slowly turns to a look of sadness and regret. 'I didn't mean any harm,' he says. 'When I came round to the house, I just wanted to say hello, find out a bit more about what happened. Rosemary's disappearance, it was so sudden. But there was no announcement in the paper.' He gives a small grunt. 'Course, she and her mother never wanted anything to do with me, but I always hoped that there might one day be a visitor to the house. Or even a guest at the funeral, come to that. But nothing. Next thing I knew, the house was being done up, new owners. You and your family had moved in and that's when I realised all trace was gone. No more links to the past.'

Iris retracts her hand and takes a step back. This man is telling the truth, she realises. His voice, his eyes show genuine sadness, the shine of veracity.

He goes on: 'I don't know what you mean about money. Or games.' As he says this, his features retain a look of fear and caution at the crazy, outraged woman standing in front of him.

She takes another step back. Her mouth is suddenly filled with saliva as though she might be sick. Her vision shifts for a moment and she puts a hand up to the whitewashed wall, which is filled with notices and posters. The caretaker tentatively reaches out to help her.

'And, so you don't know anything … it wasn't you that sent the Christmas card?' she manages to say.

He shakes his head slowly, apologetically.

'No, perhaps that would have been better than turning up on the doorstep like I did. I can see now that it frightened you for some reason. But it was just an excuse to knock on that same front door once again, to see if I could come inside. The place holds a lot of memories for me. I lost two people the day June left. Her and my child. I still don't know what happened to either of them. She just left, never to be seen again.'

Iris nods her head, ashamed. She feels terrible, is about to apologise when a clear, crisp voice carries along the corridor towards them.

'Mrs Simmonds?'

It is Ben's head of year, Mrs Khan, and it is unclear how long she has been standing there and what she has heard.

35

Laura blinks into the bright winter sun, raising a hand to shield her eyes but also because she instinctively wishes to protect herself. Self-preservation is a primeval thing, even more so when you are pregnant and she clutches her other hand, which is holding the shopping bag, to her stomach.

'I'm sorry to startle you but I'm right, aren't I?' The man continues speaking to her despite her mute response. 'You are Laura Peters? You and Iris—your sons go to the same school, I believe?'

Oh, that must be the connection, thinks Laura with relief. Quite often she finds that she is on so many people's radar though she hasn't got a clue who they are. Or perhaps it's a friend of a friend who's thinking of sending their kid to Toppingham. It's amazing how many people come out of the woodwork when they think you can be of use to them.

'Yes. Sorry, that's right, I am,' she finally responds. 'How do you know Iris?'

The man's face falls, his features stern. It is at odds with the category into which Laura has neatly inserted him and she wonders for the first time whether this is in fact bad news rather than good.

'It's complicated,' he says with a lopsided smile.

Laura frowns. This man is starting to worry her. 'How so?' she asks. 'And what's it got to do with me?'

The constant tide of pedestrians on the high street washes past them. The old woman who was standing at the bus stop has upped and left. The pigeons continue to swoop down for titbits from the pavement or congregate on the tops of street furniture, cooing to themselves in a conspiratorial huddle. Laura senses the urge to edge away from it all; the exhaust fumes, the germ-ridden feathers, this man who has assailed her out of nowhere.

'Look,' he says. 'It might be easier to explain everything somewhere quieter. I know you don't know me from Adam and trust me, I wouldn't blame you for running a mile, but your friend Iris is in a lot of trouble. And I mean a lot.'

'What kind of trouble?' says Laura, her interest piqued.

'The serious kind. As deep as it gets. The sort where she could go to prison for a very long time.'

She is aware that her mouth has opened, that she is gaping. Her eyes look away from his face and search the shopfronts, the awnings, the windows, as her mind races to catch up with this stranger's words and what they could mean.

'Please, would you let me buy you a cup of tea? We can sit and I'll tell you everything.' He gestures behind him at the nice little bistro that does the French onion soup that Laura loves. 'You'd be quite safe, I assure you, surrounded by staff, customers. I give you my word. I just want to talk. You might be the only person who can help your friend before it's too late.'

It is quite simply the most absurd conversation she has ever witnessed.

'This is a joke, right?' she says, though there is no sense of amusement on her features. Laura is not the sort of person to suffer fools gladly and she never likes to think that she would ever be the butt of anyone else's joke.

The man shakes his head. 'No, I'm afraid not. I'm deadly serious,' he says.

All of Laura's instincts scream that she should walk, if not run, away. That this is some stupid scam or worse, a dangerous trap. She looks about her, almost expecting a film crew or some hidden camera she hadn't noticed before. But there is nothing out of the ordinary. In fact, everything about this man appears to be normal, respectable and honest. Indeed, something about his words ring true for her on another level.

Laura has been so sidetracked, so distracted by the all-encompassing matter of her own personal drama – the affair, the pregnancy, the tests, the risks – that she's taken her eye off the ball where everyone else in her life is concerned. She knows that Iris hasn't been her usual self for many months now. But she had put it down to the stress of moving house and her continual angsting over that son of hers. The woman is more tightly wound than a Swiss clock.

Yet something has definitely been off. Out of whack, as she suspected. She hadn't allowed herself to examine it too closely at the time or to even intervene to help because her friendship with Iris had become so compromised, so tainted with guilt. So all the time that Laura had felt tied up in knots over the affair, it seems that Iris was harbouring her own guilty little secret. And she suspects that Steve hasn't got a scooby doo. Not that he's ever that quick on the uptake anyway. But what? What on earth could Iris have done that would make this person fear for her safety, her security, like this?

The man's face beseeches her again.

'Please,' he says. 'Just half an hour of your time?'

So she relents. What harm can it do, she thinks. Besides, he has her completely hooked, she doesn't mind admitting. Whatever this man knows, she needs to know it now, too. Everyone loves a secret, or even, let's just say it, outrageous gossip. Laura looks towards the bistro with its linen curtains, its steam bent wooden chairs, the gold lettering on the window advertising *plats du jour*. And she looks back to the stranger standing in front of her, his expensive suit, his white teeth, his earnest expression.

'Tell me more,' she says, and they make their way inside.

36

Iris slumps into the chair in front of Mrs Khan's desk while the teacher slots herself into the seat opposite. Drawing her long fingers into an elegant steeple, elbows resting on the wooden surface, Mrs Khan's voice is a smooth, honeyed balm.

'How can I be of help, Mrs Simmonds?'

Iris looks round the room, taking in the flourishing plants, their fronds well-tended and healthy, the tall filing cabinet, the mug, which is turned away from her but clearly reads, *The Boss*.

'I'm sorry,' she says. Again, she feels incredibly hot and then cold, despite the fact that the office window is open and a pleasant breeze is filtering through. Sweat bathes her upper lip, floods her armpits. 'Is that radiator on?'

Mrs Khan rests a hand gently on the metal ribs next to her. 'I expect so. The heating is quite antiquated here along with the original building. It has two settings, I'm afraid: boiling or frigid.'

'I feel terrible. I realise I'm disturbing you on your lunch,' says Iris, catching a glimpse of the utilitarian clock on the wall, a half-eaten sandwich on the desk.

'Not a problem. As I said before, happy to help, although,' she gives a slight chuckle, 'we would normally expect parents to schedule an appointment in advance. But as you're here now, we should have another chat about Ben. I have concerns.'

Iris leans forward and takes up a piece of paper from the desk, begins to fan herself with it. Mrs Khan's eyes follow her movements but she says nothing. 'Can I be frank?' she continues and

Iris nods. 'How can I put this? I'm sorry, there's no easy way and please don't be offended. But am I right in thinking that you and your husband are experiencing money worries of some kind?'

Iris's hand slows, the makeshift paper fan falling to her lap.

'No. Why would you think that?'

Mrs Khan sighs, shifts her behind in its seat and leans forward. 'It's just that we've noticed that Ben isn't eating at lunchtimes. I know he has to be careful around food but normally he brings a packed lunch as you know. For several weeks now, our staff on lunch time duty have noticed that he is going without, not eating. When questioned about this, he seems shy, embarrassed. When urged to go to the school canteen, to buy some food on credit, as we always allow our students to do if they are without funds, he refuses.'

'He isn't without funds. We have plenty of money. I don't know why he's not eating. Perhaps he already ate his food at break time?'

Mrs Khan nods, her face a mask of obsequious concern. 'Sure, sure. I know that's possible. But we have also noticed his uniform is becoming less presentable. Ripped, stained, not up to the usual standards we expect here. And of course there was the issue with the missing boots. I understand our Mr Maddox very kindly went out of his way to return them to you and yet Ben has repeatedly skipped PE lessons due to missing equipment, refusing to wear spare kit when provided. He seems to be unwilling to get changed in front of the other boys as well. Is he worried about what they might think?'

Iris's face grows hotter still. She can feel a red tide of heat or anger, she's not sure which, rising up from her chest to her neck to her cheeks.

'Why don't you know where he is?' she snaps. 'When he's at school, you're supposed to be in loco parentis. I'm trusting you to take care of him. And yet somehow, you've allowed him to go missing, to disappear from the school grounds this morning. I can't get hold of him and it's your responsibility. You have a duty of care. If anything happens to him, I'm holding you personally liable.'

The wobble in Iris's voice belies her fear and she has to forcibly hold back the tears as her throat tightens.

'Mrs Simmonds, please. I can see you're distressed.' The teacher stands and moves to a water cooler, pours out a measure into a paper cup which Iris gratefully seizes and drinks.

She continues: 'I only say this because there is provision made – a hardship fund, as such – for the less privileged pupils among our student body and we are happy to make that available to you and your husband …'

'That won't be necessary, thank you,' says Iris through gritted teeth. 'We're not a charity case.'

'If there's anything else you'd like to share with me, offload so to speak, please know that we are here to help. All in strictest confidence, of course.' The teacher eyes her beadily, as though trying to transmit some secret meaning to her.

'What are you saying?' demands Iris, her anger suddenly rising again. 'What do you mean by that?'

'I only meant that—'

'You think that my son doesn't belong in this school, isn't good enough? That we don't have a right to send him here? That we don't deserve to live in our house, in this catchment area?'

Mrs Khan opens her mouth to speak but appears, possibly for one of the few times in her professional career, lost for words.

Iris bangs her fist down on the desk.

'Ben has every right. Just as much right as every other snotty-nosed, jumped-up kid here.'

'Mrs Simmonds. If you don't calm down, I'm going to have to call for assistance and you will be removed from the premises.'

'Don't bother,' says Iris, standing abruptly, knocking her chair backwards so that it falls to the floor behind her. 'I'm going. And I'll be the one lodging a formal complaint against you.'

37

Laura's mouth falls open into another appalled 'O' shape as she squeezes the lemon into her tisane with a teaspoon.

Len, as he has informed her is his name, sits opposite her and raises his shoulders into an 'I told you so' shrug.

'Fucking hell,' says Laura on a long, slow outward breath. 'I can't believe Iris, anyone for that matter, would do such a thing. Steal someone's property. And all for a house in the right postcode? Jesus!'

'Don't underestimate what people will do to get their hands on the right house. As a property developer, I've seen it all. You can pick up a lot just buying houses at auction, witness feuding families, contested wills. And that's before you have to deal with subletters, squatters, warring neighbours, fraud, arson.'

Laura sits back in her chair, her hand flying to her mouth in shock.

'But how? Why would Iris go to such lengths to take a house that doesn't belong to her?'

Len rolls his shoulders and gives a protracted sigh, weighing up his response.

'I don't know. She's your friend. Has she been under a lot of stress? Could she be suffering from any mental health issues?'

Laura shakes her head in mystified silence and then replies. 'No. Well, yes, maybe. I don't know, to be honest. She's a dark horse but I never thought she'd be capable of something like this. It's so outrageous!'

'Maybe it wasn't her idea. Could it be the husband? Iris might not have planned this. Or she might be acting under duress?' he suggests.

'Oh God, I hadn't thought of that,' says Laura. 'Y'know, that might actually be it. Steve, he's … Well, let's just say I've seen a very different side to him in recent months and he's got a bit of a temper, I can tell you. Doesn't like it when he can't get his own way, if you know what I mean?'

Len raises his eyebrows at her in response.

'Who knows,' she continues. 'Maybe he's coerced Iris into doing this and she feels like she's got no other choice than to go along with it?'

'Look,' says Len. 'All I know is what I saw. I've been keeping a watchful eye on Riddleston Road and Rosemary for a while now, ever since I moved back to the area. It was hard at first to visit the street, the house, knowing what I know about how the whole family treated me and my mum, June. What happened as a result.'

'June?' asks Laura.

'Rosemary's elder sister and her only sibling,' explains Len. 'It's quite a story really.'

Laura leans forward, inclining her head in enquiry and Len smiles ruefully.

'I was adopted when I was an infant. Taken in by a wonderful couple, I should say, who were childless and brought me up as their own. I was very fortunate in the end. But I'll never forgive Rosemary and her mother for what they did.'

He takes out a packet of letters – handwritten, dog-eared and yellowed with age – and drops it onto the table between them. Laura resists the urge to fall on them, to open them up and read them. She can tell how sensitive a matter this is to him.

'My birth mum, June, was a young, unmarried mother. The family disowned her. She tried to raise me all by herself, with no financial support. There wasn't quite the same social care or benefits system available back then.'

Laura nods, solemnly. 'Go on.'

He places a hand on the wad of correspondence. 'These are all the letters that Rosemary sent to June while they were estranged. It looks like my mum was staying at a women's boarding house while she was pregnant, and working at a factory. But it seems she lost her job when she began showing and her landlady chucked her out. A lodger friend, Fran, took pity and let June share her bedsit after I was born. It's down to her that I even have these letters. And this.' He reaches into his wallet and takes out a small photo. 'My only picture of her.'

Laura picks up the photo. A young woman, sitting with a baby swaddled in her arms, stares out of the image defiantly.

'She was beautiful.'

'Yes,' he says and swallows.

'What happened to her?' Laura asks quietly.

'It was all there in the hospital records. Apparently, I became very sick not long after I was born. Not surprisingly when June was struggling to feed herself and me. The family refused to send her any money, any help whatsoever. To quote one of Rosemary's letters, they felt she had made her bed and must lie in it. They were punishing her for bringing shame on them all.'

He shakes his head and gives a hollow laugh.

'Apparently it was touch and go for a while whether I would make it. Somehow I pulled through. But June caught pneumonia while she was in hospital with me. And, well, she died ...'

'I'm so sorry,' says Laura into the laden pause that ensues. She looks around at the busy activity surrounding them in the bistro, the animated faces, the noisy chatter. The way the fairy lights twinkle benignly. She can't quite assimilate it with the story she has just heard, this sad tale harking back to another generation that feels so alien now.

'And so you were put up for adoption?' she prompts.

'Yes,' he continues. 'Fran had supplied the hospital with Rosemary's address as next of kin and they tried contacting the family to see if they would take me in …' He trails off.

'But they refused to,' supplies Laura.

He nods.

'Oh my God,' she says, shaking her head in disbelief. 'I know they say it was a different time back then but this … it's brutal.'

Len gives a tilt of his head.

'I understand from Rosemary's letters that their father died suddenly from a stroke not long after June left and that their mother blamed the scandal for bringing on his untimely death. There must have been a lot of grief and pain and resentment, I guess. But still, I find it difficult to understand. Or forgive.'

'So, what made you return to the area?' asks Laura, trying to bring the conversation back to the present.

'Curiosity, I guess. I was surprised that Rosemary had remained there by herself for all of these years. She is my only blood relative, after all. I've never been able to trace my biological father. And in a weird way that house still holds meaning for me. It's a link to the past, my birth mother …'

'For a long time I used to walk past it,' he continues. 'I couldn't bring myself to knock on the door or introduce myself for fear of what I might say or how I might act. Quite honestly, I could have happily strangled the old battleaxe myself.' He looks up, catches Laura's eye and smiles. 'Only kidding. In the end, all I could do was send flowers, on occasion. Anonymously, of course. I think my Christmas wreath might have caught Iris unawares, by the way. I forgot that I had it on order at the florist's.'

He checks her face again and she nods at him to go on.

'But the thing is, Rosemary was an old woman, in ill health, reclusive. I guess a part of me felt responsible for her. Love and hate can be two sides of the same coin,' he says wryly. 'I used to try and keep an eye on things from time to time, when I was in the area. Keep a look out for her. Though she does always seem to have been stubbornly independent. Sometimes I wondered whether I should just forget about her and leave it all well alone.' He shrugs apologetically. 'I'd been away on business, travelling a lot for a few months. Hadn't been able to visit the neighbourhood as regularly as I would have liked. And then, not long ago, I was just checking in on the place and that's when I first saw Iris.'

'What do you know of Iris and her situation?' asks Laura, latching on to this last statement.

'Like I said, I'd noticed some changes. The house had been spruced up. Rosemary was nowhere to be seen and this new family appeared to have moved in. It was baffling. I checked the records but there was no notice that she had died so I thought maybe the old biddy had had enough. Upped and left and sold it in a quick deal. It happens sometimes. But then, well, I happened to be walking past the gate one day when Iris came out of the house. I took my chance and had a word with her. She was so shifty. Obviously not well. And she was lying through her teeth, making out that she was related to Rosemary, was taking care of her.'

Laura feels her eyes widen at this.

'I was very tempted to go to the police right then and there but something about her, her sadness and desperation, the way she was with her son. You could feel it. And I thought maybe I needed some more evidence before I began accusing people.'

'So what do you think really happened then? With Rosemary?'

Len takes a deep breath and lets it out with a long, low huff. 'Maybe Rosemary did leave. But I don't know. I've done a search of all the local hospitals and care homes within a fifty-mile radius and nothing. She has no other friends or family. None of the neighbours or locals know anything. It's like she just vanished into thin air. But Iris and her family somehow knew the place was vacant and took it for themselves. I can't help thinking that something is most definitely not right there.'

Laura takes a swig of her drink. She's been absentmindedly pummelling the lemon slice in her glass for the last ten minutes and the water is now sharp and bitter. She winces, choking on her words.

'No shit,' she agrees.

'I'm sorry to say it, Laura, but the more I think about it, the more I suspect foul play of some sort. As I said, Iris does not seem like a well woman. And as for her husband, he looks like a bit of a wrong'un to me as well. I've seen them together. Weird, aggressive behaviour. I just feel sorry for that young lad of theirs. Whatever they've done, he's been caught up in the middle of it all.'

At this, Laura leans forward in her seat.

'And what, exactly, do you think they've done?'

Len looks at her for a moment, his face serious.

'I don't know. I can't be sure, of course. I've got no proof. But I think Iris and her husband are somehow responsible for Rosemary's disappearance.'

Laura gasps, unable to control herself.

'No. Surely not. Iris isn't capable of that.'

'Well, it's one explanation. Rosemary has disappeared without a trace. No notice of death, no coroner's report, no funeral. Nothing.'

She shakes her head in denial, trying but failing to imagine how her friend could be involved in any of this.

'I'm sorry, Laura. I'm aware that by telling you all of this, you're now implicated too. You may feel that you should go straight to the police with this information. I've wrestled with that myself. But I keep coming back to the son, Ben. I'm sure he must be innocent in all of this.'

Laura nods in agreement.

'Ben's always been a poorly kid, as well. He nearly didn't make it himself once, when he was young. He's their world. Iris, especially, is very protective as you can imagine. Would do anything for him.'

Len looks at her meaningfully and she feels herself stiffen.

'Would she? Anything?'

Laura gives her head another shake, trying to disassociate herself from all of this. It's just too bizarre, unthinkable. And yet, she knows why Len is suspicious. There is something about this situation, with Iris and the house, that has always troubled her. That doesn't add up.

'Look, I know it's a lot to get your head around,' he goes on. 'Trust me, I know. That's why I thought I'd come to you first. To see whether you can cast any light on all of this. Figured you would be able to understand Iris far better than me. And I do try to see the best in people, to give them a fair break. But something is going on here. And we have to get to the bottom of it.'

Laura pushes her drink away from her, abandoned. She looks to the table, to the pile of letters and then back to Len's face.

'Or what? You'll go to the police?'

'Yes. I will have to, I'm afraid.'

She looks to the ceiling, places a hand on her tummy. She registers an instinct to stand up and leave this stranger, this café, this whole unsavoury business and wash her hands of it. But then she thinks of her baby, the undeniable link that binds them all together; Iris, Steve, even Ben. The possible reasons behind Iris's behaviour, the decisions she has felt compelled to make. No, Laura thinks, she is already implicated. There's no denying that she must have had a role to play in all of this and she will always feel a modicum of guilt where Iris is concerned. She owes her, she realises. She can't just walk away.

'Okay,' she says finally. 'Leave it with me. I'll see what I can do. But please don't go to the police just yet. Like you said, I don't think Iris is well. I think she needs help. My help.'

Len nods.

'Thank you, Laura. I'm glad you see it that way too. And I'll be grateful for anything you can do. But …'

'But what?'

'I will have to register Rosemary as a missing person before too long. It's the only right, legal thing to do.'

As they stand outside the bistro, staking their place on the busy pavement, the bright, sunny morning has given way to a colder front and the tables and chairs up and down the high street are empty now. Laura turns to Len.

'Well, nice to meet you, I guess?' she says, putting her hand out to shake his with a wry smile.

'Thank you for taking the time to hear me out, Laura. And sorry, this will have been quite a shock. You must have thought I was a complete nutter.'

Laura laughs indulgently, never one to miss an opportunity to casually flirt.

'Oh don't worry, I've met a few of those in my time too. Especially in my line of work.'

'What is it that you do?' he enquires.

'Freelance photographer,' she returns. 'Pretty much anyone or anything: I can shoot it.'

He laughs good-naturedly at her black humour as she rummages in her wallet and takes out a business card. Len reads the front, purses his lips in approval. I'll take a look at your portfolio. I'm always in need of some good publicity shots.' He taps the card in her direction and then touches her arm gently and squeezes it.

'Thank you again, Laura. It feels so good to be able to discuss this with someone. Please stay in touch and let me know what happens.'

With that, he walks away from her, his expensive suit moving over his body in all the right places. She watches him leave for a moment, still replaying the contents of the incredible conversation they have shared in the last hour. As she turns away finally, she sees it again. The shadowy figure across the road, the one she glimpsed earlier that morning. Only this time, she can see a face clearly, recognises its features. It is Steve. No question. He stands, shoulders rounded, hands shoved truculently into his coat pockets. His face is a hard piece of stone, his eyes flashing molten anger.

38

When Steve gets home that night, Iris is standing at the kitchen sink washing pots. She could have put them through the dishwasher, but she wanted something to do with her hands. And she found that the warm suds provided a comfort to her of sorts as she slowly, methodically cleaned each cup, each plate, every individual piece of cutlery down to the last teaspoon.

Ben is still not back and she has no idea who this girlfriend, this Becky is, or where she lives. She has tried to call Laura to see if Freddie can locate Ben but she has not been returning her calls all afternoon. What is the point of all this technology if you can't actually find someone or speak to them when you really need to? She has even considered going to the police, but then she wonders if that is an overreaction. And besides, she can't. It would only alert them to the situation here, the house, the disappearance of Rosemary. Once again, she feels caught in a trap of her own making where every which way she turns, she is more ensnared.

So she has tried to busy herself, here, alone in this house. Trying to still the fears that rear up in her, to quiet the voices in her head. At one point, she had become so lulled by the washing up that she had accidentally sliced her thumb open on the bread knife that lay in wait for her beneath the foamy water. Startled by the pain, she had brought her hand up to her face and watched, fascinated, as the blood ran down her wrist, reaching to her elbow, splashing into the sink where it diluted into nothing.

Now, she turns to look at Steve as he comes through the door, broken from her trance, her hands shrivelled and sore from the long submersion. He drops his bag on the floor with a menacing slowness and pinions her in place with a cold, hard stare.

'What's wrong?' she asks, her voice already running up and down a scale, unable to stay at a controlled level. She can smell from here that he's been drinking. And that means that he has driven while over the limit.

'I got a call from the bank today.'

Iris closes her eyes in dread and reaches for a tea towel to wipe her hands. The cut on her thumb throbs as though it has its own heartbeat, her pulse beginning to canter.

'Just a friendly call, Mr Simmonds,' he says in a mocking, high-pitched approximation of the female assistant at the bank. 'We've noticed some unusual activity in the last day or so. Several withdrawals of £250 from different cash machines in your local area, all on the same day, resulting in a total of £1,000 deducted from the account in your name. I'm just confirming that you are aware of these withdrawals and there hasn't been a security breach of some kind?'

Iris feels her shoulders droop, her whole body sag. Her legs feel insubstantial, her limbs turning to jelly.

'I can explain,' she says, just as she had rehearsed it in her head previously. But the words still come out in a stuttering warble. 'I needed to pay off my credit cards. The Christmas presents for Ben. The interest has been building up and I haven't had as many shifts at the shop this month.' Iris swallows, thinking of her job. The one she has just walked out of with no other to go to.

'I don't believe you,' he says. 'There's more to this than you're letting on. You're always lying to me. Stop treating me like a bloody idiot.'

He is shouting now and she feels herself cringing from him. The weight of this terrible secret bears too heavily on her and the desire to roll the stone from her back is overwhelming.

'I needed the money for something else,' she begins in a frightened whisper. The tears are leaking from her now, undammed.

'For what? For fuck's sake, Iris. Just be honest with me for once in your miserable, little life.'

A sob escapes from her chest. Why is he being so cruel when all she's ever done has been for the good of him, their son, this family?

'Someone knows. I had to pay them. To keep them quiet. I thought I knew who it was but I was wrong. And now I'm not sure who it is or what's going on any more.' She continues to sob, her cries hiccupping uncontrollably. 'I wish I could just go back to the beginning, that day when she fell and I'd just walk away. I'd just carry on walking right past. And none of this would have ever happened.'

Steve is shaking his head, slowly advancing towards her. But he is not concerned or sympathetic. He doesn't reach out to take her in his arms and comfort her. Instead, he sticks his face into hers, forces her to focus on him and says, 'What the fuck are you talking about? You're completely mad in the head, you stupid cow, do you know that? Who fell? What woman? What are you on about?'

'Rosemary,' she spits out, eyeing him properly for the first time. 'The old woman who used to live here. This is her house. She died. So I put her out there.' She points her head in the direction of the garden, beyond the kitchen window. 'And I took the house. No one else would have wanted it, the state it was in. But we needed it, Steve. We needed it more than all the others. Ben needed it.'

Iris draws her hands up to her mouth, shaking. She covers her lips as though she might stop any more words spilling forth.

Steve merely looks at her, his eyes staring blankly, unblinking. Desperately trying to understand these sentences, as though she is a stranger who has spoken in a foreign language he cannot translate.

'What?'

Iris moves towards him.

'What are you saying?' he asks, shaking his head.

'You were away. I didn't know what to do. I panicked. It was a mistake, I know that now. But, Steve …'

He backs away, colliding with the work surface as he stumbles out of the kitchen. He holds his head in his hands, raking his hair.

'This isn't happening. This … it can't be real. I can't—'

'Steve,' she calls. But all she hears is his feet climbing the stairs, the banging of wardrobe doors in their bedroom.

A few minutes later, he thunders down the stairs with a hold-all in his hand.

'Where are you going?' she asks.

'I'm leaving,' he says, his face having now taken on a permanent look of horror. 'I can't stay here, in this house, with you. I won't be a part of this. It's insane. You're fucking insane.' He is shouting now, tapping the side of his head. The alcoholic fumes reach her along with a fleck of spit as his face leers too close. 'As soon as I'm sorted with somewhere to stay, I'm coming to get Ben and he'll be living with me. I'm not gonna leave him here with a nut job like you.'

'Ben's missing,' she starts. 'From school. He went off with a girlfriend or someone called Becky and I can't get hold of him.'

'Good. I don't blame him. I'd rather he was anywhere but here with you.'

'What? How can you say that? Steve, I'm worried.'

'Oh for God's sake, when aren't you worried? So, he skived off for a day. You and I used to do the same when we were kids.'

'But, this is serious—'

'Relax. I got a text from him earlier saying he was going over to Freddie's. What is serious, what is actually really deadly serious, is the fact that you buried a body in the fucking garden.' He gives a manic laugh, listening to his own words.

'I mean, who fucking does that, Iris? I should call the police right now.'

'Stop it, Steve,' she cries, trying to shush him, holding her finger to her lips. There is still a small part of herself that believes if they don't talk about it, don't think about it, they can pretend it never happened. 'Stay,' she pleads. 'We'll pack up the house. We'll go, find somewhere else. All three of us, somewhere new. A fresh start. I know it was wrong.' She clings to his arm now. 'Please don't leave me. I can't live without you. Without Ben.'

Steve looks at her with pity which quickly transmutes to disgust as he shakes her off. 'You're sick. I don't know you any more. I certainly don't love you, that's for sure.'

A croak of pain escapes her as he opens the door and slams it behind him. She listens to the revving of an engine as he drives the car away from outside the house, straining to hear its sound as it disappears down the road. Finally, she collapses onto the bottom stair; a rag doll with all its stuffing torn out.

39

Laura wakes early, her mind instantly leapfrogging to the meeting with Len, what he told her about Iris, as though her brain has been tracing and retracing this problem all night long. What to do? What to say? How to even broach this subject with her friend? Whether Iris might actually be a potential danger to her now. And the baby. After all, if Iris is capable of something like this, what else might she do?

In the end, the decision is made easy for her. At just a little after 8.30 a.m., as Laura has finished towelling herself down from the shower, she receives a text from Iris.

Hi can you come round asap? Steve has left me …

Laura makes a face, the equivalent of the awkward, gritted teeth emoji, and shows the phone screen to Ivo who reads it with a furrowed brow and gives a low whistle.

'Well,' he says. 'Was only a matter of time before the lid blew off that little pressure cooker.'

If only you knew the half of it, thinks Laura. She had considered telling Ivo all about it last night but on reflection had waited. Len had told her in confidence and this situation is delicate, to say the least. If Laura had blabbed to Ivo he would have hit the roof in self-righteous, civic-minded outrage and been straight on the phone to the boys in blue. And, of course, there's Ben to think of too. God knows what that boy has seen or heard living in that house for the last nine months. And now his dad has walked out, Iris is all the poor lad has got.

No, she decides. It's time for Little Miss Fancy Pants to pull on some big girl knickers. Go round there, talk it through with Iris, and try to find out exactly what happened to this old woman, Rosemary. Who knows, she might have gone on holiday, gone missing abroad. It happens. Or perhaps she went to visit someone in another part of the country and was taken ill? Maybe she just wanted to disappear, to run away from that big old house and live out the rest of her days in a nice hotel by the sea.

There might be a perfectly reasonable explanation for all of this and everything can be resolved somehow. Maybe not the marriage. And frankly, good riddance to Steve. But Laura still wants to think the best of her friend. She doesn't believe Iris is guilty of anything more than a moment of madness, brought on by stress and a bit too much of *Homes Under the Hammer*. And really, is what she did so terrible? Moving into an empty, near-derelict house? Squatting, that's hardly a new thing. Ironically, Iris has actually improved the property rather than damaging it.

After she dresses, swiftly pulling on her new go-to uniform of cashmere joggers – easy around the midriff – and crisp white shirt, she kisses Ivo goodbye.

'You know where I am,' she says. 'If I'm not back in a couple of hours, send out a search party.' She says this with a wink but Ivo seems to latch on to some deeper meaning, catches her hand as she trails past him on the way out of the bedroom.

'Hey! Everything okay?' he asks.

'Of course. Fine,' she assures him. 'Just a bit of friend maintenance. It's the least I can do for her.'

When she arrives at Iris's house, it's worse than she expected. Of course the place is still pristine. The more upset Iris is, the more she cleans. So it's no surprise that her friend's obsession has gone into overdrive in recent weeks. But as a direct counterpoint to the neatness of the cushions, the bleached sterility of the kitchen, Iris herself looks like a house that is falling down from the inside out.

Her hair is both greasy and yet frazzled like a scarecrow's – she must lend her that miraculous leave-in conditioner she discovered the other day. Her cheeks are sunken, her vacant eyes resting in shadowed sockets. Her whole body seems to have lost its inner struts of support, her arms hanging listlessly at her sides until she folds them into her trademark defensive stance.

'How are you doing?' she asks.

Iris gives her a weak smile and a shrug of her shoulders. A gesture that appears to take up all of her physical strength. She wonders when this woman last ate anything healthy or nutritious, a piece of fruit even. She is half tempted to whizz up one of her super juices but then reconsiders.

'I'll put the kettle on.'

Laura is still wondering how much Iris knows, whether she's considered if Steve might have been having an affair. But if she suspects any of these things, it doesn't show. If anything, it is Ivo who is behaving a little strangely around her. One minute withdrawn, the next over-protective. It is a reminder to stay on her guard, watch what she says. With both of them.

As she fills the kettle at the sink, she looks out of the window onto the back garden. It's a shame that the big old tree has been cut down, she thinks. It has left the lawn looking exposed, vulnerable. But something else has changed too. Something is different and she can't quite put her finger on it. She feels it then, a prickle on her neck, and when she turns it is to find Iris standing behind her, looking out at the same part of the garden.

'Oh my God,' breathes Laura, clutching a hand to her chest. 'You made me jump.' She turns back to put the kettle on to boil. 'I'm making strong tea, with two sugars,' she says as Iris collapses into a seat at the kitchen table. 'No arguments. You've had a shock.'

As she busies herself with teabags and milk, Laura wonders how she should play this. She is conscious that for the first time in their friendship, she is wary of angering Iris, of provoking her. She is frightened though she's not sure why. She puts the mug of tea down and clears her throat.

'Iris,' she says firmly. Her friend's gaze slides from the middle distance and focuses on her momentarily. 'It will be okay. I know it doesn't feel like it right now, but maybe one day, you'll come to realise that you're better off.'

Iris's face hardly even changes bar a minor flicker of comprehension that flits across her features, a minute flaring of her eyes.

'Better off?'

'Without Steve.'

She waits for a response and eventually Iris gives a slow nod of her head as tears begin to track silently down her cheeks. 'And you can stay here, in your lovely new house.' She says this carefully, aware now that she is on dangerous ground. 'Ben can carry on going to Toppingham. There doesn't have to be too much upheaval. And you've got friends. Me and Ivo.'

'Steve says he wants Ben to live with him,' says Iris. 'All the time. I'll never see him again.'

Laura pulls back in shock.

'What? Why? Why would he want to take Ben away from you? Surely you can handle this amicably? Shared custody and all that? Lots of parents manage it.'

Iris shakes her head miserably. It's clear that she's not telling Laura the full story, that there's something her friend is holding back. But then she's always suspected there were skeletons in this marriage. She just wonders which ones. She is all too aware Steve can be a nasty piece of work. Unreasonable. Aggressive. Though why on earth would that make him the better parent, the one to take care of Ben instead of Iris? What is it he has over her?

Iris has lowered her head to the table now, sobbing uncontrollably into her hands.

'Oh, honey,' says Laura, moving closer to embrace her as Iris continues to make small, stifled grunts. 'You did the right thing.'

Iris raises her snot-smeared face up a fraction.

'Really? Do you really think so?'

'Of course I do. Steve is not the man you think he is. You could do so much better than him.'

Iris's face falls, her eyes filling with tears again. 'Oh, I see.'

'Now, drink up,' commands Laura. 'I'll speak to Ivo. See who he can recommend as a divorce lawyer. Get you tooled up.'

Iris lifts her mug and swallows down the sweet tea in one long gulp like an obedient child taking its medicine. She seems to have taken on a docile faraway look again, as though she is not quite all there. Poor thing, thinks Laura. What a state she's in. As she gathers up both the mugs and takes them to the sink, she looks out at the garden once again.

'Uh-oh,' she says casually. 'The cat's back.'

Iris lurches out of her seat and comes to stand by the window. She stares at the moggy as it settles itself on the patch of grass by the tree stump.

'I'm going to throttle that thing, I swear.'

'Hey, hey,' says Laura, appalled. 'Sit down. I'll take care of this. We should probably get it checked at the vet's. Might be chipped.'

Before Iris can disagree, she opens the back door and steps down to the garden, walks slowly but confidently towards the cat which remains sitting, washing one of its paws. The grass is still frosty with dew, the plants dead and lifeless though there are some green shoots, ready to spring forth. Life will always find a way, muses Laura. Everything comes out, in the end.

The cat does not seem to be afraid of her and she bends down to stroke its soft fur, to reach around and rub the back of its neck. As she does, she realises the cat has a collar and a tag.

This is no stray. It is someone's pet. Laura lifts the dull metal disc and reads the inscription, a name: JUNE. Immediately, she drops the tag as though branded, and stands abruptly, causing the cat to flee. This is Rosemary's cat, she's sure of it. It's too much of a coincidence. Named for her long-lost sister, June. Len's birth mother. And if that's so, why is it still here hanging around the house? If Rosemary had moved on, she would have taken her cat with her, surely?

She stands there, trying to piece it all together. Looking down she becomes aware of the bumpy patch of verdant turf next to the tree stump, scattered with wild-growing winter aconite. No, it can't be. Iris would never, it's just not possible. But then she thinks back to her childhood, how her father had once dug a hole in the ground for their old, dear Labrador when it died. How the grass grew over in time, though she could never quite bring herself to play in that part of the garden again.

A shiver runs through her. Was Len right all along? Has something bad really happened to Rosemary? Could Steve be responsible and this is why he is fleeing the scene of the crime? She looks up then, towards the kitchen window. Iris is staring down at her, watching, her face a strange, inscrutable mask. Laura's hand flies to her stomach in defence, as it always does these days, and she smiles back at her friend, weakly. It is time to leave.

As she strides back up the steps and into the house, she feels her skin prickling again as she tries to keep her voice light and carefree. She realises now, in this moment, that she really doesn't know Iris, or Steve, at all. It's true that none of us ever know what anyone else is capable of and she finds her blood is pounding in her ears.

'Sorry, I'm afraid I couldn't catch it after all. Maybe it will get tired of you and move on to someone else eventually.'

'Perhaps. I don't know. It seems to like it here,' says Iris mechanically.

'Look, I've got to go,' says Laura as breezily as she can. 'I told Ivo I wouldn't be long and he'll be expecting me back.'

'How lucky you are to have a husband who loves you so much,' replies Iris. 'Lucky, lucky Laura.'

There is an edge to her friend's voice now, which she finds hard to read. But still Laura allows a rare speck of guilt to land on her briefly. She has never considered just how difficult things were for Iris, how desperate she must have been all these years. Yet, how is she one to talk? Her own life is hardly textbook right now, she concedes. And, yes, she does feel remorse for the dalliance with Steve, though it was just sex and she will never regret the gift that is now growing in her womb. She places a hand back on her tummy and gives a silent prayer of thanks yet again for her baby. Her baby, its safety: that is her priority now. Not Iris and what she or Steve might have done, if indeed she is right about what has happened here. She can't be sure. Laura's mind is reeling, unable to trust her instincts, only wishing that she could be gone now, out of the house and able to think clearly somewhere else. Somewhere safe.

As she walks down the hallway towards the front door, Laura turns and gives Iris an encouraging smile, one she hopes might mollify her.

'It will be okay. Everything will be all right in the end.'

'Will it?' asks Iris, her eyes searching Laura's face. 'You know, this house. It doesn't belong to us and it never will. We should never have moved in here.'

Laura pauses, her hand on the door latch, caught between the temptation to run and the need to hear what else Iris might admit to.

'Well, I know you're only renting but that doesn't matter. Look at what you've done to the place,' she replies, trying to conceal the quaver in her voice.

'Yes,' says Iris. 'Look at what I've done.'

Their eyes lock on to each other for a moment and Laura finds that she is holding her breath.

'I must go,' she says, turning decisively but Iris puts a hand up against the door to bar her way.

'That's not all,' says Iris, leaning over towards her bag, which is lying on the floor by the bottom of the stairs. She takes out a square white envelope and hands it over. With a frown of confusion, Laura takes out the Christmas card, opens it up to read the contents.

'Oh my God. Is this what I think it is?' Her eyes rake over and over the printed sticker with the blackmail notice, the details of the PO box number. 'Have you any idea who could have sent it?'

'No,' says Iris. 'I thought I did. The old guy who works at the boys' school. But I got it all wrong. That's why Steve has left, when he noticed the money went missing from his account.'

'Wait, what? You didn't actually send money to this person, did you?'

Iris nods sadly.

'But this is extortion. Look, I don't know what's going on here, Iris. But this could be dangerous. You should report it.'

'No,' says Iris resolutely. 'I don't want to go to the police.'

Laura sighs. 'But they can trace a PO box, you know. They might need a court order, but in time they could track down whoever's doing this.'

'Doesn't matter any more. I'll probably have to move on again soon. I can't stay here on my own, now Steve and Ben have gone.'

'I suppose not,' says Laura, tapping the card thoughtfully before inserting it back into its envelope as though it is better out of sight, out of mind. There is something about this note that has spooked her in more ways than one and she registers again the need to leave, to return to the safety of her own home, her family.

She gives Iris's shoulder a last comforting squeeze.

'I've really got to go. But call me if you need anything. I'm here if you want to talk.'

Iris nods and then looks up.

'By the way, thank you for having Ben round to stay last night. I'm so glad he wasn't here. What with me and Steve rowing and him walking out and everything.'

Laura freezes as she is about to step over the threshold.

'What do you mean? Ben wasn't at our house last night, Iris.'

40

Iris feels a fresh wave of panic wash over her. Just when she thought she was numbed to everything, couldn't feel any worse, couldn't feel anything, it turns out she can. The knowledge that Ben is lying to her and Steve about where he is, who he is with, comes as a new acute pain. The realisation that he has, in fact, been missing for twenty-four hours now.

'Iris, don't panic,' says Laura, reading the fear in her eyes. 'I'll speak to Freddie, his friends. There must have been some mix-up. A miscommunication. Steve was angry, upset last night. Maybe he read the message wrongly.'

'He had been drinking,' replies Iris distractedly. Even through this strange, dislocated sensation, she knows that they are clutching at straws.

'Who else might Ben have been with? Another friend, someone you don't know as well?'

'Apparently there's a girl called Becky. A friend. Girlfriend. I don't know. I thought they were far too young for this sort of thing. There's a chance he might be with her.'

'Right, there you go,' says Laura, brightening. 'And trust me, Iris, I don't think we know the half of it any more. Kids. They grow up quicker these days.'

'No,' declares Iris, stung. 'Not my Ben. He's always been a good boy.'

Laura appears to swallow what she is about to say and instead reminds her that there's probably a perfectly normal explanation for all of this. But Iris can tell she's bluffing. Laura's face has taken on that shrewd look, as though her brain is running counterpoint to her lips. Then an even more alarming thought occurs to her.

'What if it's something to do with this card? The blackmailer? Oh my God. They want us out of this house. They want to hurt me, my family.'

'Woah! Easy, Iris. Let's not lose our heads and get carried away,' says Laura, patting the air with her hands. 'Call the school. They might be able to contact this Becky's parents. Speak to Steve, if you can bear to. I'll get in touch with Freddie and ask Ivo what he thinks. It will be okay.'

Iris inhales deeply and tries to steady her ragged breath. She can feel her lower lip wobble and clamps her teeth down into its soft flesh, tasting blood.

'But Iris,' continues Laura. 'All the more reason to think about speaking to the police soon.'

Her friend stares pointedly into her face. She knows, thinks Iris. She knows. But how much?

Iris watches Laura stroll down the path and close the gate behind her. She always has such a spring in her step, that pert bottom, the swell of her pregnancy still subtly concealed underneath the effortlessly chic shirt. Iris can't imagine Laura ever suffering even so much as a crisis of confidence let alone an actual real crisis. And if she did, she would no doubt carry it off with panache, not a hair out of place, and all the while smelling of Diptyque.

She closes the door. Who cares? She no longer has any energy left in her to be envious and, after all, it was good of Laura to be so supportive, though she suspects there must be some underlying reason for it. But she hasn't got the headspace to try and fathom it any more. She feels paper-thin, wafer-like, as though she could dissolve in water and disappear into nothing.

Summoning all her strength, Iris pulls herself up the stairs. Her hand grasps the shining wooden handrail, the one she had so admired all those months ago, and begins to climb. Somehow, she makes it to the apex of the house and looks into the attic room, with its claustrophobic atmosphere under the eaves, the faded rose wallpaper. No matter how hard she has tried, she's never quite been able to eradicate the spirit of the house's original owner; Rosemary. This place, it really was never hers and now she must accept it is time to give it up.

She wanders back down to the next floor and peers into her bedroom. Half the room is ransacked and bare, where Steve has stripped it of his belongings, his clothes. He will never sleep on that side of the bed, will never even share a bed with her ever again. *I don't know you any more. I certainly don't love you.* The memory of his words, his pitying, disgusted face, as though he finally saw her for the terrible person she has always been, makes her double up in pain. And his threat to take Ben away from her is like a further twist of the knife in her heart. It doesn't matter what Laura suggested, about how most judges would grant custody to the mother. If Steve follows through and goes to the police, she knows she will never see Ben again. And then life really wouldn't be worth living.

With this thought, she turns and makes her way down the corridor to her son's bedroom. She opens his door gingerly as she always does now, feeling like an intruder, scared of what she might find. He is not there, of course. Her stomach turns again at the knowledge that she doesn't know precisely where he is right now or if he is in any danger. Or maybe Laura's right. He might be at school. She should call them. But then she winces when she remembers what she said to Mrs Khan, who was only trying to do her job. The woman had stared at her as if she was crazed and as Iris catches sight of her own reflection in Ben's mirror, she recoils from the aberration in front of her. She is unrecognisable even to herself these days.

Turning away, she backs out of the room but not before a small tumbleweed of cat hair wafts around her feet, whisked up by some unseen breeze. She bends to scoop it up and notices more clinging to the skirting board in drifts, like brindled candy-floss. How is this possible, no matter how much she hoovers this god-forsaken house, she thinks? Her nostrils pick up the scent of roses again as she sniffs the air.

'Okay,' she shouts. 'I get the message. We're leaving.' She slams the door behind herself and runs down the stairs. She feels faint now, the sugar from the tea that Laura made her already burned up by nervous energy. She can't remember when she last ate. Her stomach feels like it's shrunk, every morsel of food a struggle to get down.

She forces herself along to the kitchen and stands at the sink, running the cold water tap. Not bothering to find a glass she fills her hand and laps at it like a water fountain before splashing her face once, twice, three times, trying to shock herself out of this torpor.

Throwing her head back, pushing the wet hair away from her cheeks, she stares out of the window at the shallow grave in the garden. And it is now, finally, that the full realisation of what she has done truly hits her.

How could she? How could she have done such a despicable thing? No wonder Steve can't even look at her, wants nothing more to do with her. She gives a low moan when she thinks about Ben, her beautiful boy. How will he ever see her the same way, love her like he always has done, when he finds out what his own mum did? Steve was right, she is insane. They will take Ben away from her. Nothing will ever be the same again. And she doesn't think she can bear it.

41

Laura steers the Range Rover into the car park at Toppingham School. Finding a suitable space, she switches off the engine, releases her seatbelt and hunkers down into the comforting embrace of the leather upholstery. She is waiting to pick up Freddie who has stayed after school for rugby practice.

The days are just beginning to stretch out a bit further now, she realises as she casts a look around the bays of the car park, noting the odd Lexus, BMW, Porsche. But she still enjoys the softness of the gloaming at this time of year. The lights in the windows of houses with curtains not yet drawn. The oily reflections in puddles. As ever when she considers the seasons, her mind can't help but calculate her possible due date. A summer baby, she thinks, and smiles to herself. Like a summer wedding; perfectly timed after all. Bright. Warm. The longest days that will be filled with happiness and joy.

She is just basking in the glow of this idea when she becomes aware that a figure is standing beside the car, staring in at her through the window. A man, stony-faced, his mouth a thin line. Her heart skitters for a second before she recognises who it is: Maddox, the school caretaker. Clutching her chest, she breaks into a relieved smile and climbs out of the car.

'Sorry, Mrs Peters,' he says. 'Didn't mean to scare you just now.'

'No, not at all,' she replies. 'Don't worry. I was miles away.'

'You did look a little away with the fairies, I must say.' He laughs at this and Laura joins in with him. Some of the other school mums say they find him a bit creepy. And it's true, he is a bit of a strange old bird, but she likes him. She can't help feeling sorry for him. As a widower, with no family, she imagines this job is all that keeps him going. Apparently, that's why the school has allowed him to stay on for so long.

'Waiting for young master Freddie are you?' he asks her.

'Yes. As usual,' she says with a roll of her eyes. She is feeling cold standing outside the car and a spasm winds itself up through her legs and into her torso.

'I wondered,' he begins, looking a little sheepish, his eyes down to the ground.

'What is it, Mr Maddox? Have Freddie and his team mates been trashing the changing rooms again? I know they can be a messy bunch. You should see our porch at this time of year. Mud up to the eyeballs ...' She trails off.

'No, no,' he says with a quick shake of his head. 'It's not that. I wanted to ask you about your friend, Mrs Simmonds. Ben's mother. How is she?'

'Iris?' Laura baulks. 'Why do you ask about her?'

'Oh well, we had a little ... how can I put it? A bit of a run-in, I suppose you could say. The other day. Outside Mrs Khan's office. It all got a bit heated, I'm afraid. She was very upset.'

'What about?' asks Laura, her curiosity building.

'Oh, hard to say. I couldn't really make head nor tail of it at first. It seems she thought I'd been posting things through the door, threatening her. It was all a misunderstanding, of course.'

Laura nods, thinking of the blackmail Christmas card.

'Don't worry, Mr Maddox. She's been under a lot of stress lately. I don't think she meant anything personal by it.' She turns towards the car, signalling that she would like to bring the conversation to a close and get out of the cold.

'I think she must have got the wrong end of the stick,' he agrees. He looks at her with imploring blue eyes and she wonders why they seem so familiar all of a sudden. 'I'd only wanted to find out what had happened to Rosemary. The person who used to live in that house of theirs.'

Laura pauses and turns back towards him.

'You knew Rosemary?' she blurts. 'Er, I mean, the previous owner.'

'Oh yes,' he says, his face lighting up with a boyish glee. 'I knew them both, she and her sister, June. I was telling Mrs Simmonds the other day how I knew the whole family when I was younger. Though Rosemary has kept herself to herself over the years. In the end, she hardly ever spoke to anyone. Became something of a recluse.'

'Really? Why was that do you think?' she asks, trying to keep the urgency out of her voice.

He shakes his head sadly.

'I don't think she ever got over the death of her sister, June. They were thick as thieves once upon a time. Rosie idolised her older sister. We were all a bit in thrall to June back then. Myself included,' he says more quietly.

His eyes seem to take on a misty look, though they are always a little watery, and Laura feels an urge to comfort him, though she's not sure why.

'And Rosemary? She stayed in the house for the rest of her life?' she prompts. 'She never married or moved away?'

'No,' confirms Mr Maddox, wiping the end of his nose and giving a violent sniff. 'That was one of the saddest things about it all. Rosie was the scholar. The brains of the family. Always had been the brightest girl in the school. She had wanted to go off to university, do something in the world. She could have done as well, I reckon. But after June left and the father died, her mother insisted that she stay at home to keep house and look after her. Put paid to any plans of college or study.'

'Oh, I see,' says Laura, her mind running. She can feel the pieces of this picture falling into place. Out of the corner of her eye, there is a ragtag group of boys in rugby strip, their legs smeared with mud, walking across the school grounds towards the car park. Freddie is among them. She doesn't have much time, she realises.

'But Rosemary must have finally decided to move on after all these years? Do you know where she went? A care home maybe? Or perhaps she downsized?'

'I didn't see Rosemary leave. There was no sign of a house sale unless it was done privately. It must have been very quick, if so. One day she was there, the next gone.' He opens his hands like a conjuror revealing a trick.

'And when did you last see Rosemary?' asks Laura. She resists adding the word 'alive' to the end of the sentence.

Mr Maddox stares at the ground, his brow furrowing as he appears to consider this properly for the first time. Finally he looks up, his piercing blue gaze holding Laura's for a moment.

'Not long before your friend moved in,' he replies. 'In fact, I saw Mrs Simmonds one day, helping her across the road.'

Laura swallows, her mouth suddenly dry. She doesn't want to believe the thoughts that are crowding into her head. Iris is a good person, a loyal wife, a wonderful mother. But somehow she is connected with the disappearance of Rosemary. And it doesn't look good. Not good at all.

Freddie has reached the car now and is standing with his school bag on his shoulder, looking between the two of them with a querulous expression on his face.

'Thanks, Mr Maddox. I'd better go,' says Laura apologetically.

He nods in assent and walks off in the direction of the school gates.

'What are you doing talking to that old weirdo?' asks Freddie as they climb into the car. Her son takes out his phone and rests one foot on the dashboard in a rebellious act that he knows she dislikes. She bats at his leg until he moves it down. Not before she notices that he is wearing a new pair of trainers, their fluorescent colours flashing in the darkness of the car.

'Don't be mean, Fred,' she admonishes, then adds, 'Are they new?' nodding at his feet. 'Where did you get those from?'

'Dad bought them for me. Last weekend,' he answers.

'Oh, by the way,' she says, distracted. 'Have you seen Ben today? Was he at school?'

Freddie lifts his head from his phone briefly. 'Why?'

'His mum's worried about him. Apparently he said he was staying with us last night. Why do you think he'd lie about that?'

Freddie shrugs. 'How should I know? It's not like we're really friends any more.'

Laura contemplates him for a moment longer, studies his face in profile, cast in a pale blue glow from his phone. It seems their sons have been growing apart as much as she and Iris have in recent months. How wrong she has been about all the relationships in her life lately. Nothing is as it seemed.

And then she remembers what Mr Maddox had said, just before Freddie arrived. About the last time he had seen Rosemary, how Iris had been escorting her home. Her stomach turns with the realisation of what this could mean: that her friend must have known the old woman. That she had perhaps even purposefully targeted her. A new feeling of unease runs through her.

'Mum, do you think we might get home anytime soon?' says Freddie, his voice laden with sarcasm.

She is brought up short, back to herself, and she starts the car.

42

When Ben arrives home, Iris is sitting in the lounge looking out of the huge bay window. The room is now painted a plain, sludgy grey colour, as selected by Steve. Gone is the overpowering floribunda wallpaper that Rosemary had been so enamoured with and in its place is minimalist calm. The cornicing and ceiling rose are now bright and clean, standing proud against the walls that have been covered with layers of paint, hiding a multitude of sins. But it is no use, Iris can't take any pleasure or pride in this room. The panoramic sweep of the window, now hung with elegant drapes rather than dust-ridden net curtains, does not provide a better view of the world as she sits and watches it go by.

As soon as she sees Ben walking up the garden path, she stands, relief flooding her. He comes through the door, divesting himself of shoes and coat, as she tries to throw her arms around him.

'Where have you been?' she cries, angry now that he is safe and well in her arms.

He grunts a muted hello to her but rebuffs her embrace, shouldering his school bag.

'At Freddie's,' he says and runs straight upstairs to his room.

Iris wilts. Like a cut flower that has finally withered and died, she collapses onto the bottom stair again. Her bare feet are a pale milky blue, her toenails are mauve shells as she contemplates them. The Victorian tiled hall spreads out beneath her like a gaudy dress. She remembers how her eyes had glinted, her fingers had twitched, when she first saw it, albeit dusty, dirty and strewn with Rosemary's junk mail.

Looking up and around at the tall, gaping hallway that had so beguiled her, she realises. None of this matters any more. None of it makes any difference. She looks up the stairs towards Ben's bedroom door which has taken on the air of a barricaded portcullis these days.

Why is he shutting her out like this? Why can't she talk to him any more? Why does he look at her with wary eyes as though she is a wild animal or a horse run mad? She knows why. It was written all over her face, as plain as day, when she had looked at herself earlier in his bedroom mirror. This is not the face of his mother, but some strange, deranged woman; unpredictable, unknowable, dangerous.

She sighs. She has to talk to him. He still doesn't know that his father has left, their marriage over. That everything is about to change irrevocably. She can't bear the thought of causing him pain, of disrupting his world even further. And yet, how long before Steve says something to him? How much will he share with their son? Would Steve even go to the police? And now she fears that Laura is beginning to suspect her as well. The way she had looked at her as she stood on the lawn by Rosemary's grave. Iris could see it all through her friend's eyes for the first time. How incriminating it would all seem. How others might jump to the worst conclusion if they knew.

Taking a deep breath, running her fingers through her tangled bird's nest of hair, she tries to compose herself, resolves to be calm, measured. Above all, sane. Everything, all of this, can be explained. She was just trying to do the right thing by everyone, the kindest thing. Not just for themselves but for Rosemary as well. Ben will understand, she tries to reassure herself, just like Laura and Steve will in time. And then they can draw a line under it all. Forget about it. Move on.

Iris climbs the stairs as though she is scaling a mountain, one foot after another, wading through invisible mud, her body leaden. She knocks on Ben's door and after a brief pause, she enters. Ben is sitting on his bed, cross-legged, his school books fanning out around him, eating a packet of crisps. Her senses are immediately alerted.

'What are you eating? Where did you get those?'

'From the school tuck shop. Don't worry, I've checked the ingredients listing.'

She grabs them out of his hands and checks them herself, reading the packet with hawkish eyes.

'Why haven't you been eating your lunch at school?'

Ben falters for a second. 'I have. Most days. Sometimes I just want to buy my own stuff or share with others.'

'What? Don't be so stupid. You know how risky that is. I prepare your lunch for you and you alone. You know you have to be ultra-careful.'

'Yes,' he says, sighing heavily. 'I know, Mum. I can look after myself. And yes, before you ask, I have got my inhaler and my EpiPen. Between you and school, I could hardly forget.'

'And why, might I ask, weren't you at school yesterday? I know you were absent. And why did you lie about going to Freddie's house last night? I know, Ben. I know about it all.'

He turns his face away, his features hard and closed.

Iris swallows, trying to calm down and get back on track. This wasn't how she wanted this conversation to go. As she draws in the air through her nose and pushes it out through her mouth, she catches another whiff of roses.

'God, what is that bloody smell?' she asks, launching herself towards the curtains in order to heave open the sash window. As she does, she catches sight of a collection of items on Ben's bedside table; a perfumed body spray, a lip balm. None of them are his. Iris reaches for the spray; a lurid pink-coloured can decorated with illustrated flowers.

'Whose is this?' she asks, unable to keep the snobbish tone from her voice.

Ben looks sheepish but then brazens it out. 'Becky's. My girl-friend.'

Iris gives an involuntary snort. 'Aren't you a bit young for a girlfriend?'

'Okay, well she's more of a friend, who's a girl. We get on, that's all. She's nice. Nicer than most people at school,' says Ben.

'Tell her you shouldn't be breathing in toxic stuff like this,' she says dropping the spray into the bin. 'It could get into your chest. Bring on an attack.'

Ben stands, retrieving the spray from the bin.

'It's fine, Mum. Stop interfering.'

'Don't speak to me like that. I'm your mother. I've taken care of you all these years, remember? I know what's best. How to keep you safe.'

Ben looks away, his cheeks flushing, eyes shooting arrows.

Iris moves towards him, her instinct always to comfort when he looks upset. But as she does so, she hears a rustling sound from underneath the bed.

'What was that?' She stalls in the middle of the room, her instincts on high alert again.

'Nothing,' Ben says too quickly, his voice high and panicked.

They both wait, holding their breath, poised, listening. And then it comes, a small mewling sound.

'Mum. Don't freak out,' says Ben urgently.

'That bloody cat,' says Iris, lunging towards the underside of the bed. 'Did you sneak it into the house?' She begins to pull at things, catching hold of the end of a blanket and tugging. The cat hisses and then darts out. It sees that the way is blocked, the door closed and tries to hide under a chair.

'Mum, it's fine. I'm not allergic. It doesn't bother me. In fact, I like it. I think she likes me,' says Ben, pleading with her now.

'You can't have pets, Ben,' she shouts. 'Especially not a stray. Who knows what germs it could be harbouring? Dirty, stinking thing.'

She lunges towards the cat again, who launches itself against the door and begins clawing its nails at the painted wood, desperate to escape.

'Don't hurt her,' Ben says, pulling at Iris's arm.

She throws him off, oblivious. 'Get out,' she shouts, opening the door, chasing it towards the stairs. 'Get out of my house.'

She follows the cat down the stairs, determined to make sure it has really gone.

'No, Mum,' calls Ben after her. 'Let her stay. This is her home too.'

Iris ignores him, blundering down the stairs, shooing the cat towards the front door which she throws open. The cat sees its way clear and dashes through the exit but Iris continues to pursue it down the path. She will not let it hide in the garden or skulk about in the bushes. She's had enough of the thing and, driven with a purpose she hasn't felt in weeks, she chases it towards the gate, the pavement, off the premises entirely.

Of course, she never meant for it to happen, but as she herds the cat towards the road, shouting and baying at it, she doesn't think about the traffic, the cars. Opening her arms wide, like a pantomime villain, she drives the cat one last time. It hisses, ears back, its eyes like slices of glass and then it runs out into the road.

The sound is sickening; a screech of brakes, a dull thud, a pterodactyl-like cry from the cat. Iris watches, horror-struck. She turns to see that Ben has followed her downstairs and is standing at the gate, having witnessed the whole scene. The cat lifts itself from the ground, its fur standing on end, electrocuted. It emits another plaintive cry of pain and then pulls itself, limping across the road to safety and into a nearby privet hedge.

'No,' cries Ben.

Iris spins around. 'I'm sorry, forgive me,' she begs him. 'I didn't mean … don't worry, love. We'll find it. We'll take it straight to the vet, I promise. It will all be okay, don't cry.'

Ben's face is a picture of shock. It feels like a sucker punch for him to look at her this way, with such disbelieving hatred. He turns and runs back towards the porch and hastily pulls on his shoes, grabs his coat.

'No, no, Ben. Don't go. I'm sorry. Help me find it. You said it likes you. Trusts you.'

He pushes past her wordlessly.

'Where are you going?'

'Away from here. From you,' he answers and runs.

43

Opening the door to her own house, Laura breathes in the smell of expensive perfumed candle and rugger boots, reassured by the safety, the familiarity of it all. She allows herself a moment of appreciation for her own good fortune before she barrels into the hallway, intent on her mission.

She takes out her wallet and finds the business card that Len gave her, running her thumb along the embossed print that reads: Leonard Drake, LPD Property Development, CEO. He had told her she could reach him on his mobile any time, day or night. So, she texts a message to him.

We need to talk to Iris. Meet me at Riddleston road tonight.
6 p.m.? Laura

The response from Len comes less than five minutes later, her phone bleeping in her hand, as though he has been sitting, waiting patiently for her to get in touch.

Will do. See you then. Len

She finds Ivo at the kitchen table, tapping away at his laptop.

'Everything all right?' he asks, lifting his head. 'Who was that?'

'Oh, no one,' she says absentmindedly and then when she catches a wounded look cross his features, she adds, 'Iris.'

'How is she?' he asks. 'Is she going to be okay?'

'Yep, I think so. I mean, she's in a state but …'

'Trust Steve to do a runner. To be honest, I never did like the cut of his jib.'

'No,' Laura agrees. 'No, me neither.'

She holds Ivo's gaze for a second. It's as if they are trying to read one another. But then he gets up from the table, shutting his laptop lid and packing it away into his leather satchel. Coming closer, he wraps her in his arms and kisses the side of her head.

'And how are you, my love?' He puts a hand on her belly. 'Both of you.'

She smiles, relishing this feeling, something she had imagined for many years. But then she opens her eyes, reality sinking in again. 'Good, fine,' she says. 'Just got one or two things to sort out. I'm going to pop over to Iris's again. Y'know, just to check in on her.'

'Again? Must you?'

'Yes. Look, I can't go into it now but there's an issue with the house and well, Steve's being a prick and says he wants custody of Ben.'

'Wow, what a mess,' he says, shaking his head.

'It is and I'm worried about Iris's mental health. She didn't seem at all well this morning. I have a feeling she's going to need to lawyer up too. Ivo, can we do something to help her? I mean, I think we should, don't you?'

She sees her husband blanch in surprise at this but then he shrugs his shoulders and says, 'Sure. Why not? Love thy neighbour and all that. I'll see what I can do.'

'Thank you,' she says and leans in to kiss him. 'After all, not everyone is as lucky as we are.'

He pulls back for a moment.

'You would tell me,' he says. 'If there was a problem. Anything to worry about?'

Laura pauses, tempted to admit to what she knows. But Ivo will only overreact and she wants to handle this herself for now.

'I'll explain everything,' she says. 'I promise. Once I've dealt with Iris. Don't worry, I'll be back soon and then we can relax for the night.'

'Good,' he says, kissing her one last time as if sealing a document. 'You should be taking it easy. You're like a whirling dervish, woman. Slow down!'

Bundled up in her duvet coat, as though she might be able to wrap herself in protective wadding, Laura walks the short distance to Iris's house on Riddleston Road. As she traverses the street, she peers into the elegant bay windows where the softly lit interiors can be seen; a fringed standard lamp, a grand piano, lilies formally arranged on a table. She still can't believe that something so dreadful could have taken place on this street, in one of these houses, and worse that it is her friend Iris who is involved somehow.

Laura hurries to the end of the road where she sees Len is waiting, half-concealed by the hedge. He raises a hand to her in friendly greeting and she smiles though her stomach quakes at the thought of the conversation they must have, what might ensue. She knows Iris is a woman on the edge. Who knows how little it would take to tip her over.

'Thanks for meeting me,' she says.

'What have you found out?' he asks.

'First of all, you should know that Iris's husband, Steve, has left her. So, she's a bit fragile.'

'Begs the question: why did he leave, don't you think?'

'It's not that straightforward. I think they've always had debts but apparently someone is now blackmailing Iris for money.'

Len's eyebrows shoot up his forehead in surprise. 'Wow. Just when you think this situation can't get any weirder ...'

'I know,' she agrees. 'At first, I thought you were right. That perhaps Steve was involved or put her up to this, but now

I'm starting to think otherwise. The fact he's left and is demanding a divorce and custody of their son makes me think that maybe he didn't know anything after all. Otherwise, I don't know how he would have the gall to take the moral high ground on all this. Or think that a court would award in his favour. Not unless he was completely innocent of any wrongdoing. To be honest, Steve has always struck me as pretty clueless.'

Len nods. 'Well, if he didn't know something dodgy was going on, I think it's safe to say he's probably working things out now. And Iris must have done something pretty bad for him to up and leave like this.'

'She's not a bad person, Len …' begins Laura, thinking of how desperate and sad Iris had seemed the last time she saw her.

He looks at her reticently. 'That doesn't mean she isn't capable of doing bad things.'

Laura sighs. 'I should probably tell you as well … I found out that Iris was spotted walking with Rosemary not long before she disappeared.'

'What?' Len looks at her, appalled. 'Why didn't you tell me this immediately?'

'I don't know, I just can't bring myself to think of her in this way. It's insane. It's frightening.'

'But don't you see, Laura? This is proof that Iris is implicated. Your friend isn't who you think she is. I'm going to call the police. Iris could be a danger to others.'

'Wait,' says Laura, putting a hand on his arm as he reaches for his phone. 'Let's just hear her out. Hear her side of the story, eh? Then if you're still not satisfied, you can report her.'

Len shakes his head but then he reconsiders. 'Okay, I'll give her one last chance but be on your guard.'

'Don't worry, I will.'

They both nod at each other now, faces serious, mouths set as they head up the path and knock on Iris's front door. At first there is no response and Laura wonders if she should try

Iris's mobile. But she can see a dim light leaking from the glass above the door so she calls out speculatively.

'Iris? It's me, Laura. Are you there? Let me in.'

Eventually, the door slowly opens and Iris's pale face peers round it. She takes in Laura and then recoils when she sees Len standing beside her.

'What's he doing here?' she says, looking accusingly at Laura.

'This is Len Drake,' begins Laura, about to make the usual formal introductions.

'Oh my God,' wails Iris. 'I can't believe you'd go to social services, Laura. How could you? You promised me you'd help.'

Len steps forward, raising both his hands in a gesture of peace.

'Please, don't be afraid. I'm not from the local authorities. It's nothing like that.'

She stares at him, confusion and mistrust rippling across her face. 'What then? What do you want? What is this?'

'My mother used to live here,' he says plainly.

Iris's face falls, her eyes widening with dread. Then she seems to panic and tries to close the door in their faces. Before she can, Laura shoves her foot in the gap and Len places a hand on the wood to block it.

'Just let us in, Iris. We need to talk,' pleads Laura.

'Rosemary didn't have any children,' comes Iris's strangled response. 'You're lying.'

'No, she didn't. But her sister did,' says Len. 'Iris. I'm June's son.'

There is a pause as they all seem to draw a collective breath and then the pressure behind the door releases as Iris gives way.

'You'd better come in,' she says finally.

Inside, they gather around the kitchen table.

Laura is shocked at how much worse Iris looks, her physical appearance deteriorating by the hour. As they all agree to sit, she can see how her friend's hands shake before she tries to still them in her lap. There is no offer of a drink or refreshment. Iris seems to be beyond any of these social niceties now and perhaps it is just as well. Sympathy swims hand in hand with fear as Laura's mind continues to flit from the wretched woman in front of her to the knowledge of what she might have done.

Her eyes sweep the room, scouring the kitchen counters for sight of a knife block or other potential weapons. For want of anything better, her hand clenches the set of house keys in her coat pocket. How on earth has she found herself in this situation, she wonders. Ivo would hit the roof if he knew what she was doing, the risks she was taking. But she feels emboldened by Len's calm and authoritative presence.

'Iris,' he begins. 'I think you've probably guessed why we're here. Rosemary Parker, my aunt and the owner of this property, has disappeared. I haven't been able to trace her for some time now. And then I find that you and your family are living here. That you moved in several months ago. When I called by the other day, you claimed to be a relation of hers. But as we've just established, I'm Rosemary's only living relative.' He folds his arms, his face becoming sterner by the second. 'So, what exactly is going on here?'

Iris looks like a cornered animal. Her whole body seems to tense and stiffen. Only her eyes move, darting about the room, looking for escape. Laura holds her nerve, bracing for some kind of reaction and Len catches her eye in a silent warning. Iris grips the edge of the table; a coiled spring about to release. For one brief moment, it feels like it could go either way; she might lunge for the exit or lash out. She appears to gather herself, takes a breath, her mouth opening but then something changes. All the fight seems to go out of her and Iris sits back in her chair, defeated.

'Why don't you start by telling us how you met Rosemary?' says Laura. 'You were seen with her one day, not long before you moved in here.'

'Who saw me?' asks Iris, alarm returning to her face again.

'That doesn't matter. Just tell us what really happened.'

'I didn't plan it, if that's what you're thinking,' says Iris mutely. 'I'd never met her before in my entire life, I swear. But then there she was one day, lying on the pavement. She'd fallen, hurt herself. So I walked her back home, made her a cup of tea. Tried to help her. I even offered to phone someone for her but she wouldn't let me.' Iris raises her head and looks from Laura to Len. 'It's the truth, I promise. She said there was no one else. No relatives, no friends. No one.'

'And then she disappeared and you moved in. Sounds very convenient to me,' says Len.

'No, it wasn't like that,' says Iris.

Laura places a hand gently on her friend's arm. 'What happened next? Take your time.'

'I never meant for any of this …' Quietly, Iris begins to cry. 'But then Rosemary was dead. She'd banged her head, you see. And I didn't know what to do. I was just so worried about Ben and this house seemed like the answer suddenly. Almost heaven-sent.' She shakes her head. 'I wasn't thinking straight. One thing led to another and after that I just couldn't see a way out.'

'So what did you do with Rosemary's body?' asks Len.

Iris lets out a sob.

'Go on,' says Laura.

Iris looks at them both again, tears welling in her eyes as she shakes her head.

'Is it true, Iris? Is it what I think it is?' asks Laura, a tremor in her voice. 'Is she buried in the garden?'

Slowly, Iris nods, her shoulders shuddering.

There is a stunned silence and Laura waits to see who will speak, act first.

'My God,' breathes Len finally, springing up from the table. 'You must be out of your mind. I can't listen to any more of this.'

'Hang on, Len,' says Laura. For some reason she no longer feels fearful of Iris. Now that this terrible thing is out in the open, there on the table like cards to examine, a sense of practicality takes over. It turns out she is quite good in a crisis, after all. 'I think we all need to take a breath. Yes, you're right, Len. Iris can't have been in her right mind. Clearly, she's been under an incredible amount of strain. Like I told you, her son has been very ill over the years. She and her husband have struggled for money, have debts. Can you imagine what the stress of all that might do to a person?'

He shakes his head, turns a circle before coming to rest over by the kitchen counter.

'No, I'm sorry. Lots of people have health issues, money worries. They don't end up doing something like this.'

Iris continues to stare at the table, head down, but Laura can see silent tears splashing intermittently on the wooden surface.

'I think you'd be surprised, Len. What people are capable of if they feel desperate enough.'

He huffs at this, unconvinced. 'You know, I spoke to someone who knew the family,' continues Laura tentatively. '*Your* family. It sounds like Rosemary was as much a victim of this house, this situation, as everyone else involved.'

Len rears up.

'As much a victim as me and my mum? How can you say that?'

'Well, no, but it sounds like she had to make sacrifices, missed out on a career, marriage and kids, everything. Gave it all up to look after her mother and became tied to this house. In the end she had no one, Len. She was alone.'

Len tilts his head as he considers this.

Iris looks up then. 'I'm sorry,' she says. 'For all of it. I don't expect anyone to understand. I don't understand it myself really.'

There is a pause while Len gazes through the window, towards the back garden. He is silent for a long time and then he appears to come to some kind of resolution. He turns his attention back to the kitchen as if only seeing it properly for the first time.

'I can't believe this is where my mum grew up all those years ago,' he says. 'I've always wondered what this house looked like inside.'

'Iris has worked wonders with the place,' trills Laura before she realises what she's saying and blushes.

'Yes,' says Len. 'I can imagine it had become pretty run-down over the years.'

There is another pause while they all look at each other, exchanging glances as though they are passing a ball around the room, wondering who might let it fall first.

'Okay,' he says, finally. 'I'm not going to press charges. I don't really care about this house, if I'm honest. It's brought nothing but misery to people over the years and I'd bulldoze it to the ground if I had my way.' His shoulders sag and he gives a heavy sigh. 'Seems to me Rosemary got her just desserts, in one way or another. And I'll be damned if another mother and innocent child's lives are to be ruined. All because of one property.'

Iris lets out a grateful sob.

'Thank you,' she manages to say.

Len turns to Laura. 'But we still have to go to the police with this. It's a crime not to report a death. And to conceal a body. I can't be an accessory to this.'

Laura nods in agreement but then she cocks her head to one side.

'You know, Iris didn't actually hide or even dispose of the body. She buried it. Minor technicality, but an important one. Anyway, who's to say what Rosemary's last wishes were. Did she even have a will?'

'The only thing I found was the original family will,' answers Iris. 'Stating that everything, including the house, was to go to Rosemary – in the absence of any heirs.'

'Sounds about right,' tuts Len.

'There you go then,' says Laura. 'Who are we to presume? In lieu of any formal instructions, maybe Rosemary would have preferred this. A natural burial.'

Iris and Len look at her askance.

'No, Laura. Nice try but we have to let the authorities deal with this in the proper way. And as for Iris's guilt, a court of law will decide.'

Iris bows her head in silent obedience.

'Look, Ivo and I know one of the best barristers in London,' says Laura. 'We've been friends since uni. I know she'd take your case on as a favour if we asked her. Mates' rates and all that. Or we can cover the costs and you can pay us back. It might not even come to that anyway.'

'Why would you do all that for me?' asks Iris in a small, cracked voice.

'Well, what else are friends for? Besides, I owe you one.'

Iris walks Laura and Len to the front door.

'Get some rest tonight, eh?' says Laura. 'And then, when you're ready, Ivo and I will come to the police station with you tomorrow to make a statement.'

'Okay,' says Iris, weakly. She turns towards Len. 'And thank you.'

She seems to falter for a second and then she turns her gaze back towards his clear blue-eyed one, as though a thought has just occurred to her.

'Mr Maddox,' she says slowly. 'Our school caretaker. He's your father.'

Len takes a step back and looks from one of them to the other.

As realisation dawns on her too, Laura lets out a small gasp. 'Of course.'

44

Laura wakes the next morning. She wriggles her toes and luxu-
riates for a moment, relishing the soft weight of the sheets, the
smell of freshly laundered husband as Ivo wanders out of the en
suite and heads downstairs to put on the coffee.

She still hasn't said anything about Iris yet. Last night, after
she got home, she had collapsed into bed with exhaustion, the
weight of events finally overcoming her. But she will have to
broach the subject with him soon and fill him in, especially
if they are to accompany her to the police station today. But
then she sits bolt upright as another thought occurs to her. This
marble of worry has been rolling around her brain for hours,
no, days, she realises. Ever since Iris first told her about it. The
blackmail card. She pictures herself now, inserting it back into
its envelope as though, even then, she didn't want to look at it or
truly consider its existence.

Fuck, fuck, fuck, she whispers under her breath. She knows
exactly where that blackmail note came from and who sent it.
As her mind darts, wondering what the best course of action
might be, she hears Ivo calling up the stairs to ask if she wants
a decaf. She gets out of bed, pulling on her sari dressing gown
and babouche slippers, and pads downstairs.

'Coffee's on,' he says. 'What can I get you?'

But Laura finds her stomach twisting at the thought, not just
because she is pregnant but because of her growing sense of
unease.

'What's up?' he asks, reading her face.

Laura rearranges her features into an appropriation of calm. 'Nothing. Just some personal admin I need to do today.'

Ivo nods, then looks at his watch. 'Speaking of which, I've got to go to a meeting.'

'Do you need the car?' she asks.

'Nah, I think I'll take the train, actually,' he says. 'The traffic will be a nightmare right now. But I'll be back in good time. Maybe we could have a nice meal? Just us, while Fred's out at practice tonight. I'll cook you anything you fancy. You're eating for two now, remember?'

'That sounds nice,' she says, though her stomach registers another small wave of nausea.

She dips her head in agreement, watches him leave. This over-solicitousness is sweet but it's making her uncomfortable. She waits a second or two and then runs upstairs. She knows what she's looking for, knows where she will find it.

Opening the door to Freddie's bedroom, she drops to the floor and starts to search. Under the bed, or tucked away in a drawer perhaps, secreted behind the wardrobe. Finally, she finds what she has been looking for. Concealed within a Waitrose shopping bag is a box of unused Christmas cards. She knew she had recognised the design from somewhere; the cheerful robin redbreast on the front and the stamp of charitable donation on the reverse. Now for the last piece of incontrovertible evidence and then she knows it's definitely him. Sure enough, she climbs under the desk and sees the printer where it has always resided. Next to it is a ream of stationery, a sheet of plain white stickers, ready for addresses to be printed onto them. Just like the one on Iris's blackmail note.

Laura leans back on her haunches.

How could Freddie do this? Her own child? How can she and Ivo have been so blind to this behaviour going on right under their very noses? Her head spins. How on earth had he managed to get a PO box number at his age? Probably got someone to vouch for him, pretending to be an adult. And ever since she set up his own bank account for him, she hasn't thought twice about checking it, merely allowing him to deposit his usual pocket, birthday or Christmas money himself. She is mortified, her cheeks stinging with shame, her stomach lurching with fear at the possible repercussions.

She blows out a slow stream of air, trying to centre herself, imagining she is prostrate on her yoga mat and the instructor is creating a sound bath to lull her and the rest of the class. She wonders what he is doing with the money he's extorted? And then she thinks of the lurid new trainers he was wearing. Let's just hope that Iris has destroyed the evidence. And she prays that Freddie hasn't sent any more of those awful blackmail notes, which could lead back to them as a family.

She stands, takes the leftover Christmas cards and the ream of printer stickers and puts them back into the carrier bag, ready to dispose of in the rubbish bin. She must nip this in the bud now and cover the traces. When she gets hold of Freddie, she's going to kill him. That's it. He's grounded. And he can kiss goodbye to the rugby too. Mixing with some of the older lads at school has definitely not been a good influence, clearly.

Laura walks out of the room, her mind reeling. She can't quite take it in. It just goes to show, we all have our secrets, some more terrible than others. She thinks of her own indiscretions, the lies she's told, the half-truths, the way she has deceived her wonderful husband. The way she's let down her family. Would Freddie have turned into the sort of boy capable of this if she had paid him a bit more attention, set a better example? She's been so preoccupied by everything in her own world, she couldn't see what's been happening right in front of her eyes.

She wanders into her own bedroom, flops down into the cocoon of the four-poster bed. What else has she missed, she wonders? What else has passed her by? She thinks about how easily people take each other for granted, think they know one another, put their morals to one side in a moment of madness, allow themselves to indulge their dark side. Iris did it, as did she and Steve. What about Ivo?

She sits up, suddenly alert, her heart knocking at her ribs. Surely he wouldn't betray her or risk harming their family, breaking up their happy home, would he?

Laura begins to search again. This time, she has no idea what she's looking for, she only knows that she must find it, whatever it is, or she can't rest. She looks under the bed – such a rich trove of evidence in Freddie's pit of a room – but beneath theirs is just boxes of shoes, mainly hers admittedly and a few of Ivo's hand weights gathering dust. She opens the wardrobe. Again, there are no skeletons to be found here, just the expected contents: clothes. But it is a representation of their relationship, their marriage. Three quarters of the space is taken up with her various garments of every stripe while Ivo's small section contains just his suits, some shirts and a couple of pairs of jeans. She's never noticed how much space he allows her, how much she takes up. How much he sacrifices to allow her to indulge in what she wants.

Turning away from the closet, she moves to the tallboy chest. She knows most of the drawers will be filled with the frilly silk satin of her lingerie and nightwear, though of course Ivo loves them really. But one of the drawers is given over to Ivo's personal belongings: watches, cufflinks, old Father's Day and Valentine's cards he can't bear to throw away, ear pods, old photos from uni, ephemera from the rugby glory days.

Laura reaches a hand inside, sifts through this detritus, feeling all the way to the back of the drawer. She finds yet more sentimental tokens, things she didn't even know Ivo had kept; tickets from some of the gigs they attended, a candle stub from their first romantic date, one of Freddie's baby curls tied up with a thread of cotton. He had kept all these things.

She is about to withdraw her hand, aware that she is intruding on a soft, private part of Ivo that he rarely reveals, when her hand fastens around what feels like a folded envelope. She expects it's just another tatty old flyer from their student days but when she brings it out, she realises it has Ivo's name printed on the front and is stamped PRIVATE & CONFIDENTIAL. She hesitates for a split second and then opens it.

Her eyes graze over the text, registering first the logo of the private medical practice and then Ivo's details. These are test results, she realises. The results of fertility tests to which she never knew he had submitted, a long time ago. He had always been so adamant that he didn't want to be picked and poked over like a specimen. That they should just give it time, let nature run its course, accept the hand that fate had dealt them. But these tests clearly show that Ivo had become sterile – the words, 'low sperm count' and 'poor motility' clearly stated – in the years since Freddie had been born.

She had presumed their inability to conceive again was all her fault. She was the one with screwy periods, a presumably inhospitable womb, something not quite right with her ovaries, though all of her initial tests had suggested things were fine. That's why she had patiently waited all those years, hoping that another baby would come along.

All those good years when she was young, fertile, strong. When her eggs were healthy. She feels a tide of grief wash over her, tainted with anger. The knowledge that Ivo has lied to her or rather neglected to tell her the whole truth.

They could have adopted, for God's sake. Or investigated IVF, sperm donation, whatever. But his stupid, male chauvinist pride, his overly competitive nature, just like his bloody father and his father before him, wouldn't allow him to admit to anyone that there was a problem. And now she is finally pregnant again, so late in the day, but with another man's child, with this baby and all the health risks associated with it. It didn't have to be this way.

She wants to screw up this paper, ball it into a fist and smash it into Ivo's face. Tear it up into confetti and strew it over this farce of a marriage bed. Look what their lives have become. Look what he made her do.

Laura sinks back down onto the bed again and cries tears of shame, frustration and self-pity. Her life could have been so perfect. It was. Near as dammit anyway. And Ivo has ruined it. But then she relents. She listens to her own thoughts; how selfish, unfair they are. This is not his fault any more than it is hers. They are both to blame, both culpable. After all, a man's fertility can wane just like a woman's can. And, like her, Ivo has not been getting any younger either. In fact, he'd often joked about how he's had one too many groin injuries over the years, due to all the rugby. But, in the end, Laura must concede that his only sin is one of pride.

And then finally she accepts what is staring her in the face. Ivo must know that, unlike Freddie, this baby cannot be his. It is impossible, as the test results show. So he must know that she has had an affair, is carrying another man's child. And yet, and yet … he was still pleased, has stood by her, and wants to care for them both. That is how much he wants her to be happy. She realises how lucky she is, really, just how fortunate she truly is. Laura thought she knew, had always tried to practise gratitude, even journaling to write them down, all of these many gifts she has been bestowed, this embarrassment of riches. Hashtag blessed. But she is, she really is.

Standing, she refolds the paper into its envelope and stows it carefully towards the back of the drawer where she found it, replacing all of Ivo's other treasured items as though they had never been disturbed.

A sense of peace washes over her, now she finally knows the secret that she always suspected was hidden somewhere, deep in her and Ivo's relationship. She has brought it to the surface, examined it and can now relinquish it to the depths again.

Changing into her usual loungewear, she rakes a brush through her hair, applies a slick of lip balm. She takes one last look in the mirror. They will survive, she thinks, eyeing herself directly in the glass. Better still, they will thrive. They always have, they always will. This is just who they are.

And with that she walks down the stairs, taking her keys from the bowl in the hallway. A cursory glance at her phone confirms that Iris has not been in touch yet. But it's still early and besides, she can't face any more drama right now. Hers or anyone else's. She needs to get out of the house, to shake off all of this pent-up energy and emotion. Perhaps she will be able to catch a yoga class and then she'll drive out to her favourite farm shop, buy some organic food for her and Ivo's supper. She walks with the stride of a woman who knows she is loved. No, adored, in fact.

45

Iris opens the front door and looks out towards the gate, the privet hedge and the street beyond. She barely slept last night, rising and falling through layers of consciousness, fevered dreams, nightmares of being trapped, imprisoned, buried alive. At one point, she recalls coming downstairs and finding half a bottle of brandy in the cupboard and drinking from its neck. The burn of its fire choking past her throat as she welcomed the anathema, longingly craving the escape of sleep.

Now, she stares out at the cars, the people that pass by the house. None of them realise what she has done. How this normal, everyday house will soon become notorious. She imagines what people might do, say to her. When the news breaks, when she is arrested by the police and the papers get hold of the story. How it will affect Ben.

Her mind veers, thinking back to the last time she saw her son. How she had, half-crazed with fury, chased the cat into the road where it was struck by a passing car. How he had witnessed it all. She takes a couple of steps out into the front garden, peering hopefully for a flash of the cat's tortoiseshell markings. All those times she had wished it gone and now she would give anything to see it alive and well. But it is nowhere to be seen.

Standing in the porch, she looks one last time towards the gate, hoping that her son will come back. That he will reconsider, forgive her, understand. Pick her a flower or make her a cup of tea, like he used to do. But there is little chance of that. Iris had desperately tried to track him down last night and eventually she had confirmed that Ben was with his father, at a cheap hotel nearby. Steve's message should have been a relief but his words tore through her like a blade:

> Ben is staying with me. You should be locked up where you belong.

She moves as though underwater; she can't hear anything, can't see anything. She stumbles blindly back into the house and along the hall towards the kitchen. She thinks about filling the kettle, going through the motions of putting a bag in a cup, brewing the tea, adding milk and sugar. Would she feel better? Would it help her to find the strength, the courage to do what she must? To call the police, take herself down to the local station, ask to speak to the attending officer. She wishes to make an admission of guilt. To come clean.

Looking out at the back garden where Rosemary rests, she tries to understand how she has found herself here. A bitter laugh escapes her lips, glancing off the surfaces of the kitchen, echoing around the lofty ceiling.

This house has been a blessing as well as a curse.

Rosemary's words taunt her. The old woman was right. Iris finally understands. Vengeance has been served, justice has been meted out. She has already been punished for her crime. In the most complete of ways. She has lost everything and there is no way back from here. It really is just a house, as Rosemary had tried to caution her. And it really wasn't worth the heavy price she has paid for it.

All at once, Iris is cold to her bones, her skin running with a shivering fear. Her scalp prickles, her arms are goosefleshed. She feels the unnerving presence in the house, as she has done so many times before. It is clear that she has outstayed her welcome and it is time to leave. But she has nowhere else to go. She is entirely alone. She thinks about calling Laura, Len even, but she can't bear the thought of their faces, their voices. Instead, she turns to leave the kitchen and walks upstairs. She feels so cold, so empty and now all she wants is warmth, comfort, sleep. To not feel anything any more. Sitting on the edge of the old, chipped enamel bath, she fits the plug into the hole, turns on the hot water tap. It responds with a stuttering roar and steam begins to fill the room.

Iris stands and gathers toiletries from the cabinet, moving jars and bottles out of the way, until she finds the packet of razor blades. The room is a sweaty fug now. The extractor fan no longer works, the windows glued shut with ages of paint. No matter. She can disappear inside this mist, allow it to envelop her as she eases off her clothes.

The bath is nearly full, but she allows the hot tap to continue running, a thin stream of warm adding to the water level. She wouldn't want to be cold. Hates to be cold. As she lowers herself in, the bath feels like a baptism, a cleansing fire, a purification. If only it could wash away all her sins.

She takes the blade, carefully slips it from the packet and calmly applies it to her wrists, opening her flesh. The wounds are no different to the cut on her thumb from the other night. Perhaps a little deeper. They ache when she submerges them, the blood finding its way, the warm water encouraging it to flow freely.

Iris sighs, experiencing a release as her body acquiesces. She feels herself relax for the first time in days, weeks. Every tautly held muscle, every highly strung nerve, melting. She gives herself up, she surrenders. Staring at the running tap, her vision fades, growing dark. As her world finally turns from grey to black, the last thing she registers is the most intense perfume. Roses. A garden of it. Suffusing the air with its redolent scent. And as the steam clings to the cold walls, it forms rivulets, it drips and runs, as if the very house itself is weeping.

46

Laura sits in the lotus position; hips open, back straight, her hands resting languidly in her lap. She tries to be mindful, in the moment, focusing on her inner peace, the in and out of her breath.

But her mind is running parallel, a million miles an hour as usual. She will buy fresh scallops from the fishmonger stall at the farm shop. Pan-fry them in butter and garlic. Plus some asparagus spears if they have them in early. It should be coming into season, she thinks.

Her mouth begins to water at the idea. Not just at the idea of the meal, but the thought of sharing it with Ivo. Whatever challenges their relationship has faced recently, they have come through them. They have so much to celebrate, after all. And her life is truly delicious in every sense of the word. She vows to savour it all from now on, every minute of every day.

She gives a little nod of affirmation to herself and slowly opens her eyes as the class comes to a close. Slinging her rolled-up yoga mat over her shoulder, pulling on her Birkenstock mules, she leaves the dance studio. Walking out into the bright glare, she reaches for her sunglasses and then climbs into the Range Rover, still mentally planning her shopping list for tonight's feast.

The car knows its own way to the farm shop by now and she drives on autopilot, humming along to the radio. She likes to keep up, though Freddie would roll his eyes if she ever tried to discuss the latest new music trends with him. A brief ripple of consternation passes over the millpond of her forehead as she thinks about her son, before she dismisses the thought. He'll be okay. It's a phase. He's just testing the boundaries, like most bright, spirited boys.

As Laura winds the car along the quiet country lanes, the sun shafts through the branches of trees and hedgerows. She pulls the visor down to shield her eyes, focuses more carefully through her sunglasses to read the road, its bends and turns. As she does so, she casts a look in the rear-view mirror and sees that a lone car has joined her, threading its way along behind.

She slows down as the road straightens out. Just overtake, wanker, she thinks, refusing to speed up even though the driver continues to trail her, edging closer. Laura looks in the rear-view again as the car moves closer still. She can see the driver clearly now, though they too are wearing shades. She would recognise that face, the build anywhere. It is Steve and his mouth is set in a thin line.

A sliver of ice solidifies inside her as it dawns on her what this means. Involuntarily, her foot pushes down on the accelerator, the urge to run from danger primeval, a millennia's worth of instinct coursing through her veins now. The Range Rover responds obediently and her head is thrown back into the seat. Steve follows suit, his car dogging hers, matching her speed.

She is aware of the farm shop in her peripheral vision as the car hurtles on by. Where is she heading? Where will this road lead? She curses herself. If she'd thought about it she should have pulled into the market, parked in safety, run inside seeking assistance. Steve would never have followed her into a crowded space. He means to get her on her own. He has waited, she realises. He has planned this, stalking her until she was driving out here all by herself in the middle of nowhere.

This knowledge makes her heart hammer. Her left leg starts up a spasming twitch. There is too much adrenaline running around her body. She thinks of the baby and this immediately makes her panic more as tears fill her eyes, blurring her vision. Please, she thinks, just leave us alone.

She swings the car round another bend, frantically searching the horizon for a building, an outhouse, another car or roadside café, anything that might be of help. Somewhere she can seek sanctuary, a person to whom she can appeal. Any stranger would be preferable to Steve right now. Because she knows, with a deep certainty, that he doesn't want to see her, speak to her. He only means her harm now. Her and this baby.

Laura prods the accelerator again. The Range Rover is far more powerful than his shitty hunk of junk, she thinks. Maybe she can outrun him. This road has got to emerge somewhere. She will find civilisation, other people, soon. Nudging the speedometer up another notch, she knows she is driving far too fast for these twisty country lanes, but she pushes on. She has always felt invincible in this car, insulated, in her own little protective bubble.

But she isn't. She is vulnerable like everyone else. This car is just a car; metal, leather, rubber, plastic and petrol. Laura realises a millisecond too late that she has taken the corner too tightly, and in her panic, she over-corrects. The power steering, the ABS, the airbag all do their best. They fulfil their duty, respond on command and probably do save her life. But as the vehicle careers into the verge and overturns, coming to rest upside down in a ditch, Laura hangs in suspended animation. She registers the fact that she is alone. Alone and trapped. She can hear another car come to an abrupt halt nearby but then after a few moments it drives away. Steve has abandoned her. He isn't going to help her or phone for an ambulance. And there is no one else around for miles.

Laura's whole body hurts. She tastes the metallic tang of blood, as though she is sucking on an iron bar. Her head throbs, the sharp edges of her designer sunglasses cutting into her cheeks. One of her arms appears to be twisted at an abrupt angle and she can't feel her legs at all.

As she drags in a crackling breath and tries to push it out, her ribs feel as though they are on fire. Still, she tries to call out, to raise her voice, to shout for help. The only response is the buzz and twitter of the surrounding countryside; the caw of a rook as it cocks its head in speculation of the wreckage before it flies away.

Then she feels it; the slow seep. A wetness, fluid leaking from her down below, between her legs. She gives a low moan.

'No, no, no,' she whispers. 'Please. Please don't go,' she prays. 'Please. Stay.'

47

SIX MONTHS LATER

Laura sits beside Ivo in the hospital, absorbing the all too familiar smells and sounds; the disinfectant, the reheated food that reminds her of school dinners, the beep and whine of machines and monitors. She has become accustomed to the regulation NHS sheets; thin and scratchy from their millions of industrial launders.

Of course, she wasn't aware of much when she was first rushed into hospital. Drifting in and out of consciousness, veering between acute pain and blessed oblivion, her only thoughts had been for her baby, not her own life. Thank goodness for the local farmer, out ploughing his fields, who had heard the crash and came to her aid, phoning for an ambulance. She will be forever in his debt.

Apart from a broken arm and collarbone, severe bruising and some facial lacerations, she was okay. She would heal, in time. But the small rupture to the amniotic sac and its intermittent leaking had been more of a pressing concern. The baby was alive, though. Miraculously, she had clung on.

Laura was convinced it was a girl. And the emergency scan had confirmed it along with the assurance that if she took complete bed rest at home, guarded against any infection and kept her fluids constantly maintained, the pregnancy could continue until the planned caesarean operation at thirty-six weeks.

The first time Ivo had allowed her to look in a mirror, she had cried, she doesn't mind admitting. But the monstrous swelling and livid bruising have disappeared now. And the scarring is fading to ever paler shades of pink. Eventually it will hardly be noticeable; delicate silvery onion skin a little like the other war wounds on her belly. But these marks are nothing. She welcomes them. Besides, they know a guy on Harley Street who can work wonders if any of it is still an issue.

Laura turns her head to the side and watches her daughter in the bassinet. She is still so impossibly small, like a baby bird, newly hatched. One of many who have passed through this special care baby unit. She can't fault the staff here, they have been amazing. Still, Laura can't bear to drag her eyes away for a minute. But she never tires of seeing the rhythmic rise and fall of the tiny chest, the strong reflexive grip as the baby curls her fingers around Ivo's thumb. He is sitting in an armchair to the side of them both, looking at her with an expression he seems to wear constantly these days; that of a man who put it all on black and won but still looks nervous every time he thinks about what he might have lost.

When he's not making his daily visit to Laura and their baby daughter in hospital, Ivo is trying to keep the house running as well as his business. No wonder he looks exhausted. And of course, he's had to keep a much closer eye on Freddie these days.

Laura had told Ivo what their son had been up to but they have managed to keep the whole matter hushed up. Apparently, Freddie had been turning his hand to some good old-fashioned, low-level bullying at school – terrorising some of the weaker boys, including Ben, by stealing food and lunch money, tearing their clothes, as well as threatening to spread malicious rumours online. The card he sent to Iris had been his first attempt at serious blackmail; a lucky hunch that paid off although he had already identified other people in the neighbourhood he intended to target. In his words, 'everyone has a secret' – and it had started as a game to see who, if anyone, responded by sending money to the address.

Ivo has clamped down on all of this and any evidence has been destroyed. The PO box has been closed, all the search history on Freddie's computer has been wiped and his devices have been replaced. He is now a model student at school, his behaviour impeccable and still a star on the rugby field, so any previous 'failure of good judgement' has been forgiven and swiftly forgotten. The school needs pupils like Freddie Peters, after all.

She's glad that Ben and Iris have moved on though. It's better for everyone to draw a line under everything. She still thinks of her friend, though they are no longer in touch any more. What Iris was prepared to do for her son. A mother's love: it is both terrible and awesome in its strength. But now, with a little time and distance, Laura wonders if it wasn't so very dreadful really ... what she did to Rosemary. There are worse places to be, she muses, than to be buried in the back garden of your life-long home. After all, many people elect to have a natural burial these days. She was listening to a programme about it on the radio the other day. Woodlands, heaths and such like.

Laura leans towards the head of her sleeping child, admiring her soft, silky hair, her almond-shaped eyes.

'She will be all right, won't she?' she asks.

It is a question she has been asking herself – as well as all the doctors and nurses – for months now. She can't quite believe that either of them have survived this terrible ordeal. Her nightmares still come to her; the chase, Steve's face, the crash, the knowledge that she and her baby had been left for dead. She will need a lot of expensive therapy to heal those invisible wounds.

Ivo leans forward in the chair and looks into the crib himself.

'Yes, she will, most definitely. I promise,' he says with feeling, though he has had to voice this reassuring refrain to Laura for so long now. But he knows she is calmed by it and she looks at him as he continues. 'She's a fighter. Could take on the whole rugger team with spirit like that. And she'll want for nothing, will you, princess? Don't worry, darling, she's perfect.'

Laura latches on to his words, though they are so familiar.

'She is, isn't she? The most beautiful girl in the world.'

Ivo kisses the side of her head, just above her right eyebrow. It still hurts if anyone applies pressure there and, conscious of her scars, she allows a lock of hair to fall over her face.

'Of course she is,' he says. 'She looks just like her mother.'

And he kisses her face again, more gently this time, pressing his lips lightly to her skin as though he will make it all better. And it will be.

***

Iris moves around the small but neatly furnished flat, adjusting a picture frame here, straightening a cushion there. She stops to look out onto the garden; a newly paved terrace which leads towards a smartly appointed street. They are city-dwellers now.

She will be forever grateful to Len, but he says she can pay him back as soon as she is comfortably able. Living rent-free means she's already had chance for some savings to accrue and she's finally starting to pay off her debts.

As soon as she was cleared of any offences, she set up her own cleaning company. It had been Ben's idea but along with Len's entrepreneurial flair and a small investment from him, she is finding that she can command a much better wage than she was ever paid in any of her other part-time jobs.

Cleaning other people's houses might seem menial to some but not the type of residences in which she specialises. She now has a select number of clients – some of them contacts of Len's – who value her exacting standards and discreet service. Iris can just plug in her headphones and work to her heart's content. The properties are beautiful and it is a pleasure to hoover and polish them. She is her own boss, can manage her own schedule around Ben and doesn't have to mix with other people. It suits her down to the ground and she is paid well for it.

Her own little flat is nothing compared to these grand palaces, of course, but she and Ben don't need much space. Steve is never coming back into their lives. He has disappeared abroad without a trace. She suspects he must have got into some trouble – probably while driving drunk – and has lost his HGV license, having to find other work overseas. She wishes him well but after the way he treated her, she's not sorry that he is out of her and Ben's lives for good.

Her friendship with Laura has fallen by the wayside too, although it was not a surprise and neither does she mourn this loss. It was only when she had begun to recover, after the clouds had finally parted, that she remembered. The pearl earring. The one belonging to Laura. She had found it in the attic and yet, she realised, she had never shown her friend all the way up there. Which meant there was one obvious explanation for how it had been lost in that room. But after hearing about the accident, she bore her no ill-will and was pleased to know that the baby had arrived safely. She wonders if she will, one day, tell Ben that he has a half-sister.

Looking out onto the street, she admires the well-tended gardens, the woman who walks her children home, the old man out with his dog for their afternoon constitutional. It is a nice neighbourhood. There's a real sense of community, not that Iris knows many people yet, and Ben can walk to the local school. A fresh start after the long summer break, and far away from any of the rumours, has been the best thing for him and he finally seems to be settled. He's also kept in touch with his girlfriend, Becky, who regularly comes round for tea at the weekends.

Iris opens the blinds a little wider and a shaft of September sunlight falls on her face. She feels … there is no other word for it: blessed. She smiles to herself, thinking that this is the sort of thing Laura used to come out with. But she knows that she is so lucky. That she was gifted a second chance at life.

It was the strange, disjointed words she remembers right at the end. The garbled mixture of English and Italian that somehow permeated her consciousness. '*Dio mio*, Irees. *Merda*! *Cos'hai fatto*? Signora Simmonds. Please, wake up!'

Poor Gianni from next door. What a sight it must have been. But at least it wasn't Ben who found her. She is eternally thankful to her Italian neighbour for that. And for saving her life. Apparently, he had seen the injured cat skulking in his back garden. Knowing that Ben was fond of the animal, he had picked it up and brought it to Iris's house, but then noticed the front door ajar and no sign of life. By the time he had found her in the flooded bathroom, she was nearly gone. Sadly the cat didn't make it, though. Never mind, she has allowed Ben to have his first pet recently, now that some of his allergies are slowly abating. A kitten named Lucky.

Of course, the police had to be informed about the house, Rosemary's body, the whole sorry story. But along with Len and Ivo's help, plus a good lawyer, she was given a suspended sentence. The body was exhumed and Rosemary's remains were subjected to a full post-mortem. That and the CCTV footage, capturing Rosemary's fall in the road, combined to prove that she died from no other reason than her head injury, which corroborated Iris's testimony. Added to that, a psychiatrist's professional opinion claimed that Iris had diminished responsibility due to temporary insanity.

She is still amazed that Len has been so understanding, so generous. To think, for so long she had despised wealthy landlords and property developers. But he is a true philanthropist, a kind soul. As a self-made multi-millionaire, he can afford to make grand gestures but he seemed to feel only sympathy for their situation in the end. The bundle of letters buried with Rosemary's body were handed over to him. They were all written by his mother, June, and taken with the ones he already had, written by the younger Rosemary, he had an even clearer picture of his family history. How the house on Riddleston Road had caused such heartbreak, driving a wedge between two sisters and, as far as he was concerned, causing the untimely death of his mum while he was just a baby.

If anything, he seemed grateful to Iris for putting all of this to rest finally – he is the only person who visits Rosemary's grave, now that she has been properly interred in the local cemetery. And, of course, he has now been united with his birth father, Bill Maddox. A paternity test had confirmed what Iris had suspected and they are slowly becoming acquainted. Another second chance at life. As for the house, Len said he didn't want anything to do with it at first, wanted none of the money from it, but then he relented. Instead, the place has been put up for sale and the proceeds will go to the hospital which saved his life and cared for his mother.

Iris continues to stare through the window. Temporary insanity, she thinks with a shake of her head. It's true though, she had been driven insane by it all. The envy, the bitterness, the worry and stress; it was like a sickness eating away at her. And Steve had been right in that sense too. He had always said she was crazy and in the end she had been driven to do something completely mad. To bury a dead woman in a garden and take her house for yourself. Even to her ears now, it still sounds ludicrous and she can't quite believe it happened.

Often she revisits that day in her memory; meeting Rosemary, accompanying her home, coveting that house and everything it could provide for her family. She remembers the way she made the cup of tea in the dilapidated old kitchen, taking her time, thinking it over before she made her way through to the lounge, to Rosemary in her chair.

In her head, her mind's eye, she has replayed these events so many times. How the old woman appeared to be asleep and then, she had realised, was in fact dead. But there is a part that her brain has erased. What happened in between.

Iris had seen her chance. A gift of an opportunity. And really, Rosemary would probably have died of her injuries anyway. She was alone, lost, forgotten. No one would miss her. Iris was just helping her along. Putting her out of her misery. This is what she told herself as she'd taken one of the rose-patterned cushions and pressed it firmly over the old woman's face. It was an act of kindness really. It was the only right thing to do.

She turns away from the view. It was an ordeal but she has come through it and so has Ben. It's best left in the past now. They have survived. Better than that. They will now thrive.

Acknowledgements

I know for a fact that I could not have done this alone and so my thanks must first go to my brilliant agent, Kate Barker. Thank you for taking a chance on me, for sticking with me, and for reading my words more times than any sane person should be expected to do.

On a similar note, thank you to my wonderful editor, Cara Chimirri, for spotting the potential in me and my work, and for making it so much better in so many ways. My thanks also go to the rest of the fabulous team at Hodder & Stoughton, including meticulous copyeditor Cari Rosen and to Lisa Brewster for the super cover art. You all, in your own specific way, took a word document that resided on my laptop and made it into a real book, and for that I will always be grateful.

Thank you to all those people who have given me encouragement and support with my writing over the years, including but not limited to: the staff and students on the Creative Writing MA course at York St John University (special shout-outs to Naomi Booth, Adelle Stripe, Robin Gallagher, Abi Knowles and Anna Brizzolara). Thank you to Amanda Reynolds for the kind mentorship, Suzannah Dunn from Curtis Brown Creative, and to Caroline Ambrose and the team at the Bath Novel Award, who changed everything for me. Thank you also to fellow writers Caroline Collett, Molly Aitken and Johanna Robinson — you know why!

Before this book became a thing, there were the ones who have been with me right from the start.

To Louise: my queen! Thank you for always being my cheerleader. You knew this was the one, even before I did. To Karen: for your wise counsel, pep talks and fast reading, thank you! To Katie: thank you for getting cross with me whenever I doubted myself and for never letting me give up.

Thank you to my family. To my mum who, right from the get-go, instilled in me a love of reading dark domestic suspense fiction with all the Beatrix Potter stories. To my dad, who is no longer here, but would have been proud. And to my grandmother, Marie, who was the first one to ever tell me I could write.

To my amazing kids: you are three of the best things I have ever done. This is for you!

And, finally, Greig. Thank you. For everything.